AMANDA DAVIS HIGHW[illegible] AWARD

The Amanda Davis Highwire Fiction [illegible] memory of Amanda Davis.

Amanda Davis was a very gifted [illegible] passed away in March of 2003, at t[illegible] placeable person, one who created an[illegible] she went. She loved to write, loved being a writer, loved to read, loved the existence of books, and wanted happiness—personal, professional, spiritual, shoe-related—for everyone. She really did.

When Amanda was writing the stories that would become her first collection, *Circling the Drain,* she worked a number of ridiculous jobs to make ends meet. At one point she as writing copy for television ads for newspaper tabloids. Her second published story, "Fat Ladies Floated in the Sky Like Balloons," appeared in the second issue of *McSweeney's* and was everything we were looking for in fiction—it was bold, funny, experimental, lyrical, and ended without any conventional sort of resolution.

This memorial award is intended to aid a young woman writer of 32 years or younger who both embodies Amanda's personal strengths—warmth, generosity, a passion for community—and who needs some time to finish a book in progress. The book in progress needn't be thematically or stylistically close to Amanda's work, but we would be lying if we said we weren't looking to support another writer of Amanda's outrageous lyricism and heart. The first winner, in 2004, was Jessica Anthony, whose novel *The Convalescent* is now almost completed.

REQUIREMENTS AND GUIDELINES

Applicants should send a work in progress, between 5,000 and 40,000 words, and a statement of their financial situation. You may list any and all ridiculous jobs performed to facilitate your writing, and you may include two other short pieces, published or otherwise, which will be read if you feel they would help in the understanding of your work generally. The reading group will consist of McSweeney's editors and a handful of writers and readers close to Amanda.

The award will be given in one lump-sum grant, with no strings attached. The deadline is January 15, 2006. Winners will be notified May 1, 2006. Send materials in paper form, with SASE, to:

The Amanda Davis Highwire Fiction Award
826 Valencia Street, San Francisco, CA 94110

 After a couple somewhat elaborate issues in a row, we were excited to settle down, get back to basics—a paperback book, a bunch of good stories, maybe a Convergence. And for the most part this is what we did; the book is indeed paperback, the stories are certainly good, and we are excited to include the final (for now) of Weschler's giddy spin-outs, which will now be collected in a large, colorful book, due out in a couple months. But then somehow we ended up with a DVD in here as well. Which we're happy about, of course, but it leaves us still with our hunger for pure simplicity. Thus, the following vow: Issue 19 will be handwritten on a large sheet of butcher paper. There will be only one copy. We will pack up a 1991 Volvo 240, black, with tinted windows and a broken sunroof, and drive around the country, visiting each subscriber. Each will be given one hour with the text, or maybe slightly more if we're provided with lemonade or granola. Non-subscribers can visit our offices in San Francisco, where the issue will be available for viewing on our back porch. As usual, we're grateful for your faith and constancy. —*Eli Horowitz, chief editor for this issue.*

Printed in Canada by Westcan/Printcrafters.

McSweeney's 18

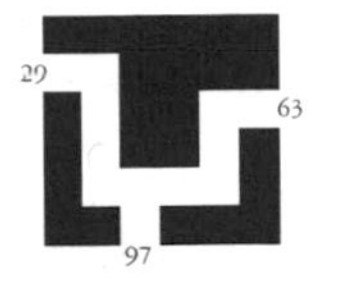

THE STEPFATHER

by CHRIS ADRIAN

OUR MOTHER WAS supposed to marry Mr. Arnold. We knew she had decided on him, we knew she was in love. She talked about him incessantly, sighed at his picture on the fridge, sat getting drunker in the kitchen after a date and sang about him. She walked differently and stood differently and ate different foods and did her hair up differently—to everyone the evidence was overwhelming, though everyone took different evidence to the same conclusion. Colm said she smelled different; Cameron said she had put on the stark Joan Crawford brows of certainty; Caroline noticed the progression of shoes—they got fancier and fancier as she got more in love and more in love; little Christopher noticed that she was already wearing her wedding lipstick—*burning sky*. Different evidence, the same conclusion: we are all very experienced, except for Little Chris, and we were all very sure. So it was a terrible shock when she married Mr. Walker, instead.

There was an order to the process, not supposed to be violated. We started with the traditional gaggle of suitors; they underwent the traditional winnowing, cast aside as mother discovered a fatal fault in them. From the dozen the four or five emerged, and then the three or four, and then the two. In the end there were always two, and sometimes it was very difficult to distinguish who would make the better stepfather, but not this time.

A shock and a disappointment—eldest to youngest, Big Chris to Little Chris, we all preferred Mr. Arnold. Who wouldn't? And of our relatives and neighbors, who didn't? The wedding was spoiled by the tense polite air. We could tell that everyone was making the same unfavorable comparisons that we were, and saw a shining, phantom Mr. Arnold standing next to Mr. Walker as he waited for my mother (escorted, as was the tradition, by her last husband, Mr. Jefferson) at the end of the aisle. The two men, real and imagined, were of a height, and had similar coloring, and both dressed in handsome suits, but despite these similarities the difference between them was striking. Mr. Walker seemed to us the corrupted and decayed reflection of the better man standing beside him; the bright blue eyes of the one man, so much a part of the constant open honesty of his expression, were darkened and hooded on the other; the lines of the face, noble on one, on the other seemed evidence that the face was habitually twisted by uncharitable thoughts; one mouth seemed constitutionally predisposed to elegant speech, the other destined to leer. Mr. Arnold stood waiting for our mother with the reverence of a man about to receive a sacrament; Mr. Walker lacked only a bib to convince that he was waiting for a messy side of ribs.

"She picked the troll," said Caroline, sitting among us on a long upholstered bench, watching our mother dance with Mr. Walker. All of us were slumped down, already exhausted—it was the days and days of accumulated disappointment, waking every morning in full disbelief of the evolving reality, and wearing out our hearts every afternoon and evening hoping we could change her mind before it was too late—though we were only an hour into the party. "Why did she pick the troll?"

"I don't know," said Calvin. "There's something sort of appealing about him." Three of us on either side of him hissed. "If you like trolls, I mean," he added.

"She's punishing herself," said Ciaran. "She woke up and said to herself, Today is a good day to poke myself in the eye with a sharp stick."

"Poor Mr. Arnold," said Colm. "He loved her. He really did."

"You love him," said Courtney. "You really do."

"Shut up," he said.

"Fag," said Courtney. "You should have married him."

"Shut up! This is serious. Don't you get it, Jokie? It's time to unroll your joints, straighten up, and put that wasted fucking mind of yours to use. There's got to be something we can do."

"It's too late," said Cameron. "What's done is done, and can't be undone. Not until the divorce."

"To the inevitable divorce," said Courtney, and we all lifted our drinks, even Little Chris, raising his Roy Roger in the palm of his hand, as if he were offering it to the ceiling."There's got to be something we can do," Colm said again. "It's a fucking disaster. We can't just sit around watching people burn and freeze to death. When somebody calls out for help from underneath a broken building, you help them. Don't you help them?"

"I know what I'm going to do," said Courtney. She stood and looked up and down the bench at our brothers and sisters, finally selecting Christina to lead to the dance floor.

"Don't you help them?" Colm asked again.

"She made up her mind," said Calvin. "It's really not our place to say. Anyway, always there's no accounting for taste."

"He is the *stepfather*," Colm said. "It's not like she was just picking out toilet paper. It's supposed to be a family decision."

He dropped his drink and clenched his fists and raised his voice, sounding angry and incredulous. "He is the stepfather!"

We murmured it up and down the bench and around the hall. This man was the stepfather. Little Chris rooted under the bench after the fruit lost out of Colm's drink. The rest of us comforted Colm as best we could—he is a smack-in-the-middle child and has always been troubled and sensitive. "They come, they go," said Calvin. "We outlast them all."

We tried to be happy for her, watching her dance with Uncle Jack and Mr. Earl and Mr. Jefferson and yes, even while Mr. Walker slouched with her around the dance floor, pawing at her and doing now a lame sort of Charleston and now an even lamer honky boogie. He was panting and sweating and from across the hall we thought we could smell his catbox breath and even feel it clinging to our clothes. But she was happy. Even those of us not close to her at all—Caitlin and Cory and Cato—could tell that she was having the time of her life out there. Wedding days were always the happiest of her life, and this one was no exception. We all tried so hard—we shut our eyes and squeezed inside, the girls Kegeling until their groins ached and the boys refluxing gin back into their mouths—but when we polled we learned that we all felt only the same sad panic.

We watched shovel-faced Aunt Ann catch the bouquet again, and endured the unholy spectacle of the garter-removal—surely traditions more suitable for a first or even second wedding, but our mother wouldn't give them up, even after no one really enjoyed them anymore, and their original meaning had become reversed; every bouquet Aunt Ann snatched out of the air seemed only to confirm more bitterly her lonely spinsterhood. Courtney still danced and Little Chris still ran all around the hall, cake on his face and his hair raised up in a sweaty perm, but we were all sinking further and further as the night went on, slumping on the bench, slipping under the tables in groups of three or four, all of us saying the same thing as we got drunker and drunker: "We should have done more, we should have tried harder." It was a half-ass job of protesting we had done in the mere week between the announcement and the wedding, and even the boldest of us—Caroline and Charles and Colm—approached her very meekly in the kitchen where she sat in her usual chair in her usual posture, chin in hand but fingers splayed except for the two that held the cigarette, hardly smoked, a long stick of ash always threatening to break from the tip. "Don't you think..." we began, over and over, never finishing the thought or voicing the complaint, only starting it over and over. Maybe you shouldn't... Have you ever considered... Doesn't it seem..." Drunk and feeling guilty, some of us indulged our bad habits, Caroline lighting her first cigarette in a month, Ciaran slipping off into the bathroom with our junky cousin Sasha, Calvin finally giving in to the longstanding salacious advances if our incestuous cousins Petra and Philip. We woke the next day, under the table or out on the street or in the park or in various beds of iniquity next to people we loathed, and wondered, How did we get here? and everyone hoped the previous night had just been a bad dream but when we stumbled home one by one he was there, waiting for us to take our seats at the breakfast table, ready to nauseate us with eggs scrambled in bacon fat and with his perpetual leer. He wore a tall chef's hat and an apron with a motto: WORLD'S BEST DAD.

Mr. Jefferson was our tallest stepfather. We liked him very much, even from the very first time we saw him, playing golf in a charity tournament organized every year by Aunt Ann. There was something in him not quite noble but merely enormously likable, and even people with all sorts of good reasons to dislike him (Aunt Ann, for instance, was both a jilted lover and victim of a bad business deal) were always surprised to find themselves, in his presence, overwhelmed by affability. "Nasty-ass bastard," Aunt Ann called him at her golf tournament. We were watching him make a putt, and we half-expected her to shout at him or throw her spiky shoe, but she sighed the insult, and crossed her arms over her belly in a way that she did when she was yearning toward something.

For most of us he was a high-school stepfather. A liar and a cheat and a philanderer, we know he was all these things and yet we still say it was a blessing to have him. During the years when organs of hatred grew fat in all our classmates, and every camping trip or post-game pizza or drug-party conversation was about the sheer awfulness of one's parents, how they were fucking morons or fucking bastards or just fucking fucks—we reached through hazes of dope to articulate our perceptions of how they were corrupt and disappointing—we always loved him, though some of us, embarrassed at the strength of feeling, mocked and dissembled. But none of us are ashamed to admit it—we have never been ashamed to love a stepfather who deserved it, and really, when you put him in his historical perspective, comparing him to preceding stepfathers, you saw that Mr. Jefferson was really just a spotted lamb and a wholesome pervert who cheated without a shred of cynicism in his heart. "I was always thinking of you," he told my mother, when it came out that he had been fellated from one end of the city to the other. "Liar!" she screamed, and tried to decapitate him with a flung china plate, but we believed him.

Mr. Walker should have been a more hesitant and tentative stepfather, given the slapdash nature of his accession to our family, and the fact that we hardly knew him, or he us. At first we couldn't tell if it was shameless effrontery or just trying too hard, the way he inserted himself so forcefully into our lives. We wanted him not to dominate the dinnertime conversation with stories of his dull life in Texas, not to show up at every PTA meeting introducing himself to everyone within reach of his long arms as our father, so people who knew the nature of our family always had to correct him: "You mean stepfather, don't you?" He'd say it was the same thing, proving how the least subtle distinctions were lost on him. We wanted him not to invade our rooms with solicitous cups of hot chocolate, or storybooks (even Little Chris was too old to be read to) or, worst of all, to sit on our bed and ask if we wouldn't like to say bedtime prayers together.

"He may as well ask us," Colm said to us later in our big circle of complaint, "to pass hooks and chains through our nipples and swing from the ceiling, or pass snakes around the breakfast table, or shit right on the carpet. How about that, Mr. Walker? How about a nice family shit before bedtime?" He was furious, but restrained himself from frankly insulting the man. "We usually just pray in our heads," Calvin said, a very diplomatic response.

"But then how does God hear you?" Mr. Walker asked. Courtney and Carla had to take him by the elbow and steer him out of the room to make him understand that he was not wanted or welcomed.

"I think we hurt his feelings," Calvin said when he came back in.

"I don't fucking care," said Colm, and he punched the wall, though not very hard. He played in the school orchestra and even in true ecstasies of fury he was always mindful of his hands. "He doesn't get it. He just doesn't get it at all." Even properly appraised and selected stepfathers who were not ugly surprises couldn't just barge into our lives.

"He smells like pickles, when you sniff close," said Carla.

"Give him some time," Calvin said, but it had already been five months. Three more passed before the night our lacrosse team played Eastport, but his behavior never changed, and our attitude congealed, so even our mother noticed, and called five of us, the night before the game, to sit with her at the kitchen table and have a drink, Colm and Calvin and Christine and Big Chris and Carla. She stared at them for a good three minutes, but even Colm could only look back for thirty seconds before he dropped his head again, glancing up again and again after multiple eternities to see her drawing on her cigarette or her gin and still doing that look, a gentle glare.

"You're sitting on my cake," she said finally.

"We're sorry," said Calvin.

"We can't help it," said Colm.

"We're not trying to upset you," said Carla.

"It's just…" said Christine.

"He's just…" said Big Chris.

"It's hard to explain," said Calvin.

"Except it's not," said Colm. He drew in a deep breath and said it. "Mother, he is a man without any redeeming qualities."

"Can't you try a little harder?" she asked, completely ignoring Colm. "He's trying so hard. Have you seen the sign he made?" He'd colored in some cardboard to carry to tomorrow's lacrosse game. KEEP YOUR HEAD UP, CARLA! it said.

"How am I supposed to see the sign if my head's down?" asked Carla. "Anyway, I never drop my head."

"You drop your head all the time," said Calvin. "You don't even look at the goal when you score, sweetie."

"That's not the point," said Colm. "A thirty-cent sign is evidence of nothing. It changes nothing."

"Honey," said our mother, gesturing toward all of them—if she'd had a free hand she would have patted an arm or a cheek. "It's the thought, don't you see? What else do you want from him?"

That got her silence. All but Carla looked at the ground; she stared past our mother's head at a portrait of Mr. Jefferson until Calvin spoke.

"It's just hard," he said.

"It's not easy at all," said Carla.

"It always takes a while, to get used to the new situation," said Big Chris.

"An apology," said Colm. "I want an apology from him."

"But honey," said Christine, "he hasn't done anything."

"Just by being, he wrongs," said Colm.

"Try harder," said our mother, still ignoring Colm. Her cigarette was nearly burned down. She set it carefully aside the ashtray and touched them, stroking Christine's soft burgundy hair, running the back of her finger over the curve of Calvin's big biceps, folding her palm against Big Chris's rough cheek, squeezing Carla's shoulder, and finally taking Colm's hand. He stared down into his drink. "All right?" she asked. He grabbed up his gin and slugged it.

"Do you love him?" he asked her, coughing and gagging—he was the least accomplished drinker of any of us, next to Little Chris. The other four gasped at the boldness of his question. It was something Courtney might ask, but only after days and days of descending intimacies, at the end of a weeklong cruise or a spa getaway or a wilderness adventure, after they'd had time and solitude to become again properly and deeply mother and daughter to each other.

"Mostly," she said, not batting an eye at his bold impropriety.

"I'll try," he said softly, not because he'd had a change of heart, he told us later in the debriefing circle, but because it was now certain that she had. The other four said it, too. "We'll try, Mother. We'll try very hard."

"Mostly!" we said to each other, erupting in the middle of breakfast and lunch and history, in the locker room while we buckled up our pads, on the field as we ran and blocked and checked. "Mostly!" Calvin said to Mina Blotyre, the lovely captain of the Eastport team, as they were about to face off. He shouted it again more as they raked and the ball flew up between them. They knocked their sticks together three times, hard and swift as saber fencers—mostly! mostly! mostly!—and then he pushed the ball toward the wing where Courtney scooped it up and passed it to Colm.

We lost the game. We didn't care. Mostly was halfway to not anymore—it usually took years to get to mostly, and even when we estimated conservatively we anticipated that Mr. Walker would be out of our lives before Calvin's next birthday. "Are you sure she hasn't said it?" we asked Courtney as we were walking to the post-game pizza party.

"Last week I was brushing her hair and she stopped me and said, 'You know, darling, sometimes...' That was it. Nothing more."

"It's a start," said Colm. It was another sign. *Sometimes I look at him and wonder what I was thinking.* She said it about Mr. Herbert and Mr. Wilson and Mr. Earl, about all of them as far back as the oldest of us could remember. It meant that the mind was changing, the heart was looking with altered eyes. "Along with the Mostly, it's practically a definite."

"You put too much on the Mostly," said Calvin. "Anyway, I'm almost getting used to him."

"Stop saying that," he said. "It's not even funny." Calvin shrugged, but even his needling couldn't ruin our good mood.

The post-game pizza party was as festive as any after a win, and the dope-break at Alanis Booker's house was blessed with a number of profitable hook-ups, and even Colm seemed at peace that night, not protesting when Calvin dragged him along to the park to ogle the shy, closeted sailors who stood around under trees or sat quietly in their cars, the very spirits of furtiveness. Maybe it was our collective happy mood—there was something universally intoxicating for us about shared happiness—that made Calvin bold enough to snag himself a sailor, and Colm curious enough to sit with one on a picnic table and talk about baseball while the sailor rubbed a hand up and down and up his leg, neither of them acknowledging the active hand. He neither liked nor disliked it—the sailor reached some sort of finish, coughing and sighing, then stood up and hurried away. Colm stood up, tied his shoe, and then looked around for Calvin—he'd only been a few benches away a few moments before—but our brother was nowhere in sight.

We did not like Mr. Herbert, though he came highly recommended by his predecessor, Mr. Wilson. He spent most of the marriage in the bathroom, and when he wasn't talking about his digestion, had little to say. There was really nothing wrong with him, but nothing right with him, either, as Courtney always liked to point out. Mother was done with Mr. Wilson, and there was no one better to marry that year. She threw him over for Mr. Jefferson at the first chance.

It had been ages since we'd had a death in the family. The days before and after Calvin's funeral were incredibly strange; all of us confused and sad and angry and horrified. Colm and Courtney and Charles and Caroline pored obsessively over the coroner's report, Colm especially reading it over and over as if the details of the crime, written on our brother's body, would, if properly apprehended, yield up an understanding of why it had happened, or what it meant, or what would come next. Others of us, not able to bear looking at the pictures or to attend one of Colm's debriefings (they escalated in detail and horror every day as he discovered more about the crime) spent days intermittently weeping and mumbling to each other. He was the nicest of us all, we said. Why him? Why us? How could anybody do something so awful?

Our mother drew her curtains and took to her bed, emerging only for the funeral, standing ataraxic, wrapped in folds and folds of black tulle, in sunglasses and a wide black hat, through the whole service. In ones and twos and threes we went knocking on her door, only to be met with silence, or a quiet "Go away." Mr. Walker was the only one she would let in. That was another miserable mystery—why did she prefer him, the man whom we were sure she had practically loaded into the dump-chute, to us, the children she'd known and loved all our lives?

"What's wrong with her?" Courtney asked as we sat gathered after the funeral for another of Colm's debriefings.

"The same thing that's wrong with us," said Carla. "Calvin is gone."

"There were one hundred and fifty-three stab wounds," said Colm. "Not one hundred and fifty, as previously reported."

"It doesn't make sense," said Christine. "It doesn't make Mr. Walker more attractive. It doesn't make him chew with his mouth closed. It doesn't make him play the piano. It should be the opposite. It should make him more of a goat, because when you look at him you think, I really need a hero now, but all I have is this fucking goat."

"And yet," said Charles.

"And yet," said Big Chris, nodding sagely.

"And yet!" sang Little Chris, knocking together a teddy bear and a robot. Though he'd already drawn a picture of Calvin's house in Heaven, we were not sure he understood that our brother was dead.

"The two largest wounds in the abdomen were found to contain semen," said Colm. "Analysis indicates the involvement of a seventh and eighth attacker, but as with the other specimens, no identification has been made."

"More and more I think you should just keep some of this stuff to yourself," said Charles.

"It would be a disrespect," said Colm. "And any one thing could make everything else fall into place."

"It's a disrespect what you're doing," said Christine. "I bet Mother would think so. It's like you're poking him with a stick, just to see if flies will come out."

"Shut up," said Caroline. "Just because you want to crawl under your bed and play with your plastic ponies doesn't mean the rest of us have to crawl under there with you."

"You shut up," said Christine. "What do you know? You didn't even cry at the funeral. What's that? You don't even care that he's dead. You never liked him. You were always scheming to get his room and..."

"The fifth metatarsal," Colm said loudly, "was not severed with a sharp instrument, as previously reported, but likely bitten off. Shear patterns and microdeposits indicate that the perpetrator wears braces."

"Stop it!" Charlotte shouted, jumping from her chair and rushing to the center of the circle to turn in place and make supplicating gestures at all of us. "Just stop it, all of you. This isn't what we should be doing now. Things like this, they're horrible, I know it. I feel it, right now, how horrible it is, but things like this make you stronger. They make you better. It's what mother is trying to tell us. She's had a vision—it's just horrible enough to redeem Mr. Walker, don't you see? That's why she'll only talk to him. Mr. Walker, you and me—we're going to come away from this thing a better family. That's it, don't you see? That's the one good thing." She darted back and forth from the center of the circle, embracing us all in turn. We all tolerated her hugs according to our dispositions—she was naïve and not terribly smart, but more than any of us she always meant what she said. Only Caroline pushed her away, and only Colm said, "Give me a fucking break" when she proclaimed, there at the bottom of our hole, that things were going to get better.

Mr. Wilson was old enough to be a step-grandfather. We were split on him, half of us finding something very appealing in him, the other half always avoiding him and referring to him, toward the end of his tenure, as "that smelly old man." He was Carl's father, and Caroline's, and Colin's. He liked to pretend to be asleep. On the front porch, in the kitchen, watching television, he would sit and snore, then exclaim delightedly, "I saw that!" if you transgressed in any way, stealing a cookie or picking your nose or fondling yourself in salute of an on-screen intimacy. His detractors declared him a pretend husband, somebody who put up a front of aged vitality when there was actually nothing there but a wrinkled shell. Alone with our mother, he collapsed, a slack puppet, to the floor, or sat quietly in his very comfortable chair in their bedroom, not bothering her with admonitions or advice or conversation. She needed a break from being husbanded, but was too much a slave to her own traditions to be single, so she took him. We who liked him said, look deeper, and see how subtle he is, hoary and powerful and sure, she loves him because he lives his life with great certainty, and is possessed of such a strength of conviction that even when he is wrong, he is right.

Things did not get better. Those of us whose hearts were lifted by Charlotte's speech, and by the incessant hopeful cheerleading she did in the months following Calvin's death, began to feel ashamed once a certain amount of unpleasantness had developed. How stupid, after all, to think that something like that could improve a family. Better and more reasonable to believe what was easier, and more sensible, that it was a ruination that would reflect through time to wreak further and greater ruin, that every one of Calvin's hundreds of wounds would reach forward to be born again into the declining future.

Even Charlotte had to agree, by our mother's birthday, months after Calvin's death, that we had not seized upon the opportunity of tragedy to transform ourselves into something better than we had been. Christine was binging and purging again, her secret habits betrayed by the fine suit of lanugo hair she'd put on and the telltale gray cast of her teeth. Ciaran made another movie, not even bothering this time to wear a leather hood. In a circle he confessed, and tore up the five hundred dollars they'd given him, and swore he'd never do it again, but not another month went by before he was hanging by chains in another harshly lit, carpeted garage. Courtney began systematically to re-date her vilest ex-boyfriends, flipping backward in her book to reverse the progress of years, and coming home with injuries of increasing severity, rug-burn to black eye to broken rib, though we begged her to be sensible and Big Chris beat the shit out of every one who touched her. Little Chris was suspended from school after attacking a classmate with a pair of safety scissors, cutting off her starboard pigtail and running with it for half a mile before he was overtaken. Colm indulged what was for him a singular vice: timidity. It was not who we were, we kept telling ourselves.

Mr. Walker's relatives swarmed at the party. Over the past few months they'd become more and more a part of our life, showing up for lunches and dinner and even for breakfast the day after a late-night party—not the kind we were used to under other stepfathers, when Tiki torches lined the lawn and clowns danced on the deck. These were affairs as somber as they were exclusive. Mother sat at a table that got larger and larger with every occasion, surrounded by her in-law cousins, aunts, and uncles, eating beef and soggy vegetables while they all spoke around her in low tones. All of us, even Big Chris, were at the children's table, staring at our portions of meat and limiting our conversation to wagering on what fruit Grandma Walker had suspended this time in her gelatin casserole.

We sat in folding chairs along the border of the lawn, listening attentively to Mr. Walker's speech: "You are a beautiful woman whose beauty is matched only by her own beauty," he said to our mother, who drooped a little in her big wicker chair, looking down mostly into her lap and never looking up at any of us. "Every birthday, you just get better. Since I married you, your hair is longer. Everyone should compliment you on the extreme beauty of your muumuu." After the speech came the dancing. Of us, only Courtney rose for it, and only when Cousin Tommy dragged her from her chair. There was something tired and sad about the way she do-si-do-'d. We all hated a square dance, anyway, but that was the theme that year. We'd already had our country Christmas and Easter and Pentecost; now it was time for a country birthday.

"I know I should be dancing," Christine said. "But I just don't feel like it."

"I'm dancing in my head," said Caroline. "But it's slow, slow."

"I'm shuffling," said Big Chris, "like a sloth on valium."

"Sloth's can't shuffle," said Colby. "They don't have the feet for it."

"It's a were-sloth," said Big Chris. "The feet aren't right but it knows how to do it because it remembers being human."

"I remember being happy," said Colm. "What's wrong with me? This is my favorite holiday. Absolutely my favorite, but even thinking about the corn roast, I just feel tired."

"It's normal," said Charlotte, whose optimism had been replaced by a clinical resignation fostered by a new habit of reading above her head in books of medicine, psychology, and philosophy. "It's part of the missing him. The holidays get hit hardest with the black rain of sadness."

"We should dance," said Ciaran. "We're going to get in trouble." Mr. Walker had instituted a system of demerits, redeemable for chores, distributed for late homework or poor grades or missed goals or sullenness or a general lack of enthusiasm or a positive drug test, a rare entity since the production of specimens was not observed, and Little Chris peed so generously.

"Fuck it," said Charles, and we were all utterly quiet. Cousin John stopped his dancing for a moment, and looked around but didn't come over. He helped Mr. Walker distribute demerits and always seemed to know even if we were thinking sullen thoughts.

"Shut up," said Caroline. "One of them's coming." But it was only little Cousin Connie. She ran up and stopped inches before colliding with Big Chris.

"I'm adopted!" she shouted.

"We know, dear," said Caroline. The little girl looked at us expectantly, twisting up her skirt with one hand and twirling a braid with another.

"And you're not," she said accusingly, then giggled and ran off.

"Come on," said Ciaran, when she was gone. "Put on your party face or Mother will be angry." He put on a frozen smile and flashed it up and down our row of chairs.

"That's hideous," said Christine.

"She won't care, anyway," said Carla. "She doesn't care about any of us anymore. All she cares about is gin and romance novels."

"Don't say things like that," Little Chris said softly, but we all heard, and we all put on our party faces, even Charles, and we all rose and participated in the square dance while Mr. Walker called out the steps and Cousin Karl sawed on his fiddle. We hooked arms with Cousins Andy and Gale and Alphonso. Courtney let Cousin Tommy dance her into a corner to smooch a little. Little Chris only rose up and kept dancing after Cousin Connie pushed him down and stole his straw boater. When we were given the smallest pieces of corn and our butter was rationed and our plates received only clawless crabs, we said nothing, only sat at our table and ate quietly. When our fireworks were confiscated as too frightening to Little Cousin Donnie, we gave them up without protest. It was only when Charles and Colm caught Cousins Donnie and Connie jumping in Calvin's bed that we were finally spurred to some sort of action. "I'm dancing!" Cousin Connie shouted as she jumped. Colm reached out and pushed her out of the bed—it hadn't been made, or touched, nothing in the room had been touched, since Calvin died. She narrowly missed cutting her face on the edge of the dresser. Cousin Donnie jumped down and socked Colm in the testicles, then kicked Charles in the shin. Neither of them struck back, and Colm even apologized to Cousin Connie, but it still earned them dozens and dozens of demerits, for laying hands upon a child, for witnessing the laying hands upon a child, for raising one's voice to a cousin, for disrespecting Cousin Connie's fragile sense of play, for going into our brother's bedroom without permission... the list of offenses, two pages long, would hang on the fridge for weeks.

"It felt... good," Colm told us later. "I know she's just a kid. I know she didn't mean anything by it, but it felt good. In as much time as it took to push her, I remembered how things used to be, and I was so angry." Charles was quiet and withdrawn for the rest of the night, and wouldn't come along when Colm organized four of us, Christine and Colby and Cara and Ciaran, into a delegation to visit our mother. He was like his old self, angry and proud, even if was only a few hours before he lapsed back into being sad, timid Colm again. After the party was over, they marched from Colm's room, past Cousin Karl passed out beneath a houseplant and Cousin Gale stuffing with ice cream in front of the television, through the dining room and the living room, right up to the door of our mother's suite. For the first time in any of their lives they opened the door without knocking. They meant to throw it open and declare, "Mother, it's time we talked!" But something about the coldness of the knob, the tallness of the door, the blackness of the wood, made them just push it open a crack, as a test, before going all the way. They opened it a hand's breadth, so all of them could see what was going on inside. Even through the narrow space they could see how the room was crowded with cousins, and Mother was plainly visible on the bed, Mr. Walker and Cousin Dickie behind her. Cousin Dickie was working, Mr. Walker's hand laid on his shoulder—tenderly or sternly, none of the five witnesses could decide which—while the crowd cheered them on, and before Cousin Elaine put her face in the door and kicked it to, our brothers and sisters saw the men switch, and heard Cousin Dickie make a crude remark—how dreadful was the smell but how exquisite was the pleasure—and they saw our mother's face, drawn and blank. It looked past them all and then the door slammed shut.

Mr. Earl was our kindest stepfather. For most of us he was the grade-school stepfather, a good man to bring your paper Thanksgiving turkeys and lopsided ceramic ashtrays—he'd praise and cherish them, though he didn't smoke. He was Charlotte's father, and Cara's, and Carl's. His detractors—mainly Big Chris—mistook his kindness for weakness, and said he didn't last long because Mother found him boring. But it wasn't mere boredom that made her throw him over. She realized that he wasn't just a good stepfather and a good husband, but a good man. Fresh from the bitter disaster of her marriage to Mr. Millhouse, she'd forgotten that she liked her husbands to be a little bad. She ought never to have recovered from Mr. Millhouse, ought never again to have desired a man who would work against her, or wanted a love tempered with hatred or bitterness. She waited and waited to discover Mr. Earl's secrets—surely someone with some a pleasant, decent surface was hiding something truly horrible and truly exciting—but he didn't really have any. He cheated only in idle daydreams, and had last sinned in his youth—innocent slights against his papa's sharecroppers. He made a better ex-husband than husband; for how quickly Mother put him off, she kept him always near at hand as an advisor and a friend. We children kept him as a refuge—the memory of a good stepfather, one who never yelled at us or punished us except fairly and gently, one who could find lasting moral lessons in the encounter between a colony of ants and a blueberry muffin, who would wait in our rooms, a hundred ghosts of him, to comfort us during one of Mr. Wilson's or Mr. Herbert's or Mr. Jefferson's rages.

* * *

We held a séance on Calvin's birthday. It was Courtney's idea. She'd been dreaming of him more and more in the past weeks, and always had the sense, in her dreams, that he was trying to tell her something. "I'll be sitting at my desk doing my homework and he comes in to say it's time for dinner," she told us. "He taps me on the shoulder and I say, 'Yeah, yeah, I'll be right there,' and it's only after he's left the room that I realize he's dead, that this was a visitation. There's something about his face, in the dreams where I see it, that tells me he wants to say something more than that it's time for dinner, or that the bus is coming, or that Cousin John needs to verify my homework. I try, really I do, to remember I should ask him what it is, but I always forget."

There was a sort of unparty—a special dessert served up by Grandma Walker after another dinner of Mr. Walker's favorite gray meat. Every cousin present wished Calvin a happy birthday. We all looked around at each other, confused, not sure why they were pretending that our brother wasn't dead. Mother sat at the head of the table, hand in hand with Mr. Walker, giving us her now customary glassy stare. We were restless all through dinner and dessert, all of us eager to get back to Courtney's room and break out the Ouija board, and though we tried not to be curt when Mr. Walker asked us in turn about our days, what we were reading in school, or our predictions about the coming game against Southport, still Colby and Corwin and Catherine all got demerits handed down the table from Cousin John. Catherine, a maker of but never an actor on bold claims, did not eat hers, like she had threatened to.

It was an old, old board, in the family for generations, made of fruitwood inlaid with mahogany and ivory, with a planchette of silver and brass. There was a family legend that anybody who dared to mess with it would within a fortnight find themselves possessed by a demon, if not by the devil himself. It wasn't something any of us except Craig, with his halfhearted satanic posing, would play with casually, and nothing that Mr. Walker would like to see us using—there'd be truckloads of demerits for us if we were caught. So we stuffed a towel underneath Courtney's door, to keep in the odor of incense and candle smoke, and whispered very softly to each other as we crowded around the board, a dozen fingers reaching to touch on the planchette. We sat waiting, our minds composed to a state of open earnest expectation, after Courtney asked the question, "Calvin, what were you going to tell me?" But it didn't move at all.

"Is your mind really empty?" Courtney asked us, after five minutes of nothing.

"Christine's mind is always empty," said Big Chris.

"This is serious," said Colm. "The spirit will never come if you make a joke out of it."

"You think you're funny," said Christine "but you're..." Just as she spoke the planchette jumped.

"I didn't push it!" said Little Chris.

"Nobody says you did," said Colm, and we waited. Very, very slowly, the words spelled out: *Mr. Walker is a butt. Mr. Walker smells like a butt. Mr. Walker smells his own butt*. Nothing profound, nothing worth a trip through the grave to speak, but we would have cherished the words nonetheless if Big Chris hadn't broken out in a giggle and confessed that he was pushing. He laughed and laughed—he always laughed when he was nervous or sad, and never even smiled on the rare occasions when he was happy—and said, "I told you it wouldn't work."

"Just get the fuck out," said Courtney. "We'll just do it without you."

"Brothers!" Christine shouted, loud enough that Colm shushed her and put his hand over her mouth. She pushed it away. "Sisters!" We noticed that though her mouth was open wide, she did not move her lips at all when she spoke. It was as if the words were playing from somewhere deep in her belly. "Listen to me," she said. It took us all a moment to recognize our brother's voice.

"What are you doing?" the voice asked us. Christine had fallen forward and was kneeling on the board, her face pointed to the ceiling, her mouth open wide enough to swallow a boot. When none of us spoke the voice asked the question again.

"Talking to you," Courtney said quietly.

"But what are you doing?"

"What is it?" Courtney asked. "What do you want to tell us?"

"What are you doing?"

"Tell us what it is," said Colm. Christine flung out a hand and smacked him in the face.

"What are you doing? What are you doing? You're doing nothing!"

"You sound upset," Cara said quietly, after a moment of silence. "Are they being mean to you there?"

"Nothing and nothing. He ruins the tradition, and you do nothing. He is a scab on our family. He is not the stepfather and has never been the stepfather, yet you feed him his beef and polish his slippers!" The voice was so angry, but Christine's face betrayed no emotion.

"I thought you liked him," said Courtney.

"Fury upon every brother, rage upon every sister. You sit and sit and say, I can do nothing, or, There is nothing to do. Why did I die, except to bring you a message of shame?"

"Are you really Calvin?" Little Chris asked. "Calvin never said stuff like that. Spirits are tricky. I read about them.

Couldn't you be the ghost of somebody else? The ghost of Amelia Earhardt? The ghost of Snoopy?"

"Is Snoopy dead, that he would speak to you from beyond the veil? Is he witness to your degradation, that he would speak against it? That man is not the stepfather. He has never been the stepfather, yet now he rules you. Undo him! Undo him! Undo him or suffer a deserved fate!"

Christine stood up, then sat down, then knelt again before falling over on her side and twitching a few beats. She sat up, rubbed her eyes, and said, "Why are you all looking at me like that?"

We spent the rest of the evening dithering, all of us chattering back and forth except Colm, who sat quietly on Courtney's bed staring into his hands. There was much to discuss: was it really Calvin, after all, who'd admonished us, or some strange pathology of Christine's, changed to a voice by the stresses of the Ouija encounter (she was more afraid of the board, and of demonic possession, for that matter, than any of us)? Maybe the words were true, but they were only what Caroline, and all of us, were afraid to say out loud. What did it mean, anyway, to undo a person?

"It means we should throw him out of the house," said Big Chris. "Him and them. Wrap them all up and throw them out. Boot every cousin, then send him out, last of all. I think we're going to need some help, but I can see it already. I can see my footprint on his ass."

"We just need to talk to Mother," said Courtney. "But in a special way. We need to get organized, people. We're subtle, aren't we? We can turn her against him over ten conversations, and she'll be kicking him out within two months. We've done it before. Doesn't anybody remember Mr. Herbert?"

"We need to rustle up new suitors," said Ciaran. "Why

didn't I think of it before? They're out there. They're always out there. All we have to do is start inviting fine specimens to dinner. She'll make the inevitable comparisons, and that'll be that."

"We'll make him look stupid," said Cara.

"We just have to steal his pants," said Little Chris.

"We have to kill him," Colm said simply.

Mr. Millhouse is a barely remembered stepfather—Caroline's father and Big Chris's and mine, too. We hear such horrible stories about him: that he nearly ruined our mother with his terrible betrayal, that he was a thief and a liar, that he once stepped on a bunny and broke its back merely for the crime of crossing his lawn. They may be true tales or false—it hardly matters to us. Those of us who can even remember him will hold him always as a dark, huge shape, his ugliness transformed by our infant and toddler eyes. Before we could discern good from bad cologne we loved his awful scent, before we understood that jowls were an unattractive feature on a face we loved his, and even dreamed of them, of his giant face, of the dark, secret, safe spaces of him. He was a bad man, we know it, we swear it just like our mother does. But look, there at the end of our memory and the beginning of our lives is the answer to our current dilemma: a bad man, but a true stepfather. What is Mr. Walker? A man who is a cynical and not an innocent cheat, a man who is boring but not good, a poseur with no substance under his pose, and a bad man who cannot put on the nobility of high, mighty evil: a stepfather who is not a stepfather.

How could we possibly… surely he didn't mean… none of us were the sort of person who could… Oh, how we dithered through the coming weeks and months. We had become practiced at it, and there was no grander occasion for dithering than the contemplation of a murder, no matter how richly it might be deserved. For weeks we met in secret circles, manufacturing distractions for Cousin John and Mr. Walker and even for Mother when she asked us one night at dinner, in the sleepy, drunk way she'd developed, what we were whispering about all the time. "A surprise," said Little Chris. Courtney kicked him.

"There are stages," said Carl, the best organized of any of us, and the one with the most systematic mind. He was a planner, not an actor—we knew he would never do it, but it was he who described to us, even as we traveled it, the path that would lead to freedom. "First, we have to consider it possible that he die at all. I know it's hard. It seems like he's been here forever, and like he will be here forever, but that's exactly what he wants us to think, how he wants us to feel. Eternity is his security, but he puts it on falsely."

"Hear, hear," said Courtney. "He is just another leaf."

"He is just another cupcake," said Little Chris.

"He is just another stepfather," said Ciaran. "Here today, gone tomorrow."

"Except he's not," said Carl.

"What was she thinking?" asked Carla and Christine and Caryn.

"What have I been doing?" asked Colm. "I've been asleep while he kicked her cake all over the house. While he made her into somebody who doesn't even like cake, or care about her cake!"

"Then consider," said Carl, "how very wrong it is, how very wrong it has been, how much more wrong it is going to get, and ask yourself, Can't I do this thing?"

"I can do it!" said Courtney.

"I can do it!" said Colm.

"I can do it!" said Christine.

"I can do it!" said Little Chris.

None of them could, though they passed the knife each to each, every one of them naming it distinctly—justice, restoration, peace, renewal—and they all had their turn. But Courtney hesitated in the pool house when he came in after a swim. From her hiding place she watched in fascinated horror as he changed out of his trunks, and he bent down as he slipped his legs into his trousers, so his neck was easily in her reach. Christine hesitated in the back of his car. He sat and sat in the driveway, smoking a cigar and muttering to himself. She had only to pop up and do the deed—there wasn't a cousin in sight. But she lay there, sniffing his cigar smoke and telling herself he wasn't so bad after all. Little Chris missed his cue. He went to him with a false story—he'd had a nightmare and was frightened. Couldn't he sleep in their bed? Mother only looked at him with her blank stare, but Mr. Walker said he could stay for an hour. The knife was in Little Chris's pajama bottoms. All he had to do was take it out and drive it—like he'd practiced with a watermelon—deep into the man's sleeping eye. There was light enough for it—the blinds were open and the moon was full—but he only sat and watched Mr. Walker sleep. Colm lurked uselessly in the bathroom sauna, ready to step out and stab through the shower curtain. We found him there hours after the appointed time, drenched with sweat, though the wooden room was cold. "I couldn't do it," he said. "Not while he was taking a shower."

Caryn, Ciaran, Charles, Carla, Big Chris, brother after brother and sister after sister we failed, and it finally came down to me. On the occasion of the anniversary of Calvin's death I stood in the wings of our home theater, hidden behind a red velvet curtain, listening to Mr. Walker speak. The little auditorium was full of cousins. Mother sat in the front row, her head lolling, falling asleep for one minute out of every five. When he finished speaking, as he walked backstage, I would catch him, wrap him in the curtain, and stab him as many times as I could.

"Calvert was a good boy," he said. Colm's hand went up in the audience—my siblings occupied the first five rows—but Cousin Dickie, sitting behind him, grabbed his hand and pushed it down. "We all miss him very much. He was a good boy. A good boy is to be missed, when he is gone. It reminds me of my youth, when I was a good boy, too. My papa used to tell me, 'You're a good boy. As good as they come, son.' I said it once to Calvert, too. 'You're a good boy, son.'" Oh, I wanted to stab him! I was practically licking the knife in anticipation while he mangled my brother's name, while he told tales, while his odious, invading cousins applauded his every third sentence, while he ducked and smirked and seemed to celebrate, not the anniversary of my brother's unspeakable rape and torture and murder, but the anniversary and the fact of his own absolute ascendancy over us. I tightened my grip on the handle while he bowed, and as he walked toward me I whispered it: "You are not the stepfather. There is a changeling in our mother's bed, but now he is leaving." He passed so close that I could smell him—catbox and cologne—and hear him muttering to himself. I raised the knife, but didn't let it fall. I felt faint and weak as I watched him walk away, his bottom swinging jauntily as he called for Cousin Dickie to attend him. I had to hold on to the curtain to keep from collapsing, knowing that my brothers and sisters were waiting for the screams and alarums that would signal our freedom, knowing that I had done nothing, that I would do nothing, and that we would forever and always do nothing.

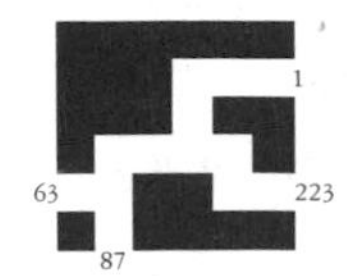

SOMOZA'S DREAM

by DANIEL OROZCO

THE PRESIDENTE-IN-EXILE is falling.

He is scuttling through the dark. His bare foot steps into something cold and slick. His leg shoots forward. He skids. The ground beneath him is suddenly gone. Synapses fire, nerve bundles twitch, and he is falling. Muscles spasm in myoclonic response. His legs jitter under the sheets. Dinorah, lying next to him, crabs away. Then an alarm, sharp and jangly. He stirs, and his tumble ceases. He reaches for the clock, kills it. Through eye slits, a vast room takes shape in the chocolate dark. Drapes thick as hides cover ceiling-high windows. Morning light bleeds in. He snorts. He hawks, swallows. He awakes, knows now where he is. His room. This world. Today: Wednesday, September 17, 1980.

The Presidente-in-Exile rises.

In the bathroom, post-shower, post-shave. He steps on the spring scale. The needle flutters shyly below one-seventy-five. Not bad. He gives his belly a small-caliber-gunshot slap. "Not bad at all," he says.

In the dressing room, his fingers glide through a kelp of neckties, fondling the Zegnas, stroking a yellow jacquard. He snaps it out, runs it through his collar. He speed-dials Bettinger, puts him on speakerphone, confirms their appointment while finishing up the knot—nine sharp, Van Damm's office at the Banco Alemán. "The fix is in, Tacho," Bettinger says. He pads to the shoe closet, selects a pair of burgundy loafers, Russia calf Henleys. "The bitch is prone," Bettinger purrs. "Knees up and ready for fucking." He drops the shoes to the carpet, kicks them parallel, steps daintily into them. He slips the heels with an ivory-handled shoehorn. Bettinger is prattling on. The Presidente-in-Exile secures his cufflinks. He moves to the dressing-room window, looks down into the courtyard two stories below, dingy and penumbral in premorning light. He can make out the white Mercedes parked under the eaves of a tree, a palsy of branches like crone's hands poised above the vehicle. His eyes adjust, and he can now see the pink turds of sticky blossoms splattered on the roof and windscreen. Bettinger is detailing financial arrangements—float risks and laundry fees and yield guarantees. He smarms and panders on speakerphone like an obscene caller. The Presidente-in-Exile cuts him off and speed-dials Gallardo. He can hear the phone ringing below, in the quarters over the carriage houses. He slips a titanium clip over the tie's face, secures a matching tie bar under the knot. When Gallardo picks up, he tells his driver to stop parking under that fucking tree, and to get that shit cleaned off the car now.

In the bedroom, he gives his suit coat a dervish-whirl and slips into it. He approaches the bed, leans down. He kisses Dinorah goodbye, reminds her about lunch. She burrows away, deep into the bedding. Body heat purls off her. She sleeps like a dead man. It is a thing about her he admires.

In the kitchen, the Presidente-in-Exile's egg is boiling. It ticks in a pot of water on the range. Cook cuts a small grapefruit in two. She Saran-wraps one half for the fridge, washes the other, and pats it dry. A timer goes ding. She reaches into the boiling water with her fingers, plucks out the egg, holds it under the cold tap for five seconds, then seats it in its special cup. Cook is a tiny woman, a Guaraní Indian of indeterminate age with jet-black hair, the hard palms of a tenant farmer, and skin dark and smooth as burnished jatoba wood. She lays out breakfast on a tray—soft-boiled egg, grapefruit, two pink packets of Sweet'N Low, two tablespoons of cottage cheese on a Rye-Krisp, six ounces of orange juice. Also, the *London Financial Times*. Also, three aspirins; he was out and about late last night. An egg spoon, a grapefruit knife, a cloth napkin. Almost ready. Cook positions a single locust-wood toothpick on a tiny copper salver. She then leans over the grapefruit, purses her lips, and releases a modest pearl of spit onto its glistening surface. Breakfast is served.

On the west patio, the Presidente-in-Exile prowls through the newspaper. The sun has just broken the ridge high above the villa. It is light and already warm. "*Buen desayuno, patrón*," cook murmurs as she places the tray before him. He rattles his paper. He does not speak to cook, who came with the villa. She retreats, returns to the kitchen to prepare luncheon. Guests are expected today—that Italian, Bettinger, and some others from the bank. No breakfast for the mistress. A late sleeper, Dinorah has yet to see the sun rise in Paraguay.

The Presidente-in-Exile repasts. He snaps a page of *El Diario*. There's been nothing about him lately, thank Christ. Since his arrival fourteen months ago the Asunción dailies have cut him no slack. Every indiscretion is rooted out and blown out of proportion—shopping sprees, drunken romps, shoving matches with cops and maitre d's, public squabbles with Dinorah. The trivia of his life as a private citizen is made public, laid out to be probed and pawed at. They went through his garbage once, and the guards caught them red-handed, knocked them around a bit, and *that* was reported—brutal suppression of the press or some such bullshit. Last year the service main in the street burst, leaving him without water for days. He called Stroessner in a fury to complain, to simply get it taken care of. The papers reported that he called the President of Paraguay to fix his plumbing. They hate him here. They think him arrogant and crass. They think he "sullies the dignity of the Republic." Sullies! That's what the papers have said! And Stroessner is no fan, either; otherwise he wouldn't let them write that shit. But Stroessner has extended his protection. And Stroessner has been well paid. But they do hate him here.

Well, fuck them. He hates them, too.

He works on his grapefruit, browses the paper. There is a full-page ad with the banner headline: *Do You Recognize This Man?* It offers a reward for information on the whereabouts of Nazi war criminal Josef Mengele. The Presidente-in-Exile snorts, flips the page. Sully my balls! Dignity of the Republic, my ass! Hideout for Nazis, haven for cocaine kings. There is an opinion piece by an Undersecretary of the Minister of the Interior railing against the feral dog population, and concluding with an appreciation of the dictator Francia, who in 1840 ordered every dog in Paraguay killed. And there is an item buried in Business Briefs, a report on unanticipated delays with a hydroelectric project down on the Argentine border, involving work stoppages and a cement embargo. Bettinger's little venture—some kind of deal with the unions that will work to financial advantage. Leave it to Bettinger: *The bitch is prone*. The Presidente-in-Exile lets *El Diario*'s pages spill to the ground. He looks at his watch. He spoons the guts of his egg onto the cottage cheese, picks up the Rye-Krisp and pushes it all into his mouth. He licks all of his fingers and wipes them with the napkin. He tosses back the orange juice and smacks his lips. "Ahhh!" He stands up, tucks the *Times* under his arm; it is air-expressed from São Paolo every morning and delivered to the villa from the airport by taxicab.

He strolls across the patio, then stops short. Something flits into the edge of his vision, and he turns. He spots it, hovering, then alighting upon the ground. He approaches. It is some kind of insect, a big one. Thin translucent wings spanning half a foot shimmer and iridesce in morning light. Perpendicular to these, a thorax over seven inches long inscribes in the air a slender and delicate arc of the deepest red—the red of arterial blood, of crème de cassis and rubies and the juice of roast meat. It is a helicopter damselfly, the rarest of the order Odonata in all the world, and far from its range in southwest Brazil. The Presidente-in-Exile would not know this. Yet he pauses. He bends down, eyes narrowed. "What the fuck," he mutters, for he has never in his life seen anything like this. He peers intently, seemingly making a study of this rare and exquisite creature—a trembling scarlet wound against the gray slate tiles. He pivots his left foot and moves the thin leather sole of his bespoke shoe centimeters above it. He taps. There is a sound like a burst of static. The insect is squashed like a bug. The Presidente-in-Exile proceeds across the patio, dragging his foot once to scrape off the gore. He cuts through the west garden, along a flagstone pathway that circles toward the front of the villa. Behind him, the discarded pages of his newspaper trip and tumble across the grounds in a zephyr that has come from nowhere on this still and windless day.

In the courtyard, Gallardo has moved the Mercedes out from

under the tree. The Mercedes is an armored vehicle custom-equipped with hardened steel body panels, 1.5-inch-thick windows of polycarbonate ballistic glass, and Kevlar-lined gas tanks. Gallardo has just finished the washing, and the car glistens all dewy in the light. He is struggling with the water hose, trying to coil it without getting his dress shirt dirty. Ten yards away, outside the gate, on Avenida España, a red Datsun blocks the driveway to the villa. Three men loll on the car, smoking cigarettes. They call to Gallardo—*maricón*, *chuparosa*, *marica chingada*. They blow him kisses. They tell him they have hoses for him to handle, if he wishes. These men are the Paraguayan bodyguards assigned by Stroessner to protect The Nation's Esteemed Guest. Gallardo snaps his wrist, flicks his finger, fires his cigarette butt. It traces an arc through the bars of the gate and lands in a burst of embers on the chest of the biggest guard. Direct hit. Beautiful. The guard leaps off the Datsun, curses, rushes the gate. But what can he do? Gallardo smiles, turns around, and waggles his ass. The guard reaches down and grabs his crotch. A piercing high-pitched whistle disrupts their *pas de deux*. From the pathway into the gardens, the Presidente-in-Exile is waving his folded paper impatiently: Let's go. The driver kicks the hose into the bushes, slips into his coat, gets in the Mercedes, and starts it up. The bodyguards squeeze into the Datsun and back the car out of the way. The gates glide open. The Mercedes exits. The Datsun follows. The gates close. Overhead, security cameras mounted atop thirty-foot poles turn slowly, taking in the perimeter with a ho-hum weariness.

In the back seat, the Presidente-in-Exile excavates his ear canal with the locust-wood toothpick. Eyes closed, he grunts blissfully. Out his passenger window, a sun-strobed flipbook of Asunción—whitewashed brick walk-ups along tree-lined avenues, nannies pushing prams, *chipa* vendors pushing carts, barefoot women with towers of folded laundry on their heads, white-suited old men walking tiny old dogs, sanitation workers in yellow coveralls sweeping dirt into the gutters. And everywhere, the guano-crowned statuary of the Republic's military heroes.

By the time they reach the Plaza of the Chaco Wars, the *señor*'s face is buried in the *Times*, and Gallardo has shaken the bodyguards. He's not supposed to do this. It pisses off the Minister of Security. But Gallardo gets bored, and it's fun, although too easy now since Stroessner's monkeys have been downgraded to that piece of shit Datsun. And besides, the *señor* doesn't care. Gallardo negotiates the traffic circle—an apocalyptic teem of limos and buses and taxicabs, dray trucks and trailer rigs, and the intrepid horse-drawn wagon. On Avenida Mariscal Lopez, he slows the Mercedes for the left onto Calle America, one of the intersections in the city with a traffic signal. The lights are his, and he would have made it but for a turquoise blue Chevy pickup that backs out of a driveway and lurches to a halt in the street. Gallardo hits the brakes. He sighs, gives his horn a toot. The truck that cuts him off is shotgunned with mud, a ferrous earth of unsettling redness. Gallardo remembers his first look at Paraguay, peering out the porthole of the Lear jet that brought them here, the Gran Chaco below him, the high desert pan that makes up the western half of this country. Flat and featureless and still, it burned red under the sun. As far as the eye could see, an ocean of blood in its doldrums. It was another world. *His* world now, he thought.

The truck does not move. Gallardo toots again, and at this moment—seconds before the rocket hits the Mercedes—he apprehends two nearly simultaneous events. The first he sees: the driver of the truck—a woman, a redhead, maybe—ducking down out of sight. And the second he hears, even with the armored-glass windows rolled up and the A/C turned up full: a brief and powerful susurration in the air like a sudden wind in the trees, or the exhalation of a thousand breaths. It is the last thing the Presidente-in-Exile's driver hears.

One block west, the red Datsun accelerates out of its turn onto Mariscal Lopez just as a fireball rises up ahead, followed by the concussion waves of the explosion. The driver of the Datsun leans on the horn, punches the gas pedal, cuts through traffic. The man next to him pounds the dashboard. The guards in the car draw their pistols, unlock and crack open the doors. They are screaming and cursing. They curse God. They curse the Minister of Security for replacing their Ford Falcons and Gran Torinos with fucking Datsuns, and curse their own mothers for bringing them into a world of bureaucrats and bean counters. And they are weeping, expelling violent and angry tears for their derailed careers, for that *puto* Gallardo smeared all over the street up ahead, and for the lost honor of the Glorious Republic of Paraguay.

In the back seat of the Mercedes, the Presidente-in-Exile looks up from his paper.

Gallardo's arms fly up over his head in a referee's goal signal of such ferocity that the arms tear off his shoulders. Gallardo's head disappears. In its place, blood-gout from the neck like a dark wet rose. Pieces of Gallardo fly up the hole in the roof, through three layers of armored steel flayed back. And the Presidente-in-Exile follows, in a geyser of metal and meat, glass and bone. Up and away.

The Presidente-in-Exile rises.

His nickname was Tacho. In history he is referred to as Tacho II—"Tacho Dos"—to distinguish him from his father, the previous El Presidente. The domestic press used to call him El

Tachito, a diminutive that implied an unfavorable comparison. This was back when the press got away with such things, before reporters started disappearing. Until the mid-nineteen-seventies, officials in the U.S. State Department called him the legitimate president of his country, for he was a vocal critic of Castro's Cuba and thus a Friend to the American People. The expatriate opposition called him *bruto*, *monopolista*, America's Fart-Sniffing Lapdog. His self-bestowed title was *jefe supremo*, and everyone in his administration referred to him as such. But he allowed the *comandantes* of *la Guardia Nacional* to address him as *señor jefe*, or simply *señor*, an informality that revealed his soft spot for the glory days, when he was once a *comandante* among them. He liked to think that this gesture put them at ease. For they were his men, his *compadres*. They drank and whored with him. But they were never at ease with him. He was volatile and petulant, a man of brittle temperament. If you brought him bad news, you were doomed. He would shove members of his cabinet, slap documents out of their hands. He would throw food at banquets, snap pencils in two, sweep the contents of laden desktops to the floor. It was said he could barely speak Spanish. This was not true; he simply preferred English, calling it his Mother Tongue. He was schooled in America, in a military academy on Long Island, then at West Point, where he was—by mandate of the Undersecretary of State for Central American Relations—a 4.0 student. He was hazed by the upperclassmen, in the name of unit loyalty and cohesion. Very often a line was crossed, and the rituals took on an erotically charged brutality. But he accepted the abuses and humiliations because he believed in the tradition of abuse and humiliation. These men did not care who he was or who his father was. He was simply a puke to them, and initiated as brutally—no more and no less—as the others were. This is what makes you a part of the whole. A puke among pukes, you become a man among men. He took little else from his formal military schooling except this, and a penchant for fancy titles and uniforms, and a love of World War II movies: *Patton*, *The Guns of Navarone*, *The Great Escape*, *The Dirty Dozen*, *Hell in the Pacific*. He was a fan of the actor Lee Marvin. He met him once at a Hollywood benefit for earthquake relief and pestered him for an autograph. The actor was drunk and belligerent, but accommodated him, and scrawled on a grimy dinner napkin:

To the President of N__________

Piss up a rope, you bastard

Lee Marvin

When his presidency was toppled, and he was run out in 1979, he was the majority stockholder of the national air and rail lines. He owned the beef ranches and the meat-processing plants, the timber tracts and the lumber mills. Coffee, cotton, bananas, sugar, tobacco, rice—from field to factory to export, it all belonged to him. Near the end, President Carter had asked him to give some of it back, to return something of his plunder—*any*thing—as a concession to history: "As a personal favor to me, Tacho." He called the President of the United States a bastard and told him to piss up a rope. His wife was an American citizen living in Miami Beach. When he joined her there, and the Carter Administration asked him to leave, she stayed. She was the daughter of diplomats, a graduate of Barnard, and had always hated his nickname. Tacho! She thought it lowborn and tawdry—a gangster's moniker. She alone among his intimates addressed him by his Christian name. Soon after their marriage she never addressed him by name at all. Within five years they lived in separate houses; within fifteen, separate countries. Yet they had five children together, who all called him *papi*. And although he was an absent father, they seemed genuinely fond of him. They were born and schooled in the United States; he joked once that he wanted them to amount to something, that the run of dictators in the family had to end. To hear an utterance such as this—wry and self-effacing—come out of a man like him was an extraordinary and unsettling event, a paradox—like a blossom from a cinder block—whose occurrence only affirmed its own impossibility. For the truth was this: he was a resolutely dull man. When he walked into a room, there was no effect. He looked liked a barber or a haberdasher, and so it was standard procedure to announce his entrances to generate the appropriate hubbub and attention. He boasted that he was a hard-ass, a control freak, a micromanager obsessed with the details. He said he wanted to know *every*thing. But when you'd tell him, he'd get bored. At cabinet meetings and security briefings he would gaze out the window at the squirrels in the trees; or release gaping yawns without covering his mouth; or intently go through his coat pockets looking for something. Then, out of sheer impatience he would cut the meeting short and hastily okay whatever was being discussed—diplomatic policy, military ops, orders of arrest and interrogation. Yet he could spend hours shopping for socks. He could fritter away an afternoon picking out the *perfect* wallet. He had health concerns. A heart attack at age forty-two scared the bejesus out of him. He was told to drop seventy pounds. He did, and he kept it off. But he bickered constantly with his doctors, fussing over his meds and his course of treatment. He obeyed them, of course. He was too scared not to. He had digestive problems—chronic intestinal gas and acid reflux—which he frequently mistook for an incipient heart attack. He brooded. He was always vaguely preoccupied or in a sulk about something. His children called him Sourpuss, Grumpy Gus, *Señor* Mopey-Pants. When he was booted from the U.S., his mistress of twelve years, a former rental-car agent and part-time model named Dinorah Sampson, joined him in the Bahamas. When denied sanctuary there, they were taken in by Paraguay. Dinorah had numerous names for him that ran the gamut of moods: Big Bear, Big Bull, *cabrón pínche*, *cabrón* Cocksucker, Lying Cocksucker Dog, My Prince, My Light, My One True Love. And swaying above him in bed, rotating gently against his decorous thrusts—for the heart attack had made him an overcautious lover—she called him *bestia*. *Mi bestia amor*, she would whisper, leaning down, the warmth of her breath in his ear, and the rasp of her cheek on his in the thick hush of the villa around them. *Bestia amor, mi corazón feroz*. My beast, my beloved. My savage, my heart.

The Presidente-in-Exile is watching his mistress swim.

He reclines in a chaise by the pool. He wears slippers and white linen slacks and a cream *guayabára*. His legs are crossed at the ankles, slim and pale as a girl's. Inside the slippers—Bergamo-silk-lined morocco loafers—his feet are bare, powdered and smooth, the heels exfoliated, the nails squared and buffed. He sips a Walker Blue Label on the rocks, and pretends to read prospectuses, a batch of them in his lap. Bettinger insists on this, Bettinger always with a hard-on for the windfall scheme, the in-and-out deal, the killing: "They all want you, Tacho." And they do. They all want his participation. Every cover letter says so: "We would be *so* pleased with your participation"; "Your participation is anxiously anticipated." He is in fact meeting tomorrow morning with people who want him, an investors group at the Banco Alemán.

The Presidente-in-Exile yawns. It is near-on dusk, too dark to read anything. But he pretends, thumbing through a folder while, from the corner of his eye, he watches his mistress swim.

She has packed on the pounds since their arrival in Asunción. He has told her: "Where is the woman I fell in love with? Where did this *cow* come from?" Sometimes he moos at her. It embarrasses him to watch her cross a room, galumphing and tottering to find her center of gravity in stiletto heels. But in the water, she is supple and dolphin-sleek. She is powerful. She laps the pool again and again, in long languid strokes that slice effortlessly through blue-black water. He marvels at her. He sips his whisky. Ice cubes shift and clink in his glass. It is humid, late winter in Paraguay—the damp immersive heat of the barber's towel, of evenings in jungle encampments and in the kitchens of childhood. On the edge of his vision, lightning bugs shimmer and weave in the twilight. He can hear the distant music and tinny laughter of a TV somewhere, the clatter of parrots in the trees, the puling of a ship's whistle on the river.

From out of the shadows, a guard steps in, salutes, approaches. And just like that, a spell is broken. He sends a message, a reminder about his engagement tonight. "Yeah, yeah," the *señor* snaps. "Go tell Gallardo." The guard salutes again, retreats.

The Presidente-in-Exile drains his whisky. He must shower and shave and dress for dinner. But he pauses. In the *cañón* behind him, beyond the wrought-iron fence, he can hear the dogs scrabbling through thick brush. (Rottweilers, he's been told. Attack dogs trained not to bark.) Far above, the roar of an airliner approaches, crescendos, recedes. All around, the sudden thrum of bush crickets revving up like evening's engines. And the bug zappers, cerulean maws afloat in the enfolding dark, and the sputter and snap of their every tiny kill. And the slap of water and the delicious insuck of Dinorah's breath at the near turn, where the Presidente-in-Exile sits, his slender ankles crossed, shaking up the ice in his empty glass, and secretly watching his mistress swim.

* * *

The Presidente-in-Exile is telling a dirty joke.

Two whores come to the handsome young priest for absolution. The priest invites them both into his tiny confessional. Sins are detailed, passions are stirred, and contortions ensue, followed by the sudden appearance of a guileless and comely young nun, and then the village idiot, who is hung like a bull. The Presidente-in-Exile is mucking up the joke, but his audience is a forgiving one. Aurelio and Méme on leave from the counterinsurgency back home; Lucho, in from Rio; and Luís and Humberto and Papa Chepe from Miami—some of the old *comandantes* down for a visit, in a private dining room at Bolsi, the toniest of Asunción's downtown restaurants.

The Presidente-in-Exile's joke careens brakeless down its narrative tracks, the confession stall impossibly stuffed with one character after another—concupiscent anarchy, a Marx Brothers porn flick. The *comandantes* bark and roar with laughter. They are tossing back carafes of wine, pounding the table and one another's backs. These are big men, and the cozy private room is a crush of humped backs and meaty forearms and big ruddy faces. In the world of the joke, the *alcalde*'s virgin daughter has just entered the confessional. Papa Chepe runs out of the room and returns dragging the maître d'hôtel, a regal gray-haired woman in her fifties. The archbishop has now arrived for a surprise inspection, and Méme rushes into the kitchen, rousts a busboy, a Guaraní Indian who speaks no Spanish. Papa Chepe kisses the maître d' on the mouth and pushes her to the carpet. Méme shoves the busboy on top of her. The restaurant proprietor, accompanied by three male diners, enters to attempt a rescue of the maître d'. Papa Chepe pulls a pistol and puts the muzzle in the proprietor's mouth. The proprietor pisses his pants. Exit male diners. A vengeful pimp has arrived at the church and approaches the ruckus in the confessional, whereupon the proprietor is thrown to the carpet and compelled to gyrate at gunpoint against the busboy. Then the police arrive. Aurelio snatches Papa Chepe's gun and submerges it in a tureen of *bori-bori*. The police are nervous. Their captain approaches the Guest of Honor warily. But the Guest of Honor is in a good mood. He laughs and cajoles. He peels bills off a wrist-thick wad and moves through the cadre of cops, tucking the money into shirt pockets and cap bands. The police officers talk amongst themselves for a moment, then arrest the proprietor, close the restaurant, and post guards outside.

Lucho raids the bar, returns with bottles of Chivas and Rémy. The men drink, sated and suddenly quiet, pensive. Luís takes a pull and passes the bottle and begins to reminisce about his first skirmish, against coffee farmers in rebel territory. His story, of a green recruit, of a boy compelled by duty to become a man, has the rest of them nodding wistfully, until more stories come—liquor-stoked recollections of the bunkhouse and the whorehouse, chronicles of love and war, and of the lusts of blood both literal and metaphoric. They regale each other with tall tales of jungle work and counterintel, and with anecdotes from the interrogation arts—stories of baseball bats and needle-nosed pliers and toilet bowls filled with excrement, stories of the light socket and the copper wire, of the salt and the wound, of the flesh and the spirit. Nostalgia like an emetic disgorges from them one dewy reminiscence after another until they are left weeping and hoarse, and Papa Chepe totters off the floor and caroms into the arms of the Presidente-in-Exile and tearfully kisses him on the lips. "*Maricones!*" Luís shouts. They all laugh. The Presidente-in-Exile stands up and speaks haltingly. He stammers something about family and comradeship, and discipline and duty, about his father and his legacy, and justice and reckoning and getting fucked in the ass by history. It goes around and around and then goes nowhere at all and although it makes little sense, it is heartfelt. And so his men are moved. They cheer and curse and roil around their Presidente. They hoist him upon their shoulders and carry him about, and as they pass him across the threshold into the main dining floor, they whack his head on the lintel. Blood laces down his face and into his eyes, where it stings and mingles with his tears. For the Presidente-in-Exile is crying—a happy man, wobbly and unsteady upon the shoulders of his men, struggling for balance with one outstretched arm, and with the hand of the other pressed to his chest, attending to the barreling pulse of a damaged, brimming heart.

Two men meet at the newsstand in the lobby of the Hotel Méridien in Dakar. They greet each other effusively, hugging and kissing and clasping hands. "*T'as l'air super bien, mon ami!*" "*Non, non, c'est toi qui a l'air bien!*" They step outside, walk arm in arm. The plaza they cross hums and bustles on this clear and balmy late afternoon. City workers in white coveralls crawl all over a gigantic bronze statue of Lady Liberty astride a stallion in full gallop. They are festooning her with ribbons and garlands of green and yellow and red. Bunting streams from the spear she holds aloft. In the distance, the pock of fireworks. The city of Dakar anticipates a celebration—Senegal's Independence Day. April 4, 1980.

The two men order Nescafés at a makeshift bistro. In their brief stroll from the hotel—down a narrow street off the boulevard, and into an arterial maze of dank alleys—the neighborhood has shifted from upscale to dicey. Alone, the men are much less effusive. In low and perfunctory tones, arrangements are made, and money changes hands—a fat manila envelope tucked into the folds of *Le Soleil*, pushed across the table.

Six weeks later, a freighter under Bahamian flag sails west from the Port of Dakar into the Atlantic, bound for Colombia, and laden with phosphate ore, peanuts, cotton, millet, salted fish. Among its unregistered cargo: raw heroin, duffel bags of marijuana, and a small but heavy wooden crate labeled TRACTOR PARTS, containing sixteen Chinese B-50 rocket grenades, four Soviet RPG-7 launchers, and four boxes of percussion caps.

By mid-August, the crate sits unclaimed in a warehouse in Bogotá. One moonless evening, two Lincoln Continentals filled with men arrive. Money changes hands—currency stacked, plastic-wrapped, and duct-taped into two tidy bricks. The crate is cracked open. Three launchers and twelve rockets are removed and transferred to the trunks of the vehicles. The rest is repackaged into a smaller crate, labeled HOSPITAL SUPPLIES. Some ancillary business is then transacted—two of the men are shot in the head, dismembered, and sealed into steel drums filled with used motor oil.

A week later, the crate is loaded onto a van and driven to a municipal airport in Quito, where it is relabeled TOOL & DIE and flown to Sucre. At the port of entry, a tightly rubber-banded wad of bills the size of a shotgun cartridge is slipped into the palm of a customs official. The crate is released and transferred onto a steam packet heading down the mighty, muddy Rio Pilcomayo. It arrives in Asunción by the end of the month, in the last cool days of August, when the rains have subsided and the city has been washed clean for the last time. The crate is opened by three men and two women in the basement of a rented house on the corner of Avenida España and Calle America. It has been securely sealed, and with no pry-bar they all struggle to get the box open, working methodically, quietly, so as not to alert the neighbors. They use screwdrivers and claw hammers, a fire poker and the blade edge of a shovel. They lift out the rockets and the launcher and the percussion caps. They hug and kiss. They stash their booty in a crawlspace behind the furnace, and go upstairs and toast each other with cans of Bud and Coca-Cola. They drink to truth and beauty, to Marx and Dario, and to justice and the death of tyrants. They put the hi-fi on low, mambo to Pérez Prado, slow dance to Iglesias. A bottle of rum has been pulled out, and Osvaldo plays bartender, passes drinks around. He mixes a stiff one for Annalisa. He will make the move on her tonight. She is three months pregnant, by Ramón, their *compa* just over the border in Argentina. But what the hell. She is incandescent tonight, ecstatic and receptive. And Osvaldo is charming and clever. And these are auspicious times.

The Presidente-in-Exile is taking a leak.

It's a good one, the kind you remember for the rest of your life—a bladder-dump, one of those butt-puckering gushers that makes the eyes flutter and elicits a rapturous "Ahhh!" The night is cool, and steam rises where he misses the wall he's aiming for. Where he doesn't miss, the cataract lays black washes onto the sand-colored stone. He chokes off, downshifts to intermittent trickles. He leans forward and settles his cheek onto the nubby granite wall, murmurs sweetly into the stone: "Fuck you." Over and over, like a lover's entreaty: "Fuck you fuck you fuck you..."

Gallardo waits a few yards away, beyond the hedgerow, pacing next to the Mercedes, which is parked at the curb on this quiet street. The entrance to the compound is on the main boulevard, up on Avenida Mariscal Lopez. A twenty-foot-high stone wall topped with iron pikes runs along the length of the street. Gallardo paces, smoking a cigarette. He has just gotten the Presidente-in-Exile from Bolsi—No matter what, he was told, get me out of there before midnight. And they were heading home, until the *señor* directed him here. Gallardo hates this detour. It is embarrassing for him, having to explain to whoever may come upon them. For the most part, the guards here don't seem to mind, which puzzles him. But what if they come across a guard who does, some greenhorn coming at him with guns blazing? This is not how he wants to die, on lookout while his boss pees on U.S. property.

Gallardo sucks on his cigarette, drags deeply. Up ahead, a figure appears from around the corner, backlit by street lights from Mariscal Lopez. Gallardo watches the figure see him, see the car, watches the guard draw his M-16 and move briskly toward him. He drops his butt, and with his arms outstretched walks slowly toward the advancing guard, putting distance between him and the Mercedes. "*Está bien, está bien,*" he calls out. "Is okay." Although he still holds his arms wide, hands in plain view, Gallardo relaxes a bit. He recognizes this Marine, this *negro americano.*

"Is okay." When he hears the voice, gets a better look at the car, the Marine guard stands down. It's that tin-pot dictator, pissing in the bushes. He sighs, shoulders his weapon, greets the driver. "How you doing?" He takes a cigarette from behind his left ear, where he'd tucked it for this little break. "Is good, is good," the driver responds. The Marine lights up, and the driver makes the international hand gestures for bumming a smoke. The Marine gives him one, watches him slip it into a shirt pocket. "For later," he tells him. Both men hear a sharp metallic rapping. They turn to see the dictator finish pounding on the roof of the car and climb into the back seat. The driver rolls his eyes, smiles sheepishly.

The Marine can't believe this shit is allowed. But the orders have been handed down, some unofficial understanding between nations: Let this fuck-wad piss on the United States Embassy. "*Vaya con Dios*," the Marine tells the driver. The driver returns the blessing, then says, "Yankee go home!" The Marine laughs. He finishes his cigarette. He watches the Mercedes pull out and make a three-point turn and drive past him, back toward Avenida Lopez. In the back seat, the ex-dictator is in shadow, but his head swivels as the vehicle moves past the embassy guard, who sends off our Presidente-in-Exile with the smartest salute he can muster, and the precisely mouthed words: "Fuck you, too."

Standing in front of a hand mirror hung by a nail on the wall, cook claws baby oil into her long black hair. She pulls and separates, creating three thick lustrous cords. She plaits them tightly together, interweaving a long strip of bright orange muslin. She lays the braid over her left breast. No, the right one. Yes, better. She slips on a pair of soft black flats that she has spit-polished with the inside hem of her skirt. She owns two pairs of shoes—sneakers for work, and these. Although cook's ankles are thick and sturdy, her feet splayed and rough-hewn, these shoes somehow render them fine-boned and delicate. She puts a peppermint leaf into her mouth and crushes it. She slips her bag over her shoulder. She exits her apartment—a single room, tiny and spare and very clean—and leaves the villa grounds via the rear service gate. She waves to the guard in the guard-booth. He waves back. She strolls a half mile down the road, to the *mercado*. There is a coffee bar there, open late. She sits at the counter and orders a *café con leche* and a biscotti. She pulls a *fotonovela* out of her bag. It is entitled *Por un beso*, and relates the adventures of a beautiful, innocent village girl in big, bad Rio de Janeiro. Because she cannot read Spanish, she gets most of the storyline from the actions depicted in the drawings. Cook gleans that the heroine in the picture panels seems to triumph, that she thwarts Lothario, and maintains Virtue, and gets a promotion at her office job. As she reads, she looks up from the paperback often, until—finally—her young friend Osvaldo pops in. He approaches her at the counter and smiles. "*Mba'éichapa nde pyhare, Ynez.*" Cook smiles back.

Cook's name is Ynez.

She has been with the villa for decades—sent to her great-aunt when she was a child, and trained by her, and taking over her duties when the woman died. The owner of the villa is a Guaraní, and he has insisted that whoever leases his property must also take the cook, and the two Guaraní gardeners, and the old kennel master. Her whole life has been with the villa, and it has been a *good* life. Her mother is dead, her father old and blind and alone. She visits him once a year, up in the Gran Chaco, in a desolate village that the young have abandoned. She sends him money each month. He is grateful. "You are an ugly girl," he tells her, running his chitinous palms gently over her face. "But you are a saintly girl." And she has always believed this to be so. Until Osvaldo, who gave her a second look one day. And whom she has run into in this coffee bar two nights a week for the past month and a half. And whose motives have always been transparent to her.

She doesn't care. For Osvaldo is young and handsome, all toothy smiles and barrel-chested swagger. He is much too young to be flirting with such as her. But he does. She can see him looking for her when he enters, can see him light up and put on that smile and that swagger as he comes to her. Other women glance up at him, and they watch him come to her! He is not old and dull, like the kennel master, whom she sleeps with occasionally—a kind man, but so diffident, and dull. Osvaldo is brash, voluble. He raises his voice, and then brings it down to a growl. He flings his hands and arms about as he talks. His Guaraní is really quite good for a non-native, with the trace of an accent—Argentine, most likely. He is charming. He is loud and flashy, and asks too many questions. And then there is that wig—lopsided and shiny, and a shade of brown not found in nature, a wig that shouts WIG! to everyone. He is *so* obvious. She worries for him.

Osvaldo orders a *tereré*, with two straws. He sips, asks about her book, about the story it tells. He pushes the drink toward her, and asks about her day with the *patrón*.

All her life, she has kept her head down and worked hard, knowing or caring very little about the tenants of the villa: the Germans who stayed for over a decade, quiet and monastic in their habits, until they left quite hurriedly one night; the university professors from Canada, hippie-types who spoke Guaraní and insisted on eating only native cuisine; the Colombian, of whom she was very afraid, and who lasted only a few months before Stroessner sent soldiers to put him on a plane out of the country.

And then, the *patrón*. Since his arrival he was always going on about how awful Asunción was—a backwater infested with bugs and Indians, with shitty food and crooked cops and not one decent nightclub. She did not understand why a rich man who could live anywhere chose to live in a place he hated. Until Osvaldo explained to her that he had no choice. And in this way she learned about the *patrón*—his infamy, his fall, and his exile.

She takes a deep draw from Osvaldo's *tereré*. It is ice-cold, as is the custom. It hurts going down. She tells him about her day with the *patrón*, tells him about the luncheon she's expected to prepare tomorrow, after his return from a 9 a.m. meeting at the

Banco Alemán downtown. She gives it all to him so he does not have to fish for the details. It is her gift to him.

She watches his eyes shift, sees them sharpen and glimmer for a moment as he takes in what she has just told him. And then he is Osvaldo again, brash and gay, slapping his palms on the counter, changing the subject. He tells her about a fender bender in front of the kiosk this morning, about the drivers who got out of their respective cars to confront each other. They were veterans of the Chaco War, old men in their seventies, wearing identical medals on their dark wool suits. They stumbled as they took swings at each other and missed, until—exhausted in the midday heat—they collapsed, and Osvaldo had to call an ambulance to haul them away. She loves how he regales in the telling of the incident, whether it happened or not. She is rapt, and hopes that her attention on him will keep him with her a bit longer. But she has given him what he's wanted. He glances at his watch, slaps his forehead. He remembers an urgent bit of business he must attend to, an errand for a cousin. And then, all showy and clownish, he brings Ynez's left hand to his mouth. She watches him kiss it. She feels suddenly bereft, lost. The floor beneath her seems to shift and sag. He bids her good night. "*Jajoecha peve, Ynez.*"

Until we meet again.

And then he is gone.

The evening is clear and cool. The markets and shops have closed, and the cafés are putting up their chairs. The boulevard teems with late-night strollers slowly heading home. Cook joins them. Her route back to the villa is a riot of plumeria in full bloom. The air is glutted with fragrance. Sagging branches overhang sidewalks everywhere. Spatulate petals reach down fat and heavy into her face. She swats them away.

She waves to the guard in the guardbooth. He waves back.

Inside her apartment, she drops her bag and kicks off her shoes. She stares at a piece of honey cake wrapped in wax paper on the nightstand. She picks it up and goes outside. She walks to the iron fence that borders the *cañón*, and kneels down. She squeezes the honey cake between her hands, and waits. The kennel master has told her not to risk this, has warned her that his children are unpredictable, that they can be capricious and willful. They are killers.

Soon the dogs come, pounding through brush, slamming into the fence, taking the cake from her. There is the snuffling of the dogs and the sound of their tongues on her, and then another noise, somebody speaking to her. She turns around. It is the *patrón*, barking at her in English. He stands there in his stocking feet, with his belt undone, and a chicken leg in his hand. Here is the man who tossed handcuffed prisoners out of airplanes over the Pacific Ocean, the man who invented this innovation for disappearing dissidents. Here he stands, shouting about who knows what, wagging a chicken leg at her. She watches a trickle of blood thread down his forehead. An omen, she thinks. She gazes at him. She feels nothing. She will perhaps feel nothing for a long time. Except maybe for these dogs. She turns to them now, watches their fat pink tongues flicking out of the bushes between the iron pickets, rasping at her fingers and palms, and doing a thorough job of cleaning her hands.

At dusk, the dogs are loosed. The sun dips below the ridge behind the villa, a photosensor engages an electric switch, and the kennel gate swings open. The two Rottweilers set off separately, bounding over root and tree-fall and crashing through sedge and bramble until they join each other in a defile that cuts to the top of the ridge. They piss along the perimeter of the *cañón* fence, metal chain-link topped with boas of razor wire. They gallop back and forth along the ridge—lunging, tongue-lolling lopes. Paladino, the younger, harries Cerbero, nipping and snarling at him, always testing the older dog. They settle down and linger here in the waning light, splay-legged and slit-eyed and content, their massive skulls bobbing, their damp noses twitching at the verdant rankness of Asunción—acrid smoke from distant forest fires; musks of sewage and slag from the river, and eddies of sweet decay from landfills; ooze of meat from the slaughterhouse district; the complex admixtures of blossoms and bleach, baked bread and dog shit, mown grass and motor oil. And always, intermingled, the slick and slippery undertow of the collective human scent. Only when it is full-on dark—when the sun has dissolved like a tablet into the Pilcomayo, draining the colors from dusk—only then do they descend from the highest point of the property. Until first light, when they know to return to the kennel before the gates swing shut, the dogs have the run of this *cañón*. For the next eight or so hours, they are free to romp and ramble, and hunt and kill.

Guinea pigs are abundant year-round, as are lizards and toads. In summer, animals foraging for food and water come out of the jungle, and down from the highlands. They breach the fence, attracted to the mulch of fallen fruit beneath the lime and papaya trees. Armadillo, capybara, anaconda, a feral cat or two. Once, a tapir, far from its range, a two-hundred-pound calf that broke through and in a panic could not find its way out. It took them all night to chase it down. And once there was a man, the greasy stink of him coming at them in torrents—the hot scent of prey like a desperate itching in the middle of the brain.

Once a week the master comes. He sweeps out the kennel, refreshes their bedding and their water trough. He brushes each of them, massages their hindquarters. Always Cerbero first.

Paladino—patient—waits his turn. The master looks into their ears, checks their teeth, tends the occasional wound. He examines their droppings. He runs them through their commands. *Sit! Stay! Catch! Hold! Tear! Finish! Good boy!* When they are done, he kisses each of them. He is not afraid. The dogs know this. The scent of the master is neither of predator nor prey, of friend nor foe. He is simply the master. Before he leaves, he reaches into a waxed bag and throws a slab of round steak before each of them. The dogs watch him, mouths shut, eyes steady. On his command, they fall on the meat. They take food from no other.

But, there *is* one other they are drawn to. She is redolent of blood, and deep in the fissures of canine memory lies a trace of what the tang of her blood once meant. (For Cerbero and Paladino are neutered males, and while the madness of the rut is absent, the absence is always present in them—dogs know their balls have been cut off.) It is this trace—the faint and fleeting residues of estrus and the mount—that brings them running. But they take food from her because it is the scent of the master that prevails. He whelms her, and she is steeped in him, and but for that, they would not come to her and gift her with their gentle mouthings. But for that, they would instead do all they could to clamp down on her hands and pull her in chunks through the *cañón* fence.

The Presidente-In-Exile is bleeding.

He holds a blood-dappled monogrammed hanky to his head. The cut is above the hairline, a tiny wound, but a real bleeder. He has just gotten home, flung his coat off, kicked off his pee-splashed Berluti mocs. He stands in front of the portable Sony in the kitchen, looking at a documentary—a history of the War of the Triple Alliance. In 1864, Francisco Solano López, third President of the Republic, invaded Brazil, then declared war on Argentina and Uruguay, engaging a doomed six-year campaign that wiped out two-thirds of the entire population; by 1870, there were only 30,000 men left in all of Paraguay. The debacle is rendered in history as a glorious act of national pride and will, and the ten-part documentary about it is aired on state television again and again. Aside from World Cup soccer in the fall, and Miss Universe and the Oscars in the spring, television in Paraguay is a tedious déjà-vu zone, awash in reruns of Stroessner's inaugural addresses and cooking shows from Argentina (*¡Mundo de bistec! ¡Barbacoa loco!*) and American sitcoms (*Hogan's Heroes*, *Green Acres*, *Happy Days*). And of course, the War of the Triple Fucking Alliance.

The Presidente-in-Exile sighs, flips off the TV. He cocks his head, listens. He drops the bloody hanky on a kitchen counter. He opens the refrigerator, finds a pair of baked chickens, and tugs at a drumstick until it comes off. He pads to the sliding glass door, unlocks and opens it, crosses to the iron fence a few yards away. He ratatats the chicken leg between two pales, and waits. He knows the dogs are trained not to take food. They never come. But tonight he hears them, panting and tumbling down the hill, crashing through undergrowth, then moving past him, along the fence perimeter, toward the back of the house. Could they be hunting? He has heard that the dogs once killed and ate a man. Gallardo—talking to the gardeners, or chatting up Stroessner's monkeys—has relayed such stories to him. A drug lord tossed an informant to them, for vengeance and sport. A Mossad agent prowling for Nazis got trapped in the *cañón*. Some street kid climbed over the fence on a dare. The stories are varied; they always change, and they all intrigue the Presidente-in-Exile.

He follows the dogs, along the gravel walkway that runs the

length of the house for thirty yards, toward the back. Where the cook lives. He comes around the corner, into a tiny patio area no more than fifteen feet square. A pool of light from cook's open apartment door illuminates the soles of her feet, the backs of her calves. She is on her knees, up against the *cañón* fence. Her back is to him, and her hands are moving in the gaps between the iron pales.

The Presidente-in-Exile is peeved. She is feeding the dogs. "You're not supposed to do that," he says to her. He can see their tongues, pink and sudden at her hands in the dark. "Hey!" he says. "What the fuck are you doing?" She turns, and her level gaze confuses him. He looks at the chicken leg in his hand, points it at her. "You stop that *now*." But she doesn't. She seems unfazed, perhaps even bored. There was a time when he could have done anything to her and gotten away with it. There was a time when women were afraid of him. But he sees nothing in this *indio*'s face. It is the face of a woman who wouldn't care what you did to her. She turns away, back to the dogs.

And as swiftly as it came, his anger is gone, dropping away like a stone off a precipice. He sighs, picks his way back down the gravel path toward the kitchen. He gnaws absently at his drumstick. His eye stings and he wipes at it. Blood. The cut has opened up again. Something in his stomach shifts and plops, and he grimaces. He'll need a bromo before bed, and the thought of this leaves him somehow disconsolate, and vaguely depressed, and only adds to the chain of disappointments in this life of exile.

The Assassin of the Presidente-in-Exile gets the word. Osvaldo, calling from the magazine kiosk on Avenida España, repeats the go code into the phone: *Blanco*, *blanco*, *blanco*. The Assassin of the Presidente-in-Exile loads a rocket into the launcher and sets a percussion cap. He hoists the launcher onto his shoulder and rests the barrel on the lip of the sill. Through the open window he trains the sight on a statue in a sliver of park across the street. He focuses on it—Francisco Solano López, killed at the glorious battle of Cerro Corá in 1870. He can hear Annalisa warming up the Chevy pickup in the driveway outside. The engine rumbles precariously. They've had trouble with the throttle, and she revs it up. He can see Josias at the curb watching for the Mercedes, his M-16 shielded by a topcoat draped over his wrist. He sees Lourdes across the street, minding a baby stroller filled with Browning 9mm pistols and an Ingram MAC-10. He sees Josias wave, hears the truck ease down the length of the driveway, piston-slap rattle receding. Through the sight he watches the Mercedes glide into view. He lifts the barrel of the launcher off the sill and glides with it until the Mercedes is stopped short, blocked by Annalisa in the Chevy. He seeks the trigger and finds it and nestles it into the crook of his index finger.

The Assassin of the Presidente-in-Exile inhales. He is suddenly taken with the clarity of the scene before him. What a beautiful morning! Sunshine pours into the street, filling it like a container. The Mercedes sits submerged in radiance, tense and gleaming in honeyed light, as if straining against the very weight of light itself. It shimmers within the cross-hatched field of the launcher's reticule.

The Assassin of the Presidente-in-Exile exhales. The rocket fires, and scoots waggle-tailed toward its target twenty yards away, slips into the armored Mercedes. The Mercedes levitates for an instant and disappears behind coils of black smoke. The Assassin of the Presidente-in-Exile drops the launcher, stands up, peels off his latex gloves. The sofa behind his station at the window smolders from the rocket exhaust. A black circle six feet across is seared into the wall; the paint in it bubbles and pops. He goes out the back door of the house, into the yard. He can hear the *ack-ack* of semi-automatic fire—Josias and Annalisa and Lourdes emptying their weapons into the wreckage. He passes through a gate in the property fence that opens onto an alley, turns right onto Avenida Venezuela, and strolls to a bus stop at the corner. The crowd there is looking past him, gawking upward at a column of smoke rising thickly into the blue. He turns, gawks with them. He recalls something from a book he'd been reading, a history of the North American Indians, and he tries to remember what it was Sioux warriors told each other before going into battle. The bus pulls up, and he stands on line with the other commuters. He jingles the change in his pocket. He can hear the click and pop of pistol fire, benign in the distance. The bodyguards in the Datsun have arrived. He pays the driver, moves into the press of standing passengers, situates himself near the back door. He pats the Browning pistol in his coat pocket, and says a prayer for Josias and Annalisa and the others—his *compas* for these past fifteen months.

And then it comes to him, and he smiles for remembering it. *Today is a good day to die.*

In the back seat of the Mercedes, the Presidente-in-Exile looks up from his paper.

The newspaper in his hands disappears, goes Poof! like a magician's trick. His hands smoke and glow and burst into flames. The suit he is wearing vaporizes. His eyeballs explode, and his mouth fills with gasoline. The back seat of the Mercedes becomes an arena of transformation, the effulgent white-hot heart of a flame brighter than a hundred suns, a whirlpool of shrapnel and fire taking its passenger apart. Hands—gone! Yet there is the glide of silk on the fingertips. Eyes—no more! Yet, before them hang the pale breasts of a first love, a girl from Stony Point, New York, named Amanda. The slide of gasoline on the tongue gives way to the textures of *pulque*, milky and sweet. There is the smell of Cohibas, of Tres Flores brilliantine. The scrape of a father's beard against skin, the slap of breakers on a shore like the beating of a giant's heart. The tug of an erection. Strokes and caresses. A pressing upon the chest like the vise grips of God. Gunfire in the distance. There is running, stumbling. There is falling. Freefall. And amid the onslaught of sensations without stimulus and memories without context, amid the random firing of synapses in a brain poaching inside its own skull, what is revealed and understood of a life in its last instant—as the Presidente-in-Exile looks up from his paper and mutters, "Fuck me" when his driver's head disappears—what is understood is simply this: the transformative power of weaponry and surprise.

In the back patio of a trattoria three blocks away, an old man sits hunched over the morning paper laid out on the table before him, waiting for his espresso to cool. With his right hand he flips the pages of *El Diario*. With his left he holds the crown of a gray felt fedora and fans himself with the brim. He turns a page, peers at it. The fedora in his left hand stops moving. His breath catches, stops, begins again. He throws his hat on the page open before him. He looks around with histrionic furtiveness, in the manner of a lonely old man reveling in the melodrama of the moment. He sees mostly other lonely old men. One is tearing up a croissant and feeding the pieces to a tiny yellow dog in his lap. Two others sit staring down at a checkerboard between them.

He nudges the fedora aside, revealing a full-page ad with the headline: *Do You Recognize This Man?* There is a picture, a blowup of a passport photo from some twenty-five years ago, of a glowering, beetle-browed man with black slicked-back hair and a broad, neatly trimmed moustache. The hair is now chalk white, full and untended. The moustache is ragged, and the brows have thinned out. The face is tanned. The glower is gone.

The old man reaches for his demitasse and tosses back the espresso. He shudders, gleefully. He calls to the waiter, orders another, and a crème de cassis as well. The waiter looks him in the face, bows, departs. Nothing. The old man giggles. He ponders a delightful paradox of photo portraiture—the picture in the paper is an accurate likeness of himself a quarter century ago, but so much so that no one will recognize it as him today. Remarkable. "*Ausgezeignet!*" he says aloud. He shudders again, claps his hands. His chair gives a sudden leap. He hears a muffled roar, feels movement in the ground beneath his feet. The other old men look past him, upward, and he turns, cranes his neck. Above the apartment building across the street, a column of thick black smoke jeweled with embers boils upward. The waiter arrives, sets the drinks down, stands and gapes with the others, all of them watching the smoke drape across the sky like a closing curtain. The old man squints, sniffs. He can smell diesel fuel, burning oil, the stink of molten rubber. And something else, something distant and familiar. He reaches for his crème de cassis, raises the glass, and carefully brings it to his lips. He pauses. Yes, of course—the smell of burning flesh. He sips the thick sweet syrup. The liqueur is served neat here, to the brim in a warmed cordial glass, in the style called Martyr's Blood. And although still atremble with giddiness, the old man spills not a drop as he drinks to whoever has died today.

* * *

Meanwhile, back at the villa, a bony cat rasps its tongue at a congealing smear of mashed bug on the slate tiles of the west patio. A wind from nowhere disturbs the trees and a blossom-fall erupts, sending slant flurries across the grounds. Security cameras tucked high and low throughout the compound click and whir to each other. In the kitchen, cook slathers chicken parts with mayo, dices tomatoes and onions, and puts water up to boil, going through the motions of preparing a luncheon that will not be served. And upstairs, in the master bedroom, the mistress Dinorah sleeps. Twenty years from now she will serve iced tea to fellow expats on the balcony of her modest condo in Coral Gables. She will regale them with the stories they want to hear, of her life with El Presidente—the palaces and the private jets, the fêtes and the galas, stories of jewelry and couture and thousand-dollar bottles of wine, of weekends abroad and late intimate dinners with movie stars. But she will keep to herself the details of their last shimmering days together, when the ardor of their love seemed to flower even in the ignominy of exile, when they swam and gamboled in lagoons under the stars, and made love all night and toasted the dawn with champagne, the both of them—sated and spent—taken truly aback by the remarkable clarity of light at sunrise in Paraguay.

But for now she sleeps, deep and hard, unencumbered by knowledge or memory or dream. She sleeps like a dead man.

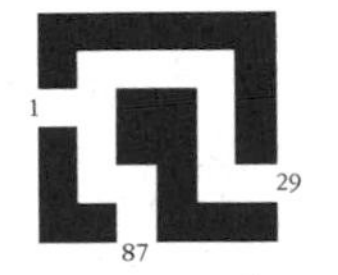

NEW BOY

by RODDY DOYLE

CHAPTER ONE
HE IS VERY LATE

He sits.

He sits in the classroom. It is his first day.

He is late.

He is five years late.

And that is very late, he thinks.

He is nine. The other boys and girls have been like this, together, since they were four. But he is new.

—We have a new boy with us today, says the teacher-lady.

—So what? says a boy who is behind him.

Other boys and some girls laugh. He does not know exactly why. He does not like this.

—Now now, says the teacher-lady.

She told him her name when he was brought here by the man but he does not now remember it. He did not hear it properly.

—Hands in the air, she says.

All around him, children lift their hands. He does this too. There is then, quite quickly, silence.

—Good, says the teacher-lady. —Now.

She smiles at him. He does not smile. Boys and girls will laugh. He thinks that this will happen if he smiles.

The teacher-lady says his name.

—Stand up, she says.

Again, she says his name. Again, she smiles. He stands. He looks only at the teacher-lady.

—Everybody, this is Joseph. Say Hello.

—Hello!

—HELLO!

—HELL-OHH!

—Hands in the air!

The children lift their hands. He also lifts his hands. There is silence. It is a clever trick, he thinks.

—Sit down, Joseph.

He sits down. His hands are still in the air.

—Now. Hands down.

Right behind him, dropped hands smack the desk. It is the so-what boy.

—Now, says the teacher-lady.

She says this word many times. It is certainly her favorite word.

—Now, I'm sure you'll all make Joseph very welcome. Take out your *Maths Matters*.

—Where's he from, Miss?

It is a girl who speaks. She sits in front of Joseph, two desks far.

—We'll talk about that later, says the teacher-lady. —But maths first.

That is the first part of her name. Miss.

—Miss, Seth Quinn threw me book out the window.

—Didn't!

—Yeh did.

—Now!

Joseph holds his new book very tightly. It is not a custom he had expected, throwing books out windows. Are people walking past outside warned that this is about to happen? He does not know. He has much to learn.

—Seth Quinn, go down and get that book.

—I didn't throw it.

—Go on.

—It's not fair.

—Now.

Joseph looks at Seth Quinn. He is not the so-what boy. He is a different boy.

—Now. Page 37.

No one tries to take Joseph's book. No more books go out the window.

He opens his book at Page 37.

The teacher-lady talks at great speed. He understands the numbers she writes on the blackboard. He understands the words she writes. LONG DIVISION. But he does not understand what she says, especially when she faces the blackboard. He does not put his hand up. He watches the numbers on the blackboard. It is not so very difficult.

A finger pushes into his back. The so-what boy. Joseph does not turn.

—Hey. Live-Aid.

Joseph does not turn.

The so-what boy whispers.

—Live-Aid. Hey, Live-Aid. Do they know it's Christmas?

It is Monday, the tenth day of January. It is sixteen days after

Christmas. This is a very stupid boy.

But Joseph knows that this is not to do with Christmas or the correct date. He knows he must be careful.

The finger prods his back again, harder, very hard.

—Christian Kelly!

—What?

It is the so-what boy. His name is Christian Kelly.

—Are you annoying Joseph there?

—No.

—Is he, Joseph?

Joseph shakes his head. He must speak. He knows this.

—No.

—I'm sure he's not, she says.

This is strange, he thinks. Her response. Is it another trick?

—Sit up straight so I can see you, Christian Kelly.

—He was poking Joseph's back, Miss.

—Shut up.

—He was.

—Fuck off.

—Now!

Miss the teacher-lady stares at a place above Joseph's head. There is silence in the classroom. The hands-in-the-air trick is certainly not necessary.

—God give me strength, she says.

But why? Joseph wonders. What is she about to do? There is nothing very heavy in the classroom.

She stares again. For six seconds, exactly. Then she taps the blackboard with a piece of chalk.

—Take it down.

He waits. He watches the other children. They take copy books from their school bags. They open the copy books. They draw the margin. They stare at the blackboard. They write.

They stare again. They write. A girl in the desk beside him takes a pair of glasses from a small black box that clicks loudly when she opens it. She puts the glasses onto her face. She looks at him. Her eyes are big. She smiles.

—Specky fancies yeh.

It is Christian Kelly.

—You're dead.

CHAPTER TWO
THE FINGER

—You're dead, says Christian Kelly.

This is the dangerous boy who sits behind Joseph. This boy has just told Joseph that he is dead. Joseph must understand this statement, very quickly.

He does not turn, to look at Christian Kelly.

Miss, the teacher-lady, has wiped the figures from the blackboard. She writes new figures. Joseph sees: these are problems to be solved. There are ten problems. They are not difficult.

What did Christian Kelly mean? *You are dead*. Joseph thinks about these words and this too is not difficult. It is very clear that Joseph is not dead. So, Christian Kelly's words must refer to the future. *You will be dead*. All boys must grow and eventually die—Joseph knows this; he has seen dead men and boys. Christian Kelly's words are clearly intended as a threat, or promise. *I will kill you*. But Christian Kelly will not murder Joseph just because the girl with the magnified eyes smiled at him. *I will hurt you*. This is what Christian Kelly means.

Joseph has not yet seen this Christian Kelly.

It is very strange. Joseph must protect himself from a boy he has not seen. Perhaps not so very strange. He did not see the men who killed his father.

The girl with the magnified eyes smiles again at Joseph.

This time Christian Kelly does not speak. Joseph looks again at his copy book.

He completes the seventh problem. 751 divided by 15. He knows the answer many seconds before he writes it down. He already knows the answer to the ninth problem—761 divided by 15—but he starts to solve the eighth one first. He is quite satisfied with his progress. It is many months since Joseph sat in a classroom. It is warm here. January is certainly a cold month in this country.

Christian Kelly is going to hurt him. He has promised this. Joseph must be prepared.

—Finished?

It is the teacher-lady. The question is for everybody.

Joseph looks. Many of the boys and girls still lean over their copy books. Their faces almost touch the paper.

—Hurry up now. We haven't all day.

—Hey.

The voice comes from behind Joseph. It is not loud.

Joseph turns. He does this quickly. He sees this Christian Kelly.

—What's number 4?

Quickly, Joseph decides.

—17, he whispers.

He turns back, to face the blackboard and the teacher-lady.

—You're still dead. What's number 5?

—17.

—How can—

—Also 17.

—No talk.

Joseph looks at the blackboard.

—It better be.

—Christian Kelly.

It is the teacher-lady.

—What did I say? she asks.

—Don't know, says Christian Kelly.

—No talk.

—I wasn't—

—Just finish your sums. Finished, Joseph?

Joseph nods.

—Good lad. Now. One more minute.

Joseph counts the boys and girls. There are twenty-three children in the room. This sum includes Joseph. There are five desks without occupants.

—That's plenty of time. Now. Pencils down. Down.

One boy sits very near the door. Unlike Joseph, he wears the school sweater. Like Joseph, he is black. A girl sits behind Joseph, beside a big map of this country. She, also, is black. She sits beside the map. And is she Irish?

—Now. Who's first?

Miss, the teacher-lady, smiles.

Children lift their hands.

—Miss, Miss. Miss, Miss.

Joseph does not lift his hand.

—We'll get to the shy ones later, says the teacher-lady. —Hazel O'Hara.

Hands go down. Some children groan.

The girl with the magnified eyes removes her glasses. She put them into the box. It clicks. She stands up.

—Good girl.

She walks to the front of the room.

What do Irish children look like? Like this Hazel O'Hara? Joseph is not sure. Hazel's hair is almost white. Her skin is very pink right now; she is very satisfied. She is standing beside the teacher-lady and she is holding a piece of white chalk.

—Now, Hazel. Are you going to show us all how to do number one?

Hazel O'Hara nods.

—Off you go.

Christian Kelly does not resemble Hazel O'Hara.

—Hey.

Joseph watches Hazel O'Hara's progress.

—Hey.

Hazel O'Hara's demonstration is both swift and accurate.

Joseph turns, to look at Christian Kelly.

—Yes? he whispers.

—D'you want that?

Christian Kelly is holding up a finger, very close to Joseph's face. There is something on the finger's tip. Joseph hears another voice.

—Kelly's got snot on his finger.

Joseph turns, to face the blackboard. He feels the finger on his shoulder. He hears laughter—he feels the finger press his shoulder.

He grabs.

He pulls.

—What's going on there?

Christian Kelly is on the floor, beside Joseph. Joseph holds the finger. Christian Kelly makes much noise.

The teacher-lady now holds Joseph's wrist.

—Let go. Now. Hands in the air! Everybody!

Joseph releases Christian Kelly's finger. He looks at Hazel O'Hara's answer on the blackboard. It is correct.

CHAPTER THREE
YOU'RE DEFINITELY DEAD

Joseph looks at the blackboard. Miss still holds his wrist. There is much noise in the room.

He sees boys and girls stand out of their seats. Other children lean across their neighbors' desks. They all want to see Christian Kelly.

Christian Kelly remains on the floor. He also makes much noise.

—Me finger! He broke me finger!

—Sit down!

It is Miss.

—Hands in the air!

She no longer holds Joseph's wrist. Joseph watches children sit down. He sees hands in the air. He looks at his hands. He raises them.

—Joseph?

He looks at Miss. She kneels beside Christian Kelly. She holds the finger. She presses the knuckle. Christian Kelly screams.

—There's nothing broken, Christian, she says. —You'll be grand.

—It's sore!

—I'm sure it is, she says.

She stands. She almost falls back as she does this. She puts one hand behind her. She holds her skirt with the other hand.

Joseph hears a voice behind him. It is a whisper. Perhaps it is Seth Quinn.

—I seen her knickers.

She is now standing. So is Christian Kelly.

—What color?

Miss shouts.

—Now!

Christian Kelly rubs his nose with his sleeve. He looks at Joseph. Joseph looks at him. There is silence in to classroom.

—That's better, says Miss. —Now. Hands down. Good. Joseph.

Joseph hears the whisper-voice.

—Yellow.

Joseph looks up at Miss. She is looking at someone behind him. She says those words again.

—God give me strength.

She speaks very quietly. She turns to Christian Kelly. She puts her hand on his shoulder.

—Sit down, Christian.

Christian Kelly goes to his desk, behind Joseph. Joseph does not look at him.

—Now. Joseph. Stand up.

Joseph does this. He stands up.

—First. Christian is no angel. Are you, Christian?

—I didn't do anything.

She smiles at Christian. She looks at Joseph.

—You have to apologize to Christian, she says.

Joseph speaks.

—Why?

She looks surprised. She inhales, slowly.

—Because you hurt him.

This is fair, Joseph thinks.

—I apologize, he says.

A boy speaks.

—He's supposed to look at him when he's saying it.

Miss, the teacher-lady, laughs. This surprises Joseph.

—He's right, she says.

Joseph turns. He looks at Christian Kelly. Christian Kelly glances at Joseph. He then looks at his desk.

—I apologize, says Joseph.

—He didn't mean to hurt you, says Miss.

Joseph speaks.

—That is not correct, he says.

—Oh now, says Miss.

Many voices whisper.

—What did he say?

—He's in for it now.

—Look at her face.

—Now!

Joseph looks at Miss's face. It is extremely red.

She speaks.

—We'll have to see about this.

Her meaning is not clear.

—Get your bag.

Joseph picks up his schoolbag. Into this bag he puts his new *Maths Matters* book and copy book and pencil.

—Come on now.

Is he being expelled from this room? He does not know. He hears excited voices.

—She's throwing him out.

—Is she throwing him out?

He follows Miss to the front of the room.

—Now, she says. —We'd better put some space between you and Christian.

Joseph is very happy. He is to stay. And Christian Kelly will no longer sit behind him.

But then there is Seth Quinn.

A girl speaks. She is a very big girl.

—He should sit beside Pamela.

Many girls laugh.

—No, says the black girl who sits beside the map.

Joseph understands. This is Pamela.

—Leave poor Pamela alone, says Miss. —There.

Miss points.

—Beside Hazel.

Joseph watches the girl called Hazel O'Hara. She moves her chair. She makes room for Joseph. She wears her glasses. Her eyes are very big. Her hair is very white. Her skin is very pink indeed.

—Look at Hazel, says the big girl. —She's blushing.

Hazel speaks.

—Fuck off you.

—Now!

Joseph sits beside Hazel O'Hara.

—Hands in the air!

Joseph raises his hand. He hears a voice he knows.

—You're definitely dead.

Joseph looks at the clock. It is round and it is placed on the wall, over the door.

—Don't listen to that dirtbag, says Hazel O'Hara.

It is five minutes after ten o'clock. It is an hour since Joseph was brought to this room by the man. It certainly has been very eventful.

—Joseph?

It is Miss.

—Yes? says Joseph.

—I'm not finished with you yet, says Miss. —Stay here at little break.

What is this little break? Joseph does not know. The other boys in the hostel did not tell him about a little break.

—Now, says Miss. —At last. The sums on the board. Who did the last one?

—Hazel.

—That's right. Who's next?

Hands are raised. Some of the children lift themselves off their seats.

—Miss!

—Miss!

—Seth Quinn, says Miss.

—Didn't have my hand up.

—Come on, Seth.

Joseph hears a chair being pushed. He does not turn.

CHAPTER FOUR
MILK

The boy called Seth Quinn walks to the front of the room. He is a small, angry boy. His head is shaved. His nose is red. He stands at the blackboard but he does not stand still.

—So, Seth, says Miss, the teacher-lady.

—What?

—Do number three for us.

She holds out a piece of chalk. Seth Quinn takes it but he does not move closer to the blackboard.

Beside Joseph, Hazel O'Hara whispers. —Bet he gets it wrong.

Joseph does not respond. He looks at Seth Quinn.

—Well, Seth? says Miss.

Joseph knows the answer. He would very much like to whisper it to Seth Quinn.

Miss holds out her hand. She takes back the chalk.

—Sit down now, Seth, she says.

—Told you, says Hazel O'Hara.

Joseph watches Seth Quinn. He walks past Joseph. He looks at the floor. He does not look at Joseph.

—Maybe we'll have less guff out of Seth for a while, says Miss.

Joseph decides to whisper.

—What is guff?

—It's a culchie word, Hazel O'Hara whispers back. —It means talking, if you don't like talking. She says it all the time.

—Thank you, says Joseph, very quietly.

—Jaysis, says Hazel O'Hara. —You're welcome.

—Now, says Miss. —Little break.

Some of the children stand up.

—Sit down, says Miss.

This, Joseph thinks, is very predictable.

Miss waits until all the children sit again.

—Now, she says. —We didn't get much work done yet today. So you'll want to pull up your socks when we get back. Now, stand.

Pull up your socks. This must mean *work harder*. Again, Joseph feels that he is learning. He does not stand up.

—Dead.

It is Christian Kelly, as he passes Joseph.

The room is soon empty. Joseph and Miss are alone. It is very quiet.

—Well, Joseph, she says. —What have you do say for yourself?

Joseph does not speak. She smiles.

—God, she says. —I wish they were all as quiet as you. How are you finding it?

Joseph thinks he knows what this means.

—I like school very much, he answers.

—Good, she says. —You'll get used to the accents.

—Please, says Joseph. —There is no difficulty.

—Good, she says. —Now.

She steps back from Joseph's desk. Does this mean that he is permitted to go? He does not stand.

She speaks.

—Look, Joseph. I know a little bit about why you're here. Why you left, your country.

She looks at Joseph.

—And if you don't want to talk about it, that's grand.

Joseph nods.

—I hope you have a great time here. I do.

She is, Joseph thinks, quite a nice lady. But why did she embarrass Seth Quinn?

—But, she says.

Still, she smiles.

—I can't have that behavior, with Christian, in the classroom. Or anywhere else.

—I apologize.

She laughs.

—I'm not laughing at you, she says. —It's lovely. You're so polite, Joseph.

She says nothing for some seconds. Joseph does not look at her.

—But no more fighting, she says. —Or pulling fingers, or whatever it was you did to Christian.

Joseph does not answer.

—You've a few minutes left, says Miss. —Off you go.

—Thank you, says Joseph.

He stands, although he would prefer to stay in the classroom.

He walks out, to the corridor.

He remembers the way to the schoolyard. It is not complicated. He goes down a very bright staircase. He passes a man. The man smiles at Joseph. Joseph reaches the bottom step. The door is in front of him. He sees children outside, through the window. The schoolyard is very crowded.

He is not afraid of Christian Kelly.

He reaches the door.

But he does not wish to be the center of attention.

He cannot see Christian Kelly in the schoolyard. He pushes the door. He is outside. It is quite cold.

Something bright flies past him. He feels it scrape his face as it passes. He hears a smack behind him, close to his ear. And his neck is suddenly wet, and his hair. And his sleeve.

He looks.

It is milk, a carton. There is milk on the glass and on the ground but there is also milk on Joseph. He is quite wet, and he is also the center of attention. He is surrounded.

—Kellier did it.

—Christian Kelly.

Even in the space between Joseph and the door, there are children. Joseph does not see Christian Kelly. He removes his sweatshirt, over his head, and feels the milk on his face. He must wash the sweatshirt before the milk starts to smell. He touches his shoulder. His shirt is also very wet. It too must be washed.

He is very cold.

There is movement, pushing. Children move aside. Christian Kelly stands in front of Joseph. And behind Christian Kelly, Joseph sees Seth Quinn.

CHAPTER FIVE
THE BELL

Christian Kelly stands in front of Joseph. Seth Quinn stands behind Christian Kelly.

All the children in the school, it seems, are watching. They stand behind Joseph, pressing. They are also beside him, left and right, and in front, behind Christian Kelly. Joseph knows: something must happen, even if the bell rings and announces the conclusion of this thing called little break. The bell will not bring rescue.

Joseph remembers another bell.

For one second there is silence.

Then Joseph hears a voice.

—Do him.

Joseph does not see who has spoken. It was not Christian Kelly and it was not Seth Quinn.

He hears other voices.

—Go on, Kellier.

—Go on.

—Chicken.

Then Joseph hears Christian Kelly. He sees his lips.

—I told you.

Joseph remembers the soldier.

The soldier walked out of the schoolhouse. He held the bell up high in the air. It was the bell that called them all to school, every morning. It was louder than any other sound in Joseph's village, louder than engines and cattle. Joseph loved its peal, its beautiful ding. He never had to be called to school. He was there every morning, there to watch the bell lifted and dropped, lifted to the teacher's shoulder, and dropped. Joseph's father was the teacher.

—I told you, says Christian Kelly.

Joseph does not respond. He knows: anything he says will be a provocation. He will not do this.

There is a surge of children, behind Christian Kelly. He is being pushed. Christian Kelly must do something. He must hit Joseph. Joseph understands this. Someone pulls at Joseph's sweatshirt. He has been holding the sweatshirt at his side. He does not look; he does not takes his eyes off Christian Kelly, or Seth Quinn. Someone pulls again, but not too hard. He or she is offering to hold it. Joseph lets go of the sweatshirt. His hands are free. He is very cold. He looks at Christian Kelly. He knows. This is not what Christian Kelly wants. Christian Kelly is frightened.

The soldier held the bell up high. He let it drop; he lifted it. The bell rang out clearly. There were no car or truck engines in the air that morning. Just gunfire and, sometimes, the far sound of someone screaming or crying. The bell rang out but no children came running. Joseph hid behind the school wall. The soldier was grinning. More soldiers came out of the schoolhouse. They fired their guns into the air. The soldier dropped the bell. Another soldier aimed at it and fired.

Christian Kelly takes the step and pushes Joseph. Joseph feels the hand on his chest. He steps back. He stands on a foot, behind him. Christian Kelly's hand follows Joseph. Joseph grabs the hand, and one of the fingers.

This is a very stupid boy indeed.

Joseph watches Christian Kelly. He sees the sudden terror. Christian Kelly realizes that he has made an important mistake. Once again, he has delivered his finger to Joseph.

It is now Joseph's turn. He must do something.

The soldiers had gone. Joseph waited. He wanted to enter the schoolhouse; he wanted to find his father. But he was frightened. The bullet noise was still alive in his ears, and the laughing soldiers, his father's bell—Joseph was too frightened. He was ashamed, but he could not move. He wanted to call out to his father but his throat was blocked and too dry. He had dirtied himself, but he could not move.

Children shout but Joseph does not look or listen. He looks straight at Christian Kelly. He knows: he cannot release the finger. It will be weakness. Seth Quinn stands behind Christian Kelly. He stares at Joseph.

The school bell rings. It is a harsh electric bell.

No one moves.

The bell continues to ring. Joseph continues to look at Christian Kelly.

The bell stops.

He found his father behind the schoolhouse. He knew it was

his father, although he did not see the face. He did not go closer. He recognized his father's trousers. He recognized his father's shirt and shoes. He ran.

Christian Kelly tries to pull back his finger. Joseph tightens his hold. He hears children.

—This is stupid.

—Are yis going to fight, or what?

There are fewer children surrounding them. The children stand in lines, in the schoolyard. They wait for the teachers to bring them back into the school. Joseph and Christian Kelly are alone now, with Seth Quinn.

—Let him go.

It is Seth Quinn. He has spoken to Joseph.

—Seth Quinn!

It is Miss, the teacher-lady. She is behind Joseph. Christian Kelly tries to rescue his finger.

—And Christian Kelly.

Miss sees Christian Kelly's finger in Joseph's fist.

—Again?

Joseph knows what she will say.

—God give me strength.

He is learning very quickly.

CHAPTER SIX
ROBBING A BANK

Miss the teacher-lady follows the other boys and girls into the classroom. She stops at the door and turns to Joseph, Christian Kelly, and Seth Quinn.

—Not a squeak out of you, she says. —Just stand there.

She is looking at Joseph. Does she think that he will run away?

She walks into the room. Joseph remains in the corridor.

—Now!

Joseph hears the noise of children sitting down, retrieving books from schoolbags. He hears Miss.

—Open up page 47 of *Totally Gaeilge.* Questions one to seven. I'll be right outside and listening out for any messing.

Joseph does not look at Christian Kelly or Seth Quinn. They do not speak. They face the classroom door but cannot see inside.

Miss has returned.

—Now, she says.

She stands in front of them.

—I didn't do anything, says Christian Kelly.

—Shut up, Christian, for God's sake.

Joseph looks at Miss. She does not look very angry.

—We have to sort this out, boys, she says.

—I didn't—

—Christian!

It is, perhaps, a time when she will say *God give me strength.*

But she doesn't. She looks at Seth Quinn.

—Seth, she says. —What happened?

—Nothing.

Christian Kelly is looking at the floor. Seth Quinn is looking at Miss.

—It was a funny sort of nothing I saw, says Miss. —Well, Joseph. Your turn. What happened?

—Nothing happened, says Joseph.

Miss says nothing, for three seconds. These seconds, Joseph thinks, are important. Because, in that time, the three boys become united. This is what Joseph thinks. They are united in their silence. They do not like one another but this does not matter. They stand there together, against Miss.

She looks at the three boys.

—You're great lads, she says.

Joseph does not think that she is sincere.

—What'll I do with you? she says.

Again, the boys say nothing.

—Seth?

Seth Quinn shrugs.

—Joseph?

Joseph looks at her. He does not speak. He will not speak. He will be punished but he is not frightened or very concerned. He is, at this moment, quite happy.

—Nothing to say for yourself? says Miss.

Joseph shakes his head. He looks at the floor. There are many loud noises coming from the classroom. Joseph hopes that these will distract Miss. She does not speak. He hears her breathe. He looks at her feet. They do not move.

She speaks.

—Right, so. If that's the way you want it—

—Miss?

Joseph looks. It is Hazel O'Hara, the girl with the magnified eyes. She is at the door.

—Yes, Hazel? says Miss.

—I seen it.

—Now, Hazel—

—But I seen it. Christian Kelly pushed—

—Back inside, Hazel.

—But he—

—Hazel!

Hazel lifts her very big eyes and makes a clicking sound with her mouth. She turns and walks back into the classroom. They hear her.

—She's a bitch, that one. I was only telling her.

Miss follows Hazel. She rushes into the classroom.

—Hands in the air!

Seth Quinn speaks.

—She thinks she's robbing a fuckin' bank.

Christian Kelly laughs quietly. Seth Quinn laughs quietly. Joseph smiles.

They listen to Miss. They cannot see.

—Hazel O'Hara!

—What?

Joseph laughs. It is like listening to a radio program.

—I heard you what you said, Hazel O'Hara!

—It was a private conversation.

He laughs because the other boys are also laughing. He hears them snort. He also snorts.

—Don't you *dare* talk to me like that!

—Like what?

Joseph looks at Christian Kelly. He looks at Seth Quinn. They laugh, with him. Their shoulders shake.

—Stand up! says Miss.

—I *am* standing.

—Hands in the air!

—She's an eejit, whispers Christian Kelly.

The three boys laugh together.

It is quiet in the classroom.

Seth Quinn whispers, —Now.

And—

—Now, says Miss, inside the room.

This is, perhaps, the funniest thing that Joseph has ever heard. He laughs so much, he cannot see. He wipes his eyes. The other boys also wipe their eyes. He tries to stop. He knows that Miss will soon reappear.

He stops.

Then he says it.

—Now.

He thinks suddenly of his father; a great weight drops through his chest. He cries now as he laughs. He feels the weight, the sadness, fall right through him. He wipes his eyes. He continues to laugh. Many times, Joseph made his father laugh. He remembers the sound of his father's laughter; he sees his father's face.

He laughs. He wipes his eyes. He looks at the other boys. They are looking at the classroom door.

Miss stands in front of Joseph.

He stops laughing. He waits.

He is surprised. She does not seem angry. She looks at Joseph for some long time.

—The three musketeers, she says. —In you go.

She stands aside.

Christian Kelly enters the room. Joseph follows Christian Kelly. Seth Quinn follows Joseph.

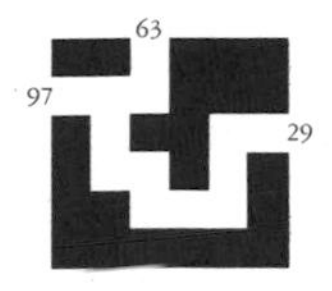

ONE DAY THIS WILL ALL BE YOURS

by PHILIPP MEYER

MY FATHER GREW UP in a mining town in West Virginia; baths outside in a coal-fired tub, missing strikers found buried in the slag piles, the vein giving out and the whole town with it. His father and twelve others died in a shaft collapse.

I went to see him after my mother left, ten years after the rest of us. My brother and sister still wouldn't talk to him. My sister got pregnant in college and married a banker; she must have played up the family saga because he treated her like a rescued bird, though she'd gotten off easiest of the three of us. I'd visited her in the Keys and she was nervous, and then the banker scolded her in front of my face for leaving the children alone with me. I headed back to Georgia that night, but my appetite was ruined and my face went gray for weeks and I told everyone I had a virus. I'm a big man. I could have wrecked that banker's jaw with one swipe.

My brother lived in Canada; he and I were on good terms. We spoke often and he asked me to visit and I wondered what he'd told his new family about me. I decided it was better if I never found out.

As for my father, he'd been alone a week before I called him. I had to work up to it. None of the others would even consider it.

"Nice to hear from you," he said. "I mean your timing."

"I was wondering how you were holding up."

"Been working on the house all week."

"Maybe you should be around people."

"Thank you," he told me.

"I was just saying."

"Did you know about this?"

"I didn't know anything," I said.

"You two didn't talk much, I know that."

"She and Melanie talked, mostly."

Melanie was my sister.

"Melanie probably knew."

"It doesn't matter," I told him.

"Things don't get easier. I thought they would, but I was wrong. In fact, they go downhill, generally speaking."

"This is just a rough spot," I said. "You'll get over this."

"My loyal son."

"Maybe we can just pretend to be nice people."

"There are things about us," he said. "There are things I've learned and you're not going to know them until it's too late."

"Come off it," I told him.

"I named Bud Mitchell executor."

"Pop."

"I'm just telling you."

"You don't even talk to him anymore."

"I called him last week. Everything is straightened out."

"Are you sick?" I said. "Tell me. Mom didn't say anything."

"I don't want your mother to find me. At first I thought I did."

We were quiet. I could hear him breathing.

"I'm calling the cops," I finally said.

"That would be best. I don't want your mother to be the one."

I had trouble staying between the lines on the road and finally I pulled over. My skin was cold and I was damp everywhere and my hands were tingling, and in my ears I could hear my blood. When I was a kid I shot a groundhog with a deer rifle from ten feet. I thought about that and how my father would look. Then I was sick.

Afterward I lay on the hood and took off my shirt to dry. The sun felt close and bright and the hood burned my back but I was shivering. I touched the padding on my gut—the softest it had ever been. Trucks went by and the air shook but I didn't hear anything.

I called my father to tell him I was on the way.

"You're not coming," he said. "I knew it before you called."

"I just had to pull over a minute."

"Sure."

"Are you outside? It sounds like you're outside."

"The neighbors are all looking at me. These people are afraid of everything."

"Wait for me," I told him. "I'll be there in ten minutes."

When I was younger I would hold broken glass in my hand and squeeze it until I couldn't think about anything else. Even now I can spin a carving knife into the air and catch it by the handle. In college I went to a palm reader, and she took one look and refused to say anything.

I pulled back onto the highway and called my brother and

sister but they didn't pick up. *I know you're there*, I said into their machines. I thought about calling my mother and decided against it. She would go back if she knew. She was the only one of us who deserved better.

Their house was a rancher. All the windows were closed and it was stale inside. I started sweating and the blood came back to my ears. There were unwashed dishes in the kitchen, which my mother would not have allowed. In the living room, there was a sheet on the couch and a pillow, empty beer bottles on the side table, a dirty magazine, unopened and still wrapped in plastic. The dining-room table was bare except for a piece of paper with my address and phone number in careful print. *Son*, it said. My father was outside, at the edge of the pond with a skeet gun across his lap.

He didn't look up when I walked out.

"Pop?"

There were dozens of new homes. I could see faces of the people inside. Their fences ran to our lawn. Long rectangles of orange dirt lay where the sod in their yards had died, and the sky beyond our house looked immense and empty where it had once been blocked with trees.

"Sorry about the lawn," he said.

I looked around for a sign that the gun might be unloaded, but there was a box of shells on its side in the grass, half scattered.

"You mind if I hold that," I said.

"I lent the mower to the woman down the street and she drove it off a curb. It's at the shop."

"Have you called Tim or Melanie?"

"You can't trust women with complex machinery," he said. "Their brains get all haywired."

"A riding mower isn't really a complex machine," I told him.

"All you're doing is agreeing with me."

"I'm not trying to fight."

"You didn't have to come over. You haven't come over for nine years and all of a sudden here you are."

"Let me hold the shotgun," I said.

He didn't let go of it, but he didn't tighten his grip, either.

"Notice anything different about the yard," he said. "Other than the woods are gone."

"No."

"Look carefully."

I thought I could wrestle the gun from him. I looked around the yard. It was the nicest part of the house, an acre with the pond at the center, a white pergola running up one side, dogwoods and apple trees. There were tulip beds around the pond. When my father was a kid, he'd seen something like it in a magazine. We pulled the weeds by hand, cut the grass around the flowers with scissors, watered sunup and sundown. There were gophers, and the poison killed our dog. When my brother left for college he filled his truck with rock salt and was going to dump it everywhere. My sister and I stopped him.

But, standing there with my father, I noticed something new. There was a sandbox, as if for children.

"Where'd that come from?"

"You guys all seem to be spawning. I thought it might come in handy."

My sister's four children, the oldest nearly twelve, had never met him. My brother and his wife had their third on the way but they'd insisted he not know.

"You need to talk to someone. I'm worried about you."

"You bought a house yet?"

"No. I put in for a transfer to Denver."

"Shack up the road just went for two hundred thousand. Believe that?"

"You'd probably get half a mil with all the land. Move someplace smaller."

"The house would be full enough if it weren't for your mother."

"Don't."

"She doesn't know how stupid she looks," he said. "Running around at her age."

"Let's not do this."

"Be glad you never married."

"I'm thirty-two."

"Your grandfather passed when he was thirty-four."

"That's a nice thing to tell someone."

"I keep thinking about that Cadillac I bought her. She drove it right out of here."

"She could have taken more," I said.

"I'd kill her before I let her have this house."

I didn't say anything.

"She's a whore. I'm not afraid to say it."

"I'm going home now."

"Come on. I've got steaks in the freezer."

"You are fucking impossible."

"I'm just lonely, Scotty. I worked so hard to make her happy."

"You don't really think that."

"I gave her that car last year. And a goddamn plumber. It burns me up, that guy riding around in my Caddy."

"Actually," I said, "he's a steamfitter."

"What?"

"Not a plumber."

"What the hell," he said.

"I want to stop this," I said. "I'm sorry."

"You know I took baths in an outdoor tub that we heated over a coal burner? That's how much we had."

"I know you had it rough, Pop."

"You had everything you asked for."

"Pop," I said.

"Your grandfather could do a hundred pushups. He'd cuff me and my ears would ring all morning."

I didn't say anything.

"It's in the blood."

"That doesn't mean anything," I told him.

We watched football for two hours without speaking. My father correctly predicted the final score. I'd been a guard at Michigan for a season, then quit to spite him.

As for the shotgun, I'd unloaded it and pocketed the shells.

"Plenty more where they came from," he said about the shells.

"Clemson is on fire this year," is what he said about football.

"They seem fine," I said.

"They're a lot better than fine."

"You need someone to talk to. Other than the guys at the trap range."

"Let me ask you a question, Scott."

"Probably not."

"Are you mad at your mother?"

"Dad."

"Well. Are you?"

"Off-limits," I said.

"Do me the favor," he said. "For ten years of not seeing you."

"That's not on me," I said. "That's on all of us."

"Just answer it. I want to hear you say it."

Of course I was mad at her. At eighteen you can look at your father and know you'll never be anything like him. At thirty it's a different story. All three of us blamed her for not seeing it when she married him, but in the end we'd paid her back. We'd escaped to colleges in different states, stayed away summers and holidays. I was the youngest and the last to leave and my mother couldn't look at me when she dropped me at the airport. *I guess I won't be seeing you much*, she said. *I guess not*, I told her. Then I disappeared like my brother and sister. I've always known it was the worst thing I've ever done.

"I'm not mad at Mom," I told him.

"Sweet Jesus Christ," said my father. "Now I've heard it all."

He picked up the remote to turn the TV back on, but I stopped him before he could.

"I used to think you did everything on purpose," I said.

"Everything what?"

"But now I'm not sure. I think it comes from someplace you don't understand."

He didn't say anything.

"I liked it better when it was on purpose."

His fists balled up like the old days and his face got dark.

I left him on the couch and got a case of beer from the kitchen.

"I'm going outside," I told him.

The sun was going down when my father came onto the patio. I don't know if he saw all the neighbors. I watched him load his gun. Then I looked away.

Where the people stood with their children and fences I imagined everything as it had been before, land unbroken all the way to the river, pigeon hawks hunting the clearings, foxes and deer, owls at night. When we were kids we would camp in those hills, my father and brother and I, and I thought about the feeling of the cold air on my face and the warmness inside the sleeping bag and the sound of my father's soft breathing as he slept.

I threw my beer into the pond. I could feel him watching me. I threw the rest of the bottles one by one. They skittered across the grass, cracked on the slate path. I expected to hear a shot. When the case of beers was empty I went into the garage and dragged back a trashcan full of bottles. I aimed them against the rocks in the pond, against the pergola and the flagstone in the yard.

The neighbors stood at their fences and watched.

"Do you want us to call the police," one of them said.

My father didn't answer. I kept throwing. The sun was getting lower and the glass on the lawn was glowing like embers from a wreckage.

"You can stop now," he said.

I barely heard him.

"Scotty," he said.

Then there was a noise, a gunshot, and a bottle cracked apart in the air. Something cut me on the face. The neighbors started away from their fences. My father had the gun shouldered and the pieces of the bottle were spinning and falling over the yard and I touched my check and it was sticky hot. We're even, I thought quickly, but then I knew we weren't and that we couldn't be. I watched him and he couldn't hold my eyes, and I saw the thinness in his arms and legs, the slouch in his back.

"That's enough," he said, but it was a whisper. It was so quiet I could barely hear it. I didn't know what it meant, or what he wanted me to do.

Then he was leaning and I caught him and held him up. I was lifting him from under his elbows and he was sagging back against me.

He doesn't want me to see him like this, I thought, but after that we didn't move. The sun was in our faces. I could hear the sound of his breathing, soft like I'd remembered it, and the light was spread across the hills and trees as if the land had been set on fire.

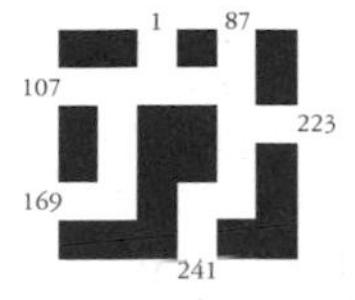

NO CRY OF DISTRESS IN OUR STREETS

by ALAN ACKMAN

REVEREND DANIELS WASHES all his fruit in baby soap, because his doctors recommend it. It will keep his soul from chafing, they explain. When he belches, out will come small puffs of absolution, which will clean his ceiling too, when they explode. So everybody wins. Daniels adheres to this advice, which has arranged his life since childhood, as faithfully as all his other truths, which tout the impermanence of worldly wealth, and harmony between vast and intimate hardships, and the unseen, mythic battles that engage all living things, and steadily destroy them—truths defining the reality of Evil. He is reading about these forces, these foes, these demons, one cool Arizona evening while, across the bed, his secretary, his angel, his heart, his Deborah, looks up from her work. She is reading catalogs of lawn tractors. She has the firmest breasts that he has ever seen, and her glasses perch atop her ski-jump nose like they are contemplating immortality. Once she told him how, on impulse, she had wrapped her purse around her mother's throat. Some things just can't be trusted, she'd explained.

Reverend Daniels loves her inconsolably, but certain things come first.

We are at war, you know.

Yesterday, he sensed another demon in his shower drain. He caught its dusky scent, like the mercenary black of sulfur cut with the glossy red of raspberry sorbet, and he dropped to his knees, ratcheted the faucets, flooded all the pipes, and muttered whatever he could remember. Then, as swiftly as reality attacked, it vanished, and it left him with the drip of water onto water, cool linoleum beneath his knees. Only then did he allow Deborah to enter. She has never understood these fits of fear and certainty, but she tolerates them, as have all the women in his family, back to the wife of Jonathan Edwards Daniels, in the days of boots and buckled hats, who would comfort and console her husband following his wheezing, blazing hours of platitudes and scorn. Today, across the bed, his Deborah pouts a pout that blossoms him like napalm.

"I think that we should take a trip," she says.

He thinks that he agrees.

Outside the window, Phoenix shimmers, wrapped in puzzling, milky snow. Deborah seems content, but the demons have dimmed the dimmer switch down on the fiery globe above them, and now it hovers like a rotting orange, dripping little gobs of heat that splatter Dallas, Rome, and Scranton, where they slop like chocolate dripped into a vat. This is a new development. Throughout the years, of course, there have been phases when the demons swelled their ranks, and threatened them with grand, imaginative annihilation, but since his Deborah came along they mostly mismatched shoes, or soured the milk, their malice leveled out to boyish pranks. But now, like gods, they thwart the heavens, and they gloat. And their insidious strength is building.

And they'll come for Deborah next.

"Your major problem," doctors tell him, periodically, "is that you're still enthralled with notions of concoction, plans. You have the gall, in fact, to believe that something cares enough to be against you. And the only cure is cleansing. Mix your milk in a solution one part water, two parts turpentine, to wash yourself of the corrosive agents. You can still be free."

His doctors, he believes, are learned, learned people.

"Oh, and abandon your secretary, your lover, your tart, your baggage. Throw her off a bridge. Sir, all she does is fuel you."

Yes, Daniels agrees, she does.

As Deborah flips her pages, which are stained with shots of poker chips, dart boards, short rubber/plywood paddles, and a thousand party games, Reverend Daniels remembers when they had first discussed his family's plight, over a lazy match of backgammon. Deborah had been younger then, quite new to guilt, to him. Her legs were sleek and toned. She'd been deliciously naïve, and gobbled up his truths like sour candy. He told her how they'd always been at war, back to the glory days of Stanford Parris Daniels, who—tired of being cowed, and of waiting for attacks to doom his life—had sniffed the demons from his congregation like a blind dog hunting felons. Back in these glory days (she'd smiled, and nodded), days of pumpkin pie and smallpox, clear-drawn lines and woeful, cheerful penitence, he'd pressed a man. The man had been afflicted. He had withered the colony's crops with his mind, but Stanford Parris Daniels isolated the problem, and then stretched that farmer across two jagged blocks of wood, stacking twenty-pound slabs of stone across his chest like pieces of fresh bread on a board. At the seventh stone, the man had babbled incoherently. At ten, he'd shit streams like a river. The afflicted man, their family legends told, had been about seventy-five years on this earth. It was, admittedly, a lot to live up to.

Deborah touched his cheek, and rolled her dice. She told him, "Everybody comes from somewhere."

Some years later, on the night that she suggests their trip, Deborah is distracting him with willowy accounts of Paris and Bhutan, Estonia and all the vast, repeating arctic places they could run. Daniels considers abandoning his fight, and asks himself if she is worth it, then awakens in the middle of the night, sees stars beyond the halo of his city, and he is overrun with joy. Nighttime, in these moments, is as still as the smell of rain. But then, across the desert, like the shower-curtain wisp of an approaching storm, a phantom cloud of insects swoops itself down hungrily along the buttes and valleys, gnashing, clenching, scraping. Daniels barricades himself, and shelters Deborah (who sleeps, unaffected, with her almond eyes fluttering, small without their frames) then mutters as he watches fury gliding past his windows, like the flickering brown static on a television. In the morning, written in the cumulus-amber of the flaking sky, he sees whole fields of cattle, skeletonized, their husks now kneeling in surprising supplication. And he understands there's no way they can win this. Ever.

Beside him, Deborah's torso twists as she scours the bedsheets, searching, and her leg slips out the sheet, up to her creamy thigh. Daniels remembers playing chess with Deborah, back in the early days of their courtship, when they played games almost daily. She had moved her pieces brazenly, with no regard for safety, or security. She played chess like a woman flipping country stations. Seventy-three moves in, he said, "You shouldn't move your bishop."

"Why?"

"I'll beat you in three moves," he said. "My forces are massing. If you move your bishop there, I'll go for the throat. I'll bury you. That isn't what you want."

"Okay," she said. "It's not."

Around him, Daniels felt transparent demons squat and watch, intrigued, already plotting, and he had beaten her handily, long into the night. To raise the stakes, they decided to remove one article of clothing for every back-row piece their opponent captured, and one article of clothing for every two pawns. Three moves in, he captured her bishop; she took off her shirt. Four pawns later, her socks lay in a puddle by the bed. By forty-one moves in, Deborah was stretched out languidly, her long legs dreamily extended, breasts concealed beneath the white silk of her bra, and Daniels couldn't concentrate. He lost the game. The demons chattered, voices like the seven-year thrum of locusts, and he and Deborah made love long into the night. In roughly four to six weeks, she presented him with a Revolutionary War chess set carved from ivory and obsidian; he told her, idly, that the Aztecs used obsidian to cut hearts from their sacrificial victims.

Three weeks later, they were married.

How long ago was that again? He doesn't know. And yet he sees their marriage as the latest union in a stretching, shaking line of fatally selected pairings, with none of them lasting very long. Demons had seen to that. Four centuries ago, Elizabeth Proctor Daniels (rest her) had been torn apart by wolves, who'd ambushed her and left her entrails dangling from a spindly, yellow maple. Some time later, Florence Bennett Daniels slipped in a hardware store, and her carotid artery connected with a four-and-seven-eighths-inch nail. Her blood, as they discovered when examining the paint cans, was exactly Candy Apple Red. Harriet Beecher Daniels, some time later, had slipped on the deck of a steamboat. Her hem connected with the rough slat of a paddle, and down she went, into the gears, arms flailing, strong voice howling, martyred to the cause. God rest them. Over the ages, some wives understood their struggle. Some had joined their noble fight. Some even yearned for peace enough that they'd proclaimed the battle finished, while others (he and Deborah?) simply ran. And some escaped. On the night they were united, Deborah cooed, "You know, I understand the risks here. You should too: I just don't see us ever having a normal life." She told him that she'd once shaved her cousin's infant, only to see what lurked beneath. Then she buried into Reverend Daniels's body, and the world was quieter than it had ever been before.

Around him, on that wedding night, doctors had wagged their heads, beards flailing. "Don't you understand," they said, "how foolish it is to ascribe patterns to these collisions? All the magnitude you see is simply *post hoc, ergo propter hoc* projection. There is no God, no demons, and the sooner you can see these things, the quicker you can shed the shackles of this sheltered, simple state. Just think it over. Oh, and jam that penknife in your lover's eye. We think it will do you some good."

He is always hearing things like this, today. He is always barely catching the acrid snap-wisp (cloaked in other sounds) of something sliding into this world from the next. He is always envisioning his Deborah baking in the desert outside Tucson, unsure how she got there. He is always glimpsing an elusive clue to their malevolent orchestrations, in the dewy glint in the eyes of passersby, in the shadowy knife of a storm front. Daniels tries to fend these demons off, but on the night of the apocalyptic locust swarm his fear becomes intolerable. And so they run.

The pair abandons Arizona. They take a pilgrimage along the Appalachian Trail, where they meet a group of camping Buddhists, whose tent radiates a dizzy, quiet calm against the rustling, hidden creatures. Then they journey to Seattle, and he takes her grainy picture on the blasted husk of Mt. St. Helens. When Manhattan leaves them both exhausted, they expand their small horizons, head to Europe, with the glitter of Paris, and the wild excess of Amsterdam, and the boggy British Isles. During the clomping changing of the guard in Stockholm, Deborah (who likes to think she's got some Nordic in her) is almost overwhelmed with tears. "It's just so nice," she says, as though relieved, "to have some sense of where you came from, right?"

She smiles. She thinks they're on vacation. But unlike Deborah, who comes from nothing, really, Daniels understands his legacy. Once—his father told him—demons froze the fields of Europe. That was in one of their more commanding stages, and the sloping Tuscan vineyards to the fertile, bloody Somme became nothing but a stretching film of ice. Children could slide a watermelon eighty yards with just one push. They did. Ten thousand people glazed in place while making love, or washing shampoo from their hair, or slinging tiny metal darts at manhole-hard boards, the darts now shattered at their feet. It was a glassy, terrible Pompeii. And on this brittle warfront, Stanford Patton Daniels (the current Reverend's father) had encountered a fellow soldier walking point along the underside of an expressway, with the convoys rolling like centipedes above him. He was a demon, that much could be said. Full grown. This elder, more powerful Daniels crept behind the man, who had stopped to warm his hands by a blazing steel drum, and he snapped his soldier brother's neck like a kindling branch. The soldier's thin spine twisted backward, and Daniels caught him as he fell, skull bouncing off the solid, jet-black ground. Wind howled. This elder Daniels, like his forefathers, scrambled for a verse or two, some absolution, but in this moment all that came back were some snatches of Psalms, which he would later share with his son—the latest Reverend Daniels—over lemonade and checkers, with the old man's palms shaking quietly. *The enemy shall not outwit him*, old Stanford had muttered, over the tweeting robins, *and the wicked shall not humble him; The Lord says to my lord, "Sit at my right hand until I make your enemies your footstool"; May there be no breach in the walls, no exile, and no cry of distress in our streets.*

Years later, during this same checkers game, the elder Daniels rustled around for a piece to make a king, while another liver-spotted hand steadied the board, which was (as always) balanced on the tombstone of Originia Daniels, the current Reverend's mother, who had been thrashed to death by a combine in a wide Nebraska field. On the day of her death, old Stanford said, there'd been an unforeseen eclipse, great signs, and the attacks had started freshly. It was important, he said, as he coughed in his hand, that they not forget these things.

Now Daniels cannot understand why no one seems to remember.

"I have not yet reached the point," his Deborah booms as they strut the streets of their adopted Budapest, cathedrals gleaming, "of believing things are not connected. My cousin Jacob earns his living buying skeletons from India. My niece Alice was born, and lives, without a heart. These things do not strike me as separate incidents." Behind them, a footbridge crumbles off into the water. Later that evening, Deborah scorches the pages of her catalogs (which seem to follow her as they travel) with slapdash flipping, convinced that existential security, if properly modulated, costs less than $3.75 shipping and handling. She has many catalogs—for coffees, ledgers, backyard statuary, and even one for cardboard cutouts of the more nefarious politicians. You can buy a six-foot cast of Huey Long. For an extra seven dollars, he will wave. Last week, out of love, she presented him with a jade-encrusted letter opener made from the finger of an Indonesian cannibal, where the finger's nail was six inches of metal, rigid as a Lilliputian surfboard. They haven't paid a bill in months, but their adventures are only beginning. Reverend Daniels wants to take her places, all kinds of places: hideous, stately castles; calming oceanfront hot-dog stands; Greece. He defends himself as best he can. But sometimes hope is overwhelming, and he falls.

How can he make her see it? This is war.

Someday she will understand, he thinks. As they travel, he glimpses smaller demons peeking behind curtains, waiting on the buses, lurking in confessionals. In Acapulco, he imagines Deborah slipping on a loose tile, tumbling down the cliffs like a flopping diver, cracking on the bottom. In Japan, he thinks he sees the oceans rumbling, beaches stretching forward as the surf retreats to rush back at them, screaming. In a Moscow cathedral, he imagines, vividly, that he should grab a censer from its hanging perch and club her, laughing, as her howls shoot up and bounce around the copulas, before he wrings his hands in horror. Deborah said that once, on impulse, she had twirled her brother's cat around her head, and launched it over the balcony, just to see how it would fly. But there is no such thing as impulse now: only sly, inescapable fear.

And someday, when the time is right, she'll see it.

In the evenings, in their cities, they make love, and when they've finished, Daniels sinks into bed. As Deborah slumbers, Daniels recollects one moment in war, at war, through war, that has stayed with him throughout the years. It is an image of himself, a boy of twenty, waiting at a train station in Germany. He thinks, for a moment, that it might have been his father, really, or some other vestigial wisp, but the oh-so-potent sensations make distilling facts irrelevant. He and another soldier, Daniels knows, were bound for the same front, with their rifles slung across their chests like a peasant's satchel of wheat, and while they waited they had played a game. They bought one bottle of tequila, one of whiskey, and poured a dozen shots of each, then lined them up in rows of four across the cool tile of the station platform, in the dimensions of a checkerboard. And they played, claiming the other player's pieces, the warm fire sliding down their throats. Daniels played to win, as always, and he snatched the pieces greedily before the world began to tilt and rearrange. He sees it happening now, perfection at his side. The things he knows, the strategies he recognizes, blur to formless shades and—far from focusing on heavy things, on loneliness, on time, on love, on things that might just save him—Daniels squints his eyes, and wills the round, warm pieces back into existence. He is certain, if he sees the pieces clearly, things can still make sense. He's certain, if he sees them, he can win.

HOT PINK

by ADAM LEVIN

MY FRIEND JOE COJOTEJK and myself were on our way to Nancy and Tina Christamesta's, to see if they could drive to Sensei Mike's housewarming barbecue in Glen Ellyn. Cojo's cousin Niles was supposed to take us, but last-minute he got in his head it was better to drink and use fireworks with his girlfriend. He called to back out while we were in the basement with the heavy bag. We'd just finished drawing targets on the canvas with marker. I wanted small red bull's-eyes, but Joe thought it would be better to represent the targets like the things they stood for. He'd covered a shift for me at the lot that week, so I let him have his way; a triangle for a nose, a circle for an Adam's apple, a space for the solar plexus, and for the sack a saggy-looking shape. The bag didn't hang low enough to have realistic knees.

When my mom yelled down the stairs that Niles was on the phone, I was deep into roundhouse kicks—I wanted to land one on each target, consecutively, without pausing to look at them, or breathing, and I was getting there: I was up to three out of four (I kept missing the circle)—so I told Cojo to take the call, and it was a mistake. Cojo won't argue with his family. Everyone else, but not them. He gets guilty with them. When he came back down the basement and told me Niles was ditching out, I bolted upstairs to call him myself, but all I got was his machine with the dumbass message: "You've reached Niles Cojotejk, NC-17. Do you love me? Are you a very sexy lady? Speak post-beep, baby."

I hung up.

My mom coughed.

I said, "Eat a vitamin." I took two zincs from the jar on the tray and lobbed one to her. She caught it in her lap by pushing her legs together. It was the opposite of what a woman does, according to the old lady in *Huckleberry Finn* who throws the apple in Huck's lap to blow his fake-out. Maybe it was Tom Sawyer and a pear, or a matchbox. Either way, he was cross-dressed.

The other zinc I swallowed myself. For immunity. The pill trailed grit down my throat and I put my tongue under the faucet.

"What happened to cups?" my mom said. That's how she accuses people. With questions.

I shut the tap. I said, "Did something happen to cups?"

"Baloney," she said.

Then I got an inspiration. I asked her, "Can you make your voice low and slutty?"

"Like this?" she said, in a low, slutty voice.

"Will you leave a message on Niles's machine?"

"No," she said.

"Then I'm going away forever," I said. "Picture all you got left is bingo and that fat-ass Doberman chewing dead things in the gangway. Plus I'll give you a dollar if you do it." I said, "You can smoke two cigarettes on that dollar. Or else I'll murder you, violently." I picked up the nearest thing. It was a mortar or a pestle. It was the empty part. I waved it in the air at her. "I'll murder you with *this*."

"Gimme a kiss!" she sang. That's how she is. A pushover. All she wants is to share a performance. To riff with you. It's one kind of person. Makes noise when there's noise, and the more noise the better. The other kind's a soloist, who only starts up when it's quiet, then holds his turn like it'll never come again. Cojo's that kind. I don't know who's better to have around. Some noise gets wrecked by quiet and some quiet gets wrecked by noise. So sometimes you want a riffer and other times a soloist and I can't decide which kind I am.

I dialed the number. For the message, I had my mother say, "You're rated G for Gypsy, baby." Niles is very sensitive about getting called a Gypsy. I don't know what inspired me with the idea to have my mom say it to him in a low, slutty voice, but then I got a clearer idea.

I dialed the number again and got her to say the same thing in her regular voice. Then I called four more times, myself, and I said it in four different voices: I did a G, a homo, a Paki, and a Dago. I'm good at those. I thought I was done, but I wasn't. I did it once more in my own voice, so Niles would know it was me telling people he's a Gypsy.

My mom said, "You're a real goof-off, Jack."

Cojo came upstairs, panting. "Tina and Nancy," he said.

I thought: Nancy, if only.

Cojo said, "They might have a car."

It was a good idea. I called. They didn't know for sure about a car, but said come over and drink. I kissed my mom's head and she gave me money to buy her a carton of Ultralights. I dropped the money in her lap and pulled a jersey over my T. Cojo said it was too hot out for both. It was too hot out for naked, though, so it wouldn't matter anyway. Except then I noticed Joe was also wearing a jersey and a T, and I didn't want to look like a couple who planned it, which Joe didn't want either, which is what he meant by too hot out, so I dumped the jersey for a Mexican wedding shirt and we split.

Five minutes later, Cojo and myself were feared, and soon after that, I learned something new about talking and how to use it to intimidate people.

How I knew we were feared was a full-grown man walking the other way on the other side of the street looked at us and nodded. It's a small thing to do but it meant a lot. My lungs tickled at the sight of it. I got this tightness down the center of my body, like during a core-strength workout. Or trying to first-kiss someone and you can't remember where to put your hands. Even thinking about it, I get this feeling. This stranger, nodding at you from all the way across the street.

It was late in the afternoon by then, and tropical hot, but overcast with small black clouds. And the wind—it was flapping the branches. Wing-shaped seed-pods rattled over the pavement and the clouds blew across the sun so fast the sky was blinking. It opened my nose up. The street got narrow compared to me. The cars looked like Hot Wheels. And in my head, my first thing was that I felt sorry for this guy who nods. It's like a salute, this kind of nod.

But then my second thing is: you better salute me, Clyde. And I get this picture of holding his ears while I slowly push his face into his brains with my forehead. I got massive neck muscles. I got this grill like a chimney and an ugly thing inside me to match it. I feel sorry for a person, it makes me want to hurt him. Cojo's the same way as me, but crueler-looking. It's mostly because of the way we're built. We're each around a buck-seventy, but I barrel in the trunk. Joe's lean and even, like a long Bruce Lee. He comes to all kinds of points. And plus his eyes. They're a pair of slits in shadow. I got comic-strip eyes, a couple black dimes. My eyes should be looking in opposite directions.

I ran my hands back over my skull. It's a ritual from grade school, when we used to do battle royales at the pool with our friends. We got it from a cartoon I can't remember, or a video game. You do a special gesture to flip your switch; for me it's I run my hands back over my skull and, when I get to the bottom, I tap my thumb knuckles, once, on the highest-up button of my spine. You flip your switch and you've got a code name. We were supposed to keep our code names secret, so no one could deplete their power by speaking them, but me and Cojo told each other. Cojo's special gesture was wiping his mouth crosswise, from his elbow to the backs of his fingertips. Almost all the other special gestures had saliva in them. This one kid Winthrop would spit in his palms and fling it with karate chops. Voitek Moitek chewed grape gum, and he'd hock a sticky puddle in his elbow crooks, then flex and relax till the spit strung out between his forearms and biceps. Nick Rataczeck licked the middle of his shirt and moaned like a deaf person. I can't remember the gestures of the rest of the battle-royale guys. By high school, we stopped socializing with those guys and after we dropped out we hardly ever saw them. I don't know if they told each other their code names. They didn't tell me.

Cojo's was War, though. Mine was Smith. It's embarrassing.

I coughed the tickle from my lungs and Joe stopped walking, performed his gesture, and was War.

He said to the guy, "What," and the guy shuddered a little. The guy was swinging a net-sack filled with grapefruits and I hated how it bounced against his knee. I hated he had them.

It made everything complicated. My thoughts were too far in the background to figure out why. Something about peeling them or slicing them in halves or eighths and what someone else might prefer to do. I always liked mine in halves. A little sugar. And that jagged spoon. It's so specific.

The guy kept moving forward, like he didn't know Joe was talking to him, but he was walking slower than before. It was just like the nod. The slowness meant the exact opposite of what it looked like it meant. I'm scared of something? I don't look at it. I think: If I don't see it, it won't see me. Like how a little kid thinks. You smack its head while it's hiding in a peek-a-boo and now it believes in God, not your hand. But everyone thinks like that sometimes. I'm scared my mom's gonna die from smoking, the way her lungs whistle when she breathes fast, but if I don't think about it, I think, Cancer won't think about her. It's stupid. I know this. Still: me, everyone. Joe says "What," to a guy who's scared of him, the guy pretends Joe's not talking to him. The guy pretends so hard he slows down when what he wants is to get as far the hell away from us and as fast as he can.

Joe says, "I said, 'What.'"

"I'm sorry," the guy says.

"Sorry for what?" Joe says, and now he's crossing the street and I'm following him.

I say, "Easy, Cojo," and this is when I learn something new about how to intimidate people. Because even though I say "Easy, Cojo," I'm not telling Cojo to take it easy. I'm not even talking to Cojo. I'm talking to the guy. When I say "Easy, Cojo," I'm telling the guy he's right to be scared of my friend. And I'm also telling him that I got influence with my friend, and that means the guy should be scared of me, too. What's peculiar is when I open my mouth to say "Easy, Cojo," I *think* I'm about to talk to Cojo, and then it turns out I'm not. And so

I have to wonder how many times I've done things like that without noticing. Like when I told my mom I'd kill her and waved the empty thing at her, I wasn't really threatening her, it was more like I was saying, "Look, I'll say a stupid thing that makes me look stupid if you'll help me out." But that was different, too, from this, because my mom knew what I meant when I said I'd kill her, but this guy here doesn't know what I mean when I say "Easy, Cojo." He gets even more scared of Joe and me, but he gets that way because he thinks I really *am* talking to Joe.

I say it again. I say, "Easy, Cojo."

And Cojo says, "Easy what?"

And now the guy's stopped walking. He's standing there. "I'm sorry," he says.

"'Cause why?" Cojo says. "Why're you sorry? Are you sorry you nodded at me like I was your son? Like I was your boy to nod at like that? I don't know you."

"I'm sorry," the guy says. The guy's smiling like the situation is very lighthearted, but it's like yawning after tapping gloves on your way back to the corner. A lie you tell yourself. And I'm thinking there's nothing that's itself. I'm thinking everything is like something else that's like other something elses and it's all because I said "Easy, Cojo" and didn't mean it, or because this guy nodded.

I think like this too long, I get a headache and pissed off.

I put my arm around Cojo. I say, "Easy, Cojo."

"Fuck easy," Cojo says to me. And when Cojo says that, it's like the same thing as when I said "Easy, Cojo." I know Cojo isn't really saying "Fuck easy" to me. He wouldn't say that to me. He's saying "Fear us" to the guy. But I don't know if Cojo knows that that's what he's doing with "Fuck easy." That's the problem with everything.

"Give us your fruit," I tell the guy.

"My—"

"What did you say?" Joe says.

"Easy, Cojo," I tell him.

Then the guy hands his grapefruits to me.

I say to him, "Yawn."

He can't. Cojo yawns, though. And then I do.

Then I tell the guy to get out of my sight and he does it because he's been intimidated.

Nancy Christamesta is no whore at all. And I'm no Jesus, but still I want to wash her feet. Nancy's so beautiful, my mind doesn't think about fucking her unless I'm drunk, and even then it's just an idea: I don't run the movie through my head. Usually, I imagine her saying, "Yes," in my ear. That's all it takes. Maybe we're on a rooftop, or the sixty-ninth floor of the Hancock with the restaurant that spins, but the "Yes" part is what counts. It's a little hammy. I've known her since grade school, but I've only had it for her since she was fourteen. It happened suddenly, and that's hammy too. I was eighteen, and it started at the beach—sunny day and ice cream and everything. Our families went to swim at Oak Street on a church outing and I saw her sneak away to smoke a cigarette in the tunnel under the Drive. There's hypes and winos who live in there, so I followed her, but didn't let her know. I waited at the mouth, where I could hear if anything happened, and when she came back through, she was hugging herself around the middle for warmth. A couple steps out of the tunnel, her left shoulder strap fell down and, when she moved to put it back, a bone-chill shot her posture straight and a sound came from her throat that sounded like "Hi." I didn't know if it was "Hi" or just a pretty noise her throat made after a bone-chill. I didn't think it was "Hi," because I was behind her and I didn't think she'd seen me. I wanted it to be "Hi," though. I stood there a minute after she walked away, thinking it wasn't "Hi" and wishing it was. That was that. That's how I knew what I felt.

Now she's seventeen, and it's old enough, I think. But she's got this innocence, still. It's not she's stupid—she's on the honor roll, she wants to be a writer—but Joe and I were over there a couple months earlier, at the beginning of summer, right when him and Tina were starting up. They went off to buy some beer and Nancy and I waited in her room. Nancy was sitting in this shiny beanbag. She had cutoff short-shorts on, and every time she moved, her thighs made the sticking sound that you know it's leg-on-vinyl but you imagine leg-on-leg. I had it in my head it was time to finally do something. I laid down on the carpet, next to her, listening, and after a little while, I said, "What kind of name is Nancy for you, anyway?"

Nancy said, "Actually, I think Nancy's a pretty peculiar name for me. But I always thought that was because it's mine."

See, I was flirting. I was teasing her. It was my voice she was supposed to hear, not the words it said. But it was the words she heard, and not my voice. It was an innocent way to respond. And I didn't know what to do, so I told her she was nuts.

She said, "No. Listen: Jack… Jack… Jack… Does it sound like your name, still?"

It completely sounded like my name, but I didn't say that because hearing it was as good as "Yes" in my ear and I wanted her to keep going. I wanted to tell her I loved her. Instead, I said "it." I said, "I love it." She said, "Jack… Jack… Jack. I'm glad, Jack Jack."

If she didn't have innocence, she'd have heard what my voice meant and either shut me down or flirted back at me.

When we got to their house on the day of the nodding guy, she was sitting on the stoop with a notebook, wearing flip-flops, which made it easy to admire the shape of her toes. Most people's toes look like extra things to me, like earrings or beards. Nancy's look necessary. They work for her.

Joe went inside to find Tina.

Nancy said, "What's with the grapefruits?"

I said, "We intimidated a man. It's all words."

"I don't like that spoon," she said. "I clink my teeth. It chills me up." She was still talking about grapefruits.

"They're not for you," I said. "They're for your parents."

"What's all words?" she said.

I said, "You don't say what you mean. You pretend like you're talking about something else. It works."

"A dowry goes to the groom, not the other way around," she said.

I said, "What does that have to do with anything?"

She said, "Implications. Indirectness. And suggestion."

Was she fucking with me? I don't even know if she was fucking with me. She's a wiseass, sometimes, but she's much smarter than me, too. And plus she was high. I would've taken a half-step forward and kissed her mouth right then, except I wasn't also high, and that's not kosher. Plus I probably wouldn't have stepped forward and it's just something I tell myself.

"Come inside with me," she said.

She kicked off her sandals and I followed her to the kitchen. It's a walk through a long hallway and Nancy stopped every couple steps for a second so that I kept almost bumping her. She said, "You should take your shoes off, Jack. And your socks. The floor's nice and cold."

That was a pretty thought, but getting barefoot to feel the coldness of a floor is not something I do, so I told her, "You're a strange one." Nancy likes people to think she's strange, but she doesn't like people thinking that she likes them to think that, so it was better for me to say than it sounds, even though she spun around and smacked me on the arm when I said it, which also worked out fine because I was flexed. I was expecting a smack. I know that girl.

In the kitchen, Cojo was drinking beer with Tina and Mr. Christamesta. Mr. Christamesta was standing. He's no sitter. He's 6'5" and two guys wide. I can't imagine a chair that would hold him. He could wring your throat one-handed. If there was a black-market scientist who sold clones derived from hairs, he'd go straight for the clog in Mr. Christamesta's drain whenever the customer wanted a bouncer. That's what he looks like: the father of a thousand bouncers. Or a bookie with a sandwich-shop front, which is what he is. But it's a conundrum after you talk to him, because you don't think of him like that. You talk to him, you think: He's a sandwich-shop owner who takes a few bets on the side. Still, he's the last guy in Chicago whose daughter you'd want to date. Him or Daley. But a father-in-law is a different story.

He said to me, "Jack Krakow! What's with the grapefruits?"

I didn't want to think about the grapefruits. The grapefruits made me sad.

I said, "They're for you, Sir, and Mrs. Christamesta."

"You're so formal, Jack. You trying to impress me or something? Why you trying to impress me, now? You want to marry my daughter? Is that it? My Nancy? You want to take my Nancy away from her papa? You want to run away with her to someplace better? Like that song from my youth? If. it's. the. last. thing. you ev-er do? You want to be an absconder, Jack?

With my daughter? So you bring me grapefruits? Citrus for a daughter? What kind of substitute is that? It's pearls for swine, grapefruits for Nancy. Irrespectively. It's swine for steak and beef for venison. You like venison? I love venison. But I also love deer, Jack. I love to watch deer frolic in the woods. Do you see what I mean? The world's complicated. It's okay, though. I am impressed with your grapefruits. You have a good heart. You're golden. I like you. Just calm down. We're standing in a kitchen. It's air-conditioned. Slouch a little. Have a beer."

He handed me a bottle. I handed him the grapefruits. He's got thumbs like ping-pong paddles, that guy. He could slap your face from across the country.

What sucked was, grapefruits or no, I *was* trying to impress him, and I *did* come for his daughter, and he wouldn't be so jolly about it if he knew that, so I knew there was no way he knew it. And since he didn't know it, I knew Nancy didn't know it, because those two are close. So I was like one of these smart guys like Clark Kent that the girl thinks of like an older brother. Except I'm not smart. And my alter ego isn't Superman, who she loves. At best I'm Smith, who no one knows his name but Cojo.

The one good thing about Mr. Christamesta going off on those tangents was it got Nancy laughing so hard she was shaking. She pushed her head against my shoulder and hugged around me to hold my other shoulder with her hands. For balance. And I could smell her hair, and her hair smelled like apples and girl, which is exactly what I would've imagined it smelled like in my daydreams of "Yes," if I was smart enough to imagine smell in the first place. I don't think I have the ability to imagine smell. I never tried, but I bet I can only do sound and sight.

An unfortunate thing about Nancy's laughing was how it drew her mom in from the living room. She's real serious, Mrs.

Christamesta. So serious it messes with her physically. She's an attractive woman, like Nancy twenty years later and shorter-haired—see her through a window or drive by her in the car, it's easy to tell. If you're eating dinner with her, though, or at church, and she knows she's being looked at, the seriousness covers up the beauty. It's like she doesn't have a face; just her eyebrows like a V and all the decisions she made about her hair-style. My whole life, I've seen Mrs. Christamesta laugh at three or two jokes, and I've never heard her crack a one.

"You, young lady," she said, "and you, too," to Tina, "have to quit smoking those drugs."

That got Nancy so hysterical that I had to force myself to think about the grapefruits again, about that guy coming home with no grapefruits and acting like he just forgot or, even worse, him going back to the store and getting more grapefruits and then, when he got home, making this big ceremony around cutting them or peeling them, whatever his family did with them. I had to think about that so I wouldn't start laughing with Nancy. If I laughed, it would look like I was laughing at Mrs. Christamesta. And maybe I would be.

"It's because you give them beer," she said to her husband.

"Is it you want a beer, honey?" he said to her.

She bit her lip, but took a seat.

He got up real close to her and said it again. "Is all you want is a beer?" He crouched down in front of her chair so his shirt rode up and I saw his lower back. His lower back was white as tits, and not hairy at all, which surprised me. He held her neck, and touched those paddles to her ears. "Is it you want a grapefruit?" he said. "I'll cut you a grapefruit. I'll peel you a grapefruit. I'll pulp it in the juicer. I'll juice it in the pulper. Grapefruit in segments, in slices, or liquefied. And beer. All or any. Any combination. All for you. Am I not your husband? Am I not a good husband? Am I not a husband to prepare you citrus on a sunny weekend in the windy city? Have I ever denied you love in any form? Have I ever let your gorgeous face go too long unkissed? How could I? What a brute," he said. "What a drunken misanthrope. What a cruel, cruel man," he said. "I'll zest the peel with the zester and cook salmon on the grill for you. I'll sprinkle pinches of zest for you. On top of the salmon." Then he kissed her face. Thirty, twenty times.

That was the fourth time I ever saw Mrs. Christamesta laugh. Or the third. And thank God because I was done feeling sorry for that nodding guy. I lost it so hard that when the laughter was finished with me I was holding Nancy's hand and she was tugging on the front of my shirt and I didn't remember how we got that way.

I made a violent face at her, all teeth and nostrils. For comedy. Then she pinched me on my side and I jumped back fast, squealing like a little girl.

"Fucken girl," Cojo whispered. But he didn't mean it how it sounded. It was nice of him to say to me. Brotherly.

Mr. Christamesta threw a key at me. "You okay to drive?" he said. "You're okay," he said. He kissed his wife's neck and we went out the back door. To the garage.

The Christamestas have two cars. Both of them are Lincolns and both Lincolns are blue. I tried the key on the one on the left. It was the right choice.

Cojo called shotgun, but he was kidding. I held the shotgun door open for Nancy and Cojo tackled Tina into the back seat.

We stopped at the Jewel for some patties and nacho chips, and then we were on our way.

* * *

I forgot to mention it was furniture day. Two Sundays a year, Chicago's got furniture day. You put your old furniture in the alley, in the morning, and scavengers in vans take it to their houses and junk shops. If no one wants it, the garbage trucks come in the afternoon and they bring it to the dump. That's what makes it furniture day—how the garbage trucks come. That's why there were garbage trucks on a Sunday.

One of them had balloons tied to its grill with ribbon. We got stopped at a light facing it. Grand and Oakley. We were going south on Oakley. That light takes forever. Grand's a main artery. It's dominant. Grand vs. Oakley? Oakley gets stomped.

There were white balloons and blue ones and some yellows. I don't know what color the ribbon was, but I knew it wasn't string because it shined.

Nancy said, "Do you think it's a desperate form of graffiti, Jack?"

Jack. I checked the rearview. Tina had her feet in Joe's lap. Joe was pretending to look out his window, but what he was doing was looking *at* the window. It was tinted, and he was looking at Tina's legs, reflected. Tina has good legs. You notice them. You feel elderly.

I said to Nancy, "It's probably the driver had a baby."

She said, "I think maybe some tagger got his markers and his spray-cans taken, and he was sitting on the curb out front of his house, watching all the trucks making pickups and feeling worthless because he couldn't do anything about it. He didn't want to write "wash me" with his finger in the dirt along the body since there's nothing original about that, and he didn't want to brick the windshield because he wasn't someone who wanted to harm things, but still he found himself reaching down into the weeds of the alley to grasp something heavy. He needed to let the world know he existed, and without paint or markers, bricking a windshield was the only way he could think to do it. Except then, right then, right when he gets hold of the brick—and it's the perfect brick, a cement quarter-cinderblock with gripping holes for his fingers, it fits right in his hand—he hears his little sister, inside the house. She's singing through the open window of her bedroom, above him. She's happy because yesterday was her birthday and she got all the toys she wanted, and it reminds the boy of the party they had for her, how he decorated the house all morning and his sister didn't even care because all she really wanted was to unwrap her presents—the party meant nothing to her, not even the cake, much less the decorations—and so this boy races inside, to the hallway in his mom's house, and tears a balloon cluster from the banister he tied it to, then races back out front, decorates the grill of the garbage truck."

Finally, the light turned green. If you're Oakley, you get about seven seconds before Grand starts kicking your ass again.

I said, "It could be the driver got married."

Nancy said, "And maybe it wasn't even today. Maybe it was sometime last week. Maybe those balloons have been there for nine, ten days because the driver thinks it's pretty. Because he understands what it means, you know? Or maybe because he doesn't understand what it means, because it's a conundrum, but it's a nice conundrum, something he wants to figure out."

"It could be his son," I said. "It could be it was his son got married or had a baby," I said.

Nancy said, "Oh." And I knew I shouldn't have said what I said. She was trying to start something with me and I kept ending it. She wanted me to tell her a fantasy story. I'm a meathead. A misinterpreter. Like hot pink? For years I thought it was regular pink that looked sexy on whoever was wearing it. And that Bob Marley song? I thought he was saying that as long as you stayed away from women, you wouldn't cry. Even after

I figured it out, it's still the first thing I think when it comes on the radio. It's like when I'm wrong for long enough, I can't get right. I had a fantasy story in my head, but I didn't say it. And why not?

We were merging onto the Eisenhower when this guy in a Miata blew by us on the ramp and I had to hit the brakes a little. Everyone cussed except Nancy, who was spaced out, or pretending to be. Then we got quiet and Joe said, "What kind of fag drives a Miata?"

And Tina said, "Don't." Tina goes to college at UIC. She was a junior, like I would have been. "Don't say fag," she said.

"Fag faggot fag," Cojo said. "It's just words. It's got nothing to do with who anyone wants to fuck." He took out a cigarette. He said, "This is a fag in England." He lit the cigarette. He said, "I know fags who've screwed hundreds of women. I know fags who screw no one. Have a fag," he said. He gave the cigarette to Tina and lit a second one for himself. He said, "That rapist Mike Tyson's a fag. And my cousin Niles. He's screwing his girlfriend even as we speak to each other here in this very car. There's fags who like windmills and fags on skinny bicycles. I know fags who fix cars and fags who pour concrete. Regis Philbin's a fag. Kurt Loder and that fag John Norris. Lots of TV and movie guys. Rock stars. Pretty much all of them. So what? It's a word. It means asshole, but it's quicker to say and more offensive cause it's only fags who say asshole like it's any kind of insult. Even jerk's better than asshole. Asshole's a fagged-out word, and fag's offensive. And it should be offensive. I want it to be offensive. Someone calls me a Polack? I'm offended. But I'm a fucken Ukrainian, you know? I don't give a shit about the Polish people. No offense, Krakow, but I don't give a fuck for your people. Someone calls me Polack, though, I'll tear his jaws off at the hinge. And cause why? Cause he's saying I'm Polish? No. Cause he's saying Polish people are lowlifes? No. He's trying to offend me is why. When he's calling me Polack, he's calling me fag. He's calling me asshole. So fine. You're pretty. Okay. You smell good. You say smart things to me when you're not telling me the right way to talk. Good news. I like you. I want to spend all my money on you. I want to take you on vacation to an island where there's coconuts and diving. Miatas are for assholes if it makes you more comfortable. But the asshole in that Miata's got fagged-out taste is what I'm telling you."

Tina said, "You've thought about this a lot, Cojo."

"I got a gay cousin," he said. "A homosexual. Lenny. He fucks men, and that's not right and it makes me sick, but that's not why he's a fag. He's a fag because whenever someone calls him fag, it's me who ends up in a fight, not him. He's a fag because he won't stand up for himself. Imagine: your own cousin a fag like that. That's how it is to be me. Not just one but two fags in the family—Lenny the homofag and don't forget about Niles the regular fag who all he does is chase girls—but I'm the only one can say it, right? About how my family's got some fags in it, I mean. Don't you ever bring it up to me. It's like a big secret, and tell the truth it makes me uncomfortable to talk about, so let's just stop talking about it, okay?"

Joe was always talking to girls about Lenny. Sometimes Lenny had cancer and sometimes he was a retard. In 1999, he was usually Albanian. But there wasn't any Lenny. I know all Joe's cousins. So do the Christamestas. Lenny was fiction. But I didn't say. If he did have a cousin Lenny, and this Lenny was a gay, Cojo would defend his cousin Lenny against people who called Lenny fag. So Cojo was telling a certain kind of truth. And it never really mattered to Tina, anyway. She'd just wanted to know Joe cared what she thought of him, and the effort it took him to come up with that bullshit about fags and assholes—

that made it obvious he cared. And Joe is definitely crazy for Tina. He discusses it with me. All the things he wants to buy her. Vacations on islands with sailboats and mangos, fucking her on a hammock. They'd still never fucked, but they mashed pretty often. So often it was comfortable. So comfortable they started in the back seat of the car, which was not comfortable for me, sitting next to Nancy, who's staring at the carton of patties in her lap while the sister gets mauled. I hit as many potholes as I could. The Ike's got thousands.

Finally we arrived at the wrong barbecue. We were supposed to go to 514 Greenway and we went to 415. It was my fault. I wrote it down wrong when Sensei Mike told us at the dojo on Friday.

But 415 was raging. Fifty, forty people. Mostly middle-aged guys, wearing Oxfords and sandals. Some of them had wives, but there weren't any babies, which always spooks me a little, a barbecue without babies. It's like if you ever had a father who shaved off his mustache.

It took us a few minutes of looking around for Sensei Mike before we noticed this banner hanging off the fence. It said, "Happy Tenure, Professor Schinkl!" By then, we all had bottles of beer in our hands. The beers tasted yeasty. They were from Belgium. That's what set the whole thing off.

The four of us were half-sitting along the edge of the patio table, trying to decide if it was more polite to finish the beers there or take them with us to look for Sensei Mike's house when this guy came up and made a show of adjusting his sunglasses. First he just lowered them down the bridge of his nose so we could see one of his eyebrows raise up. But then he was squinting at us over the frames and he had a hand on his hip. He stayed that way for a couple of wheezy breaths, then tore the sunglasses off his face with the other hand and held them up in the air behind his ear like he was gonna swat us. Instead, he let the shades dangle and he said, "Hmmmmmm." The sound of that got the attention of some other people. They weren't crowding up or anything, but they were looking at us.

The guy said, "Hmmmmmm," again, but with more irritation than the first time. Like a whining, almost.

"How ya doin'?" Cojo said to him. Nancy leaned into me, but it was instinct, nothing to make a big deal of. Tina held her beer close. Cojo was smiling, which is not a good thing for him to do around people who don't know him. His smile looks like he's asking you to stop making him smile. It's got no joy. It's because of his smile that I retrieve the cars when we work the lot together. If customers tip, it's usually on the way out.

Real slow and loud, the guy said, "How's. Your Belgian. Beer?"

So the beer was his and he was attached to it in some sick way. Like fathers and the end-piece of the roast beef. He wasn't anyone's father, though, this guy. He was being a real prick about the beer is what he was, but it was the wrong barbecue and he was harmless so far. He was tofu in khakis. About as rough as a high-school drama teacher. Still, he could've been Schinkl for all we knew, so he didn't get hit.

"You want one?" Cojo said. He said, "I think there's one left in the cooler by the grill."

The guy stared at Joe, just to let him know that he'd heard what Joe said, but was ignoring him. Then he spun on Nancy. He said, "Is that *ground chuck* in your lap, young lady? Do you mean to wash down those patties of *ground chuck* with my imported. Belgian. Beer?" He poked the meat.

I said, "Hey."

"Hay's for horses," he said, the fucken creep.

A woman in the crowd—they were crowding up, now—said, "Calm down, Byron."

He poked the meat again, hard. Busted a hole in the plastic wrap. Nancy flinched and I had that fucker in an arm-lock before the meat hit the ground. Joe dumped his beer in the lawn and broke the bottle on the table edge. We moved in front of the Christamestas, like shields. I had Byron bent in front of me, huffing and puffing.

I didn't want the girls to see us get beat down, but I thought about afterwards, about Nancy holding my hands at my chest and wiping the blood from my face with disinfected cottonballs, how I could accidentally confess my love and not be held responsible since I'd have a serious concussion.

Byron said, "Let go."

"You got a thin voice," I told him.

I pulled his wrist back a couple degrees. His fingers danced around.

Every guy in that yard was creeping toward us, saying "Hey" and "Hey, now." There were too many of them, broken bottle or no. All we had left was wiseass tough-guy shit. "Hey," they said. And Joe said, "Hay's for horses," and I forced a laugh through my teeth like I was supposed to. They kept creeping. Little baby steps. Tina whispered to Nancy, "Can we go? Let's just go."

"Just let go of me!" Byron said. "Let go of me!"

I said, "What!"

He shut his mouth and the crowd stopped moving. They stopped right behind where the patio met the grass. That's when it occurred to me the reason they weren't pummeling us was Byron. They didn't want me to damage him. And that meant that I controlled them. I thought: We got a hostage. I thought: All we have to do is take him out the gate on the side of the house, get him to the car, then drop him in the street and drive off. I was gonna tell Joe, but then Nancy started talking.

"Do you guys know Sensei Mike?" she said.

This chubby drunk guy was wobbling at the front of the crowd. He said, "What?" But it sounded like"Whud?" That's how I knew he was a lisper, even before he started lisping. Because he had adenoid problems. The first lisper I ever knew in grade school had adenoid problems. Brett Novak. He said his own name "Bred Novag." Mine he said "Jag Gragow." When people called him a lisper, I didn't know what a lisper was, so I decided he was a lisper not just because of what he did to *s* sounds, but because of what he did to *t* sounds and *k* sounds, too. So I thought this chubby drunk guy was a lisper, because I used to be wrong about what a lisper was and so "lisper" is the first thing I think when I hear adenoid problems. But since the chubby guy turned out to be a lisper after all, my old wrongness made it so I was right. It was like if Nancy wore hot pink. The color would look sexy on her, and because it would look sexy on her, I'd say it was "hot pink," and I'd be right, even though I didn't know what I was saying. I'd be right because of an old misunderstanding.

"Sensei Mike?" said Nancy. "We came for Sensei Mike." Her voice was trembling. I could've killed everybody.

The guy said, "Thenthaimigue? Ith that thome thort of thibboleth?"

This got laughs. The crowd thought it was very clever for the lisper to say a word like shibboleth to us.

But fuck them for thinking I don't know shibboleth. Some people don't, but I do. It's from the Old Testament. In CCD they told us we shouldn't read the Old Testament till we were older because it was violent and confusing and totally Christless, so I read some of it (I skipped Leviticus and quit at

Kings). The part with shibboleth is in Judges: there were the Ephrathites who were these people who couldn't make the sound *sh*. They were at war with the Gileadites. The Gileadites controlled all the crossings on the Jordan River, and the main thing they didn't want was for the Ephrathites to get across the river. The problem was the Ephrathites looked exactly like the Gileadites and spoke the same language, too; so if an Ephrathite came to one of the crossings, the Gileadites had almost no way of telling that he was an Ephrathite. Not until Jephthah, who was the leader of the Gileadites, remembered how Ephrathites couldn't make the *sh* sound—that's when he came up with the idea to make everyone who wanted to cross the river say the word shibboleth. If they could say shibboleth, they could pass, but if they couldn't say it, it meant they were an enemy and they got slain. So shibboleth was this code word, but it didn't work like a normal code word. A normal code word is a secret—you have to prove you know what it is. Shibboleth, though—it wasn't any secret. Jephthah would tell you what it was. What mattered was how you said it. How you said it is what saved your life, or ended it.

I said to the lisper, "I know what's a shibboleth, and Sensei Mike's no shibboleth. And you're no Jephthah, either." It came out wormy and know-it-all sounding. I sounded like I cared what they thought of me. Maybe I did. I don't think so, though.

"Are you jogueing?" he said. "Whud gind of brude are you? Do you *offden* find yourthelf engaging in meda-converthathions?" He pronounced the *t* in *often*, the prick, and on top of it, he turned it into a fucken *d*.

All those guys laughed anyway. It was funnier to them than the shibboleth joke. It was the funniest thing they'd ever heard.

And I was sick of getting laughed at. And I was sick of

people asking me questions that weren't questions.

I pulled on Byron's arm and he moaned. Cojo slapped him on the chops and the lisper stepped back into the crowd, to hide.

The crowd started shifting. But not forward. Not in any direction really, not for too long. It swelled in one place and thinned in another, like a water balloon in a fist. It was in my fist.

I saw the lisper's head craned up over the shoulder of a guy who'd snuck to the front, and that's when I knew.

They didn't stop creeping up at the patio because they were scared of what I'd do to their friend and his arm. They stopped at the patio to give us space. They stopped at the patio so I could do whatever I'd do to Byron and they could watch.

I said to Nancy, "You and Tina go get the car, okay?"

Nancy reached in my pocket for the keys and whispered, "Be careful." Then Tina kissed Joe. The girls ran off. It could've been a war movie. It could've been Joe and I going to the front in some high-drama war movie. It was a little hammy, but that didn't bother me.

As soon as I was sure the girls were clear, I asked Joe, with my eyes and eyebrows, if he thought we should run for it.

He told me with his shoulders and his chin that he thought it was a good idea.

Then I got an inspiration. I started yelling at the top of my lungs: "AHHHHHH!"

The whole crowd went pop-eyed and stepped back and stepped back and stepped back. I got a huge lung capacity. I think I yelled for about a minute. I yelled till my throat bled and I couldn't yell anymore. Then I dropped Byron, and we took off.

Nancy was just pulling out of the parking spot when we got to the car. Some of the sickos from the barbecue ran out onto the street, and one of them was shouting, "We'll call the police!"

* * *

We still didn't know Sensei Mike's right address and the girls decided it was probably better to get out of Glen Ellyn, so we headed back to Chicago. When we got to the Christamesta house, Tina and Joe went inside and I followed Nancy around the neighborhood on foot, not saying anything. I don't know how long that lasted. It was dark, though. We ended up at the park at Iowa and Rockwell, under the tornado slide, sitting in pebbles, our backs against the ladder. Nancy opened her purse and pulled out a Belgian beer. I popped it with my lighter and gave it to her. She sipped and gave it back. I sipped and gave it back.

I've told a lot of girls I was in love with them. There's some crack-ass wisdom about it being easier to say when you don't mean it, but that's not why I didn't say it to Nancy. I didn't say it because every time I've said it, I meant it. If I said it again, it would be like all those other times, and all those other times—it went away. And silence wasn't any holier than saying it. Just more drama for its own sake. All of it's been done before. It's been in TV shows and comic books and it's how your parents met. And there's nothing wrong with drama, I don't think. And there's nothing wrong with drama for its own sake, either. What's wrong is drama that doesn't know it's drama. And what's wrong is doing the same thing everyone else does and thinking you're original, thinking you're unpredictable.

I said, "Maybe it's cause he wanted racing stri—" and the sound cut off. My throat was killing me from the yelling and it closed up.

Nancy said, "Your voice is broken."

And that was an unexpected way to put it, drama or no.

I swigged the beer again and told her, all raspy, "Maybe it's racing stripes. The guy wanted racing stripes."

"What?" she said.

"Don't what me," I said. I gulped more beer. I said, "He wanted to paint racing stripes and the city wouldn't let him. There's a code against painting stripes on city vehicles. So every day he ties the balloons on the grill. And maybe that's a half-ass way to have racing stripes, but then maybe he figures stripes on a garbage truck aren't really racing stripes to begin with, so he doesn't mind using balloons. Or maybe he does mind, but he keeps it to himself because he's not a complainer. Maybe he just keeps tying balloons on the grill, telling himself they're as good as racing stripes, and maybe one day they will be."

"That's a sad story," Nancy said. She carved SAD! in the pebbles with the bottle of beer.

"How's it *sad*?" I said.

Under SAD! she carved a circle with an upside-down smile.

"It's not sad," I said.

She said, "I don't believe that."

"But I'm telling you," I said.

She said, "Then I don't believe you, Jack."

And did I kiss her then? Did Nancy Christamesta close her eyes and tilt her head back, away from the moon? Did she open her mouth? Did she open it just a little, just enough so I could feel her breath on my chin before she would kiss me and then did I finally kiss her?

Fuck you.

MY HUSTLERS

by EDMUND WHITE

WHEN I WAS seventeen I worked for my father in Cincinnati all one summer manning an Addressograph machine. By today's standards it was a cumbersome, noisy, labor-intensive way of running off mass mailings. One device stamped out names and addresses on metal plates and these plates were then inserted in a carousel, I believe, which noisily stamped inked letters on envelopes. My father had thousands of clients' names on his list. The Addressograph clattered away to itself for hours on end.

His office was only a few blocks away from Fountain Square, which by day was the slightly seedy heart of the small city. But at night the Square (which was in reality a long oval) became still seedier and attracted a few hustlers and johns. Adolescents from across the river in Covington, Kentucky, or the outskirts of Cincinnati would perch on the metal guardrails around the central raised oval with its verdigrised fountain. The young men would spit and nurse a cigarette inside a cupped hand. They might have another cigarette tucked behind an ear, which looked like a white barrette pushed into their carded hair. Their hands were big, raw, rough-skinned working hands. They usually wore white T-shirts and beltless, low-riding jeans and ordinary lace-up shoes, scuffed and worn down at the heels. Sometimes they might have on fancier trousers of a sleazy fabric, pleated and baggy. Their spitting gave them the air and appearance of dogs marking their territory.

Cars would creep around the oval and the older male drivers would look up at the guys sitting on the rails. If the car paused, the youngster would grudgingly slip down from his perch, throw away his cigarette, spit, and lean into the open car window, his bare arm resting on the car roof. He might flash a smile that would reveal missing or ill-suited teeth. The smile was so out of character in these faces with their thin lips, gnarled Adam's apples, and crafty eyes of palest blue that it came across as incongruous, like a curtsy from a prisoner.

I knew intuitively what everyone was up to. I earned a small salary from my father. I thought I could hire one of these guys and have sex with him. Although I was seeing a shrink during the school term in order to "mature" and go straight, my treatment had nothing to do with my imperious sexual desires. I was in the grip of a compulsion that didn't have much to do with pleasure. I mean, I didn't imagine a man stroking my naked body idly or kissing me or letting me enter him. I could conjure up the idea of love—doomed, crepuscular love—but not of pleasure. I had no specific sex positions or acts in mind. My ambition was to hire a guy, to touch his erect penis, to make him come, to be able to tell myself I had been with another male and put my lips on his penis. Maybe he would love me and we'd run away.

I had expended an infinite amount of time and energy arranging to seduce the neighbor boy, then a guy at camp, later two guys at boarding school, and to jerk off a few married men in various public toilets in Chicago where my mother lived. It seemed that almost no boys my age wanted to have sex with another fellow though the one in a thousand who was willing I was always quick to spot. If someone's eyes lingered even a fraction of a second on mine, I went into instant alert.

How convenient that these young Kentucky men, smelling of beer and Camels, their bodies so lean they had no hips, a T-shirt sleeve swollen because it was folded back over a cigarette pack above a tattoo—how convenient that they were for hire.

I wasn't yet part of the homosexual subculture of the 1950s. I didn't know yet that a big penis was considered more desirable than a small one, that "we" had finicky preferences for or against circumcision, and that a straight man was viewed as the highest good and another queen as nothing but shoddy goods, a pathetic "sister." For me then almost any man would do. Not long before I'd been thrilled to be felt up in a nearby deserted Cincinnati movie theater by a man who smelled of licorice while we watched Hitler's dull, perfectly innocent home movies of Eva Braun at Berchtesgaden—innocent though the posters outside promised an orgy in the Bavarian Alps. She jerked from parapet to bench, stagily exclaiming over a new puppy or twirling to show off her new skirt as the man, consuming his long black threads of candy and never looking at me, let one pale hand travel blindly up my thigh.

I was in a fever of desire for these hillbilly boys perched on the Fountain Square railing. As the city baked and sweated and the cars pulsed light and crept around, the air refusing to stir, I looked and looked. Here was a big blond with strong arms and slicked-back hair and a square, dimpled jaw—he saw me across two lanes of cars and his eyes tightened with curiosity. When he was sure my glances were intentional he broke into a big smile and waved me over, his eyes suddenly catching the stinging smoke from his cigarette and watering.

"Hey, lil fella, har yü?" His hillbilly accent was nearly incomprehensible. He motioned me closer with an insider's sideways jerk of the head. He stood. He was wearing jeans. I noticed how his legs were slightly bowed, which made me picture him mounted on a horse. The area around his crotch was carefully bleached.

After some discussion I agreed to give him twenty dollars and I laid out another five for a room in a fleabag hotel two blocks away. I had on a short-sleeve white shirt and a black knit tie; I wore nerdy Steve Allen black glasses and had a longish brush cut. I was skinny and given to tics—my neck was always stiff and bobbing and I nodded it in little spasms that were so noticeable that I hated to sit in front of anyone at the movies. Although there were few people on the street I feared running into someone I knew—me, a seventeen-year-old nerd with a prissy way of talking and a constant tic, and he, an older, drawling hillbilly with a prominent crotch and a white T-shirt sticking to his chest.

Up in the room Hank undressed slowly, chatting away. For him tonight was typical, not transcendent. Despite the heat I pushed the wooden shutters closed but through the slatted openings the neon sign outside still kept blinking. At last Hank was naked except for his white underpants. He lay down on the bed, smiled and opened his arms.

"Whatya wanna dü?" he asked.

As I stumbled out of my suit trousers and up-to-the-knee black stockings and undid my tie and shirt, I just smiled and said, "Oh, I don't know."

"Yü gotta have sumpin' yü wanna dü," he said, smiling and stretching his tan forearms and pale biceps.

"I just—"

"What? I can't hear yü."

"I just want to be—"

"Pardon?"

"Held."

I turned off the light and hopped into bed beside him. He slipped off his underpants and so did I. A blue neon glow from below the shutters alternated with a pink light from above. He asked me if I liked his muscles. I said I did. He flexed. I manifested enthusiasm, though for me the scenario was suddenly all wrong. I wanted him to stare into my eyes and sip kisses from my lips and hold me tightly and tell me he loved me while down there our genitals would do something ecstatic and nonspecific. And I wanted him to admire me, admire my soul and my very existence, since even unattractive people (*especially* the unattractive) harbor dreams of finally being loved not for their attributes but for their essence. In love I was an essentialist.

"Want me to flex?" he asked.

I thought that if I just shrugged he'd be annoyed, so I said with extra enthusiasm, "Oh, *please* do."

He wanted to be admired and so did I, but even though I was paying I felt his need was greater than mine. Or rather my sense of self could survive rejection since it was built on it, whereas his self-esteem was at once more masculine and more fragile. My desire for love obviously had to pay an admission price—admiration for his muscles. As he flexed and I expressed my enthusiasm, a faint smile came to his lips: I was a pansy after all panting over a real man's body and that felt comfortably familiar to him.

And then it was over. He was dressing, still wearing his benign, contemptuous smile. I'm sure he thought I had nothing to complain of since we'd both come and his come had shot halfway up his chest. My youth, my innocence, my capacity for devotion meant nothing to him. I was surprised he didn't even remark on my age, for surely I was at least ten years younger than he. But maybe it didn't show.

He playfully mimed socking my jaw and said, "See yü around, kid."

Those Kentucky boys also hung out at the Greyhound bus station a block off Fountain Square or loitered around a dirty bookstore right on the Square. Once every two weeks I could afford one of them. I knew which ones I preferred—the compact blond beauties with hairless forearms and a certain spark-striking way of walking heel first and a constant need to pull their jeans up with thumbs hooked in the two front loops. They seemed to be concentrating on their crotches. They had a habit of looking me right in the eye while spitting to one side through compressed lips, as if it were a form of muttering or curse. Usually I was so flustered that I'd go with the first man who spoke to me, no matter what he looked like. I'd panic, afraid an outsider would see what was going on. I'd lower my head in shyness or assent, do anything rather than draw any more attention to my vicious desire. "Hey!" was all they'd have to say and I was helpless. Usually I got someone spotty and mocking.

One day in the park I met a tall, weedy gay man in his early twenties who had been studying me and was on to my game. "Well, hello!" he drawled, the "lo" on a rising then a falling note, as if to suggest the importance of this encounter. He sounded like Mae West. His forehead was shiny, his nose infected near the nostril. He came up to me as I was smoking a cigarette I'd stolen from home. I was standing in the doorway next to the bookstore.

"A lot of beef on the hoof tonight, wouldn't you say?"

I wasn't quite sure what he meant.

"The trade," he said.

"I'm sorry?" I said.

"Don't you even know what trade is?"

He explained to me that all these dumb hillbillies were "trade"—men who could be "serviced" though of course they'd never reciprocate since they were real men and "not at all light in the loafers." "But of course they like to be serviced. When a guy is horny he doesn't stop to wonder whether the nearest warm hole is male or female." I wondered if that could possibly be true. It sounded unlikely.

He asked me how much I was forking out.

"Twenty," I said.

"Drive a harder bargain, hon. You're ruining it for the rest of us. You can get them down to ten."

At that rate I could have one every week, though at the end of each of my previous encounters I had felt wretchedly guilty and I'd vowed never to sleep with another man. As it turned out my hustlers would form a long sequence that I wanted to end with each new addition.

"I've been watching you," he said. "You're so fearless."

"Driven," I said, smiling. It felt good to acknowledge my compulsion with stylish rue.

He laughed. "Don't you have a car?"

"Next year, but I'm just seventeen now," I said. "I'll have a car next summer."

"Gawd, real jailbait. You look—well, you don't *look* older but you're so sure of yourself, such a saucy wench."

Another friend of his drifted up, a plump young man with dark blue patches under the arms of his pale blue shirt. "Mary, the joint is hopping tonight!" he said in a bored drawl, offering me a feverish little hand when we were introduced, which he confided to me as if it were a sleeping dachshund. "So, how many of these guys have you had, Miss Thing?"

"Four," I said. "That big blond with the pompadour—"

"Oh, *her*, if she's straight she could die with the secret. Only bulldaggers are *that* masculine."

There was a bored, careless camaraderie among us as our eyes kept wandering over the beef that thrilled me, though I didn't let on. The year before in Chicago I had met a gay man in his thirties who owned a bookshop on Rush Street and he, too, had befriended me in this same offhand way. The understanding was that though I was just a kid I was in training and their job was to instruct me in the arcana of gay life, though unemphatically, certainly with no excess of sentiment. When we were alone among ourselves we formed a secret sorority of flamboyant Maenads in hot pursuit of an Orpheus to devour. We wanted a real man, a heterosexual man, but if he ever reciprocated our blandishments then he'd lose his virility and become as compromised as we were. A real man had to be primitive, angry, not too intelligent and, in conversation, a bit ludicrous, whereas we queens were clever but as sterile as eunuchs.

I didn't believe all these things, not yet, maybe I never would, but I understood that such was their view of the world. We knew that these men, these hustlers, had no interest in us physically (in fact they must despise us as sick queens, as freakish fairies). They wanted nothing but our money. So be it! At least this motive was simple, honest, and acted as an acceptable alibi for their availability. And hustling gave a lot of out-of-work people something to do in the empty summer city.

These two Cincinnati queens worked in a nearby downtown church, one as the deacon and the other as the organist. They wanted me to take a hustler down to the men's room in the basement of their church and suck him off in front of an open window. They'd be squatting in a darkened room on the other side of the airshaft outside the window. The window of their room looked out on the airshaft and was lined up with the bathroom window. They wanted me to provide them with titillation. In those days there were no gay bars except in faraway Toledo, no gay YMCAs except a fabled orgy palace of a Y in Milwaukee, no gay pornographic films, no places for gays to cruise each other ("And do *what* together?" the organist screamed: "Two big girls? Bump pussies?"). But here in Cincinnati there were only these skinny straight hillbillies with million-mile stares, boyish torsos, grease-heavy DAs, and tumescent crotches that could be opened and revealed, as in certain holy statues of Our Lord tearing open his chest to reveal his Sacred Heart.

I was burning with the desire, night after night, to see what these penises looked like, to know the size and girth and smell and taste of each one. I was possessed by literalism (I would never have been content with the description of a penis I couldn't see or touch).

I was glad to have someplace to take my hustlers, the church basement rather than hotels where I had to pay five dollars for a room and register under the contemptuous eye of the night clerk.

Nor did I mind exhibiting my tricks and talents to my invisible but attentive sisters on the other side of the airshaft. Their presence worked to make me feel more normal, a sister in a sorority. They also made me feel marginally safer, though I knew that if a hustler got tough with me they'd take to their heels and certainly never call the cops and risk probable imprisonment and exposure. But the hustlers didn't know this place and the unfamiliarity made them uneasy, just enough (we hoped) for them to take no chances.

We were alone in the big blackened brick church with its permanent smell of coal smoke and disinfectant, with its linoleum-lined halls lit by red exit signs. This unexpected solitude might have spooked the boys. They might have thought I was working for the cops. Maybe this was entrapment.

The hustlers were used to playing with themselves at a urinal and giving a john a sneak preview of what he could buy. But when I asked them to back up two paces and stand in front of the window where I could drop to my knees, they were puzzled and became uneasy, even though we were presumably alone in a silent, empty building. They were so accustomed to stepping fractionally closer to the urinal and hiding their excitement if a stranger walked in that they were reluctant to give up this useful reflex.

"Oh, Gawd, he was gorgeous!" the organist exclaimed half an hour later when I came back to the scene of the crime.

"You're such a huzzy," the deacon told me with a mild smile. "Hoovering away like that on that nice country boy, young, dumb, and I presume full of come. Where'd you learn to swallow it, girl? I usually spit it out."

The next summer when my dad let me drive a company car I picked up a half-drunk kid with beefy, freckled arms, red fuzz, jeans that smelled of beer piss, and a florid face with small, puffy eyes and lips so full they looked as if they might split open. There's no point in mentioning him—his is just a face and a body and a big dark penis. It lay there on his stomach like a blood sausage.

An older guy with mutton-chop sideburns and a worried look insisted I park in a dark alleyway just a block from the bus station. As I was going down on his soft penis the car door on my side flew open and there was another guy, ugly, angry, who was saying, "Now you're in big trouble. You're breaking the law, you know."

I sat up, rigid with fear. "Oh?" I said in a high, airy voice I didn't recognize. My heart was pounding and I was wondering how I was going to get out of this.

My hustler had already zipped up. Now I understood why he'd been limp—he was in a state of high alarm. I'd learned a valuable lesson: a soft dick means the guy is about to rob you. The hustler was looking around and in some peripheral pocket of my mind I thought that they, too, must fear the cops, for even if I had no rights or recourse surely what they were doing was illegal too, if in some lesser way.

"Okay," the partner said, sliding into the driver's seat and closing the door. I was wedged between them and for a moment I hoped that after I'd paid up they'd let me service both of them. "Damn, you're in hot water, Mister. You better show me all the money you got on you and if you hold anything back you'll be in deep shit."

I pulled out my wallet and emptied the cash flap of the forty-two dollars I had. I dug into my pants pocket and fished out a small handful of coins, mostly pennies. The guy knocked the money out of my hand and the coins splashed on the rubber floor mat.

"Shit, this all you got?" He counted the bills carelessly, as if such a small sum was beneath his notice. "If your pa knew you were out suckin' peter you'd be up the crick, wouldn't you?" I lowered my eyes. His big hand, resting on the seat behind me, knocked me hard on the back of my head. "Wouldn't you?" he asked in a loud voice that had suddenly gone redneck.

"Hey, Jumbo," my hustler said in a low voice, clearly embarrassed and miserable. "Jess lay off and let's get out of here..."

"Shit, man, that's bogue. Don' be usin' my name." A cruel smile turned his mouth up on one side. "What else you got for us, cocksucker?" He grabbed my hand and looked at my class ring. "I'll take that."

"Oh, please don't," I said in an overbred, fluty voice, which revealed to me how much of a victim I'd become. "My father will notice it's missing. I won't be able to explain—"

"Let the kid keep his ring, Jumbo," my hustler muttered. I was so irrational that I found myself liking him. I was already half-fantasizing that we'd get together some other time.

"I told you—" Jumbo shouted. But he broke off when the hustler jumped out of the car. A second later Jumbo was gone, too, and there I was in a parked car in the middle of the front seat, an empty wallet on my lap. Both front doors were open and the overhead light was glowing feebly and the cooling motor was ticking to itself as it contracted.

I was always reading novels, and I knowingly chuckled when a character was described as "foolish" or "naïve" but here I was: I was naïve, I was foolish, which until this moment I'd never suspected. The reader considers himself to be all-knowing, superior, but now I had to push this conventional flattery aside and recognize that cleverness is not a question of perspective but of accumulated experience in the world. I was slowly putting together my own fund of lived worldliness, more modest but more real than the reader's omniscience.

One could learn about life from literature—one could learn to spot a confidence man—but only if one woke up from the smug, dreamlike superiority of the reader, which blinded one to the actual slippery manifestations of vice and dishonesty in the shadowy world of reality. In the novel, at least the reassuring nineteenth-century novel, one was always privy to everyone's well-lit motives and alerted to even the first sign of corruption.

But in life—how could one navigate in an unnarrated world? Of course I was always narrating my life to myself (idea for novel), but unfortunately I had no access to the private thoughts of the other characters around me. Even my own mind was too prolific to be comprehensible. It was certainly true that I was fashioning the book of my life at all times, trying out sentences, sketching out plot lines, hoarding impressions, restaging the scenes I'd just lived through. I'd already written and typed two novels in boarding school, one about me and the other (my senior thesis) about my mother or some more driven version of my mother to whom I attributed my own sexual obsessions. At every moment I convinced myself that I was gathering material for the novel of my life—all experienced from the philosophical distance of the author. Even these humiliating occasions when I was robbed could be used as material. Life was a field trip. My writing would turn all this evil into flowers.

I mentioned just now my "sexual obsessions," but all these encounters with hustlers were as much an expression of fear as of desire, and above all they were animated by curiosity. I was swallowing the sperm of strangers and this feast convinced me I was *possessing* all these men. I was like one of those nearly insane saints who must take communion several times a day, who are driven by a desire to eat the body and drink the blood of a long-dead historical human being. That man may also have been a god, but the saint longs for the pulse and crunch of a thirty-three-year-old Jew nailed to crossed boards. In the same way I had this permanent, gnawing hunger for all these street-corner Hanks or Orvilles, for their penises fat or thin, crooked or straight, eager or reluctant.

Hustling in the gay world is quite different from female prostitution aimed at the heterosexual male world. A straight man can assume that almost every woman he meets is attracted to some man, if not to him in particular, whereas the total number of gay men is very small, never more than five percent, and prostitution is an obvious way of enlarging that proportion. In poorer populations or in those where women may not have sex before marriage even many heterosexual men are available to other men, if they're paid something. *They*, of course, don't consider themselves homosexual—only their partners are.

For me in the 1950s I could walk for hours down the beach on Lake Michigan past hundreds and hundreds of sunbathers of all ages and several races—and everywhere I saw nothing but straight couples and families. Never did faunlike eyes flicker toward me through bangs, never did a hairy brute adjust himself and look at a passing lad's butt with an open mouth. There were no gay men in the world, or just a few here and there, hissing, theatrical queens, alcoholic and suicidal. But in Cincinnati there were *hired* men and the idea that twenty—or even ten—dollars could open their flies and make them lie back with a sneer and flex their muscles. They were like dolls in a toy store that I could play with promiscuously but their mechanisms would permit them to perform only one action—turn their head or open their arms—and that would exhaust their entire repertory.

My father and stepmother wanted me to attend debutante parties. I'd put on my tux and black tie and squire Mitzi or Taffy about or stand in a ballroom at the Netherland Hilton, alone in a crowd of extra men, afraid to strike up a conversation, even more afraid to appear conspicuously alone. But after I'd driven home my buxom, freckled date to her dimly lit mansion and pecked her chastely at the huge oak door, I'd head right back downtown in the company car, still wearing all my finery and still feeling the slight buzz of the champagne punch. I'd cruise slowly around Fountain Square, the swerving car lights suddenly snapshotting a white T-shirt, tanned hand, and a thin arm raised to brush back thick hair. If I idled for a moment a guy in tight jeans and with ribs that could be counted through a T-shirt and huge, knobby shoulders standing up like epaulets would be leaning down to smile through my open window, his breath smelling of tobacco. He'd slip in on the passenger side and say, "Just get off work?" and I realized he thought I was a waiter in a monkey suit and I said, "Yeah. Where should we go?"

"What you got in mind?"

"Just a quiet place where we can relax."

"How much is me relaxin' worth to you?"

"Ten bucks."

"Twenty?"

"Fifteen."

"Deal. I know a itty-bitty little lane up the hill in Hyde Park, you'll feel you're in the country."

I reached over at the light and he spread his legs and pushed his pelvis forward. "Hmm..." I purred.

"You like that?"

"Sure do."

"You gonna take care of me real good?"

"Sure will."

When I was in college I spent one summer in Chicago. My mother went off to work in a clinic in Munich. She let me stay alone in her apartment and even gave me four postdated checks of twenty-five dollars each to see me through the month—enough to make sure I didn't starve to death but so little that I'd be forced to get a job. I worked on the South Side loading trucks, which, in that day before containerization, was all done by hand. In order to get the job I had to lie and promise I wouldn't abandon it at the end of the summer in order to go back to school. I told them I'd dropped out. But one by one the men I worked with came up to me and urged me to return to the university. "If you don't, you'll be like us, doing a shit job the rest of your life."

I have no idea how they survived that job year after year. I couldn't stand it even a week, working in the hundred-degree weather. I worked nights and got off at dawn. The loading docks weren't air-conditioned and in the Chicago heat and humidity my eyes were stung and blinded by sweat, every muscle in my body ached. Although I'd lived by the bell in boarding school, nevertheless I'd always been interested in my studies and the long afternoons, from two to six, had been free. During my freshman year at college I'd studied hard but at least I'd been exhilarated by my exotic courses (Chinese social structure, beginning Chinese, the music of Bartók, Buddhist art) and in any event I still had vacant hours for bull sessions around the dorm.

Now I was alone in a big city full of laboring, sweating adults. In my dirty work clothes I'd return at dawn from the South Side trucking district to my mother's elegant Near North apartment on the thirty-second floor overlooking the Loop and a swipe of the Lake Michigan shore. Coming home I'd walk down Michigan Avenue in my jeans and T-shirt breasting waves of executives in seersucker suits and nurses in static-clinging white uniforms and elevator men in pale brown short-sleeve shirts and secretaries in pastel dresses and matching high heels, this whole disorganized army of wage earners walking through the slanting early light projected past the office buildings, like aisles of light in a morning forest. I was exhausted but it felt disconcerting to sleep by day on my mother's gold-thread upholstered couch.

Nevertheless I curled up on the couch in the sun-bright living room, as if I were the fertilized speck inside a warm yellow yolk, anything rather than lie down on the bed in the darkened bedroom. A nap on the couch, no matter how long, felt less sodden, less resigned than a more methodical turning of day into night. Late in the afternoon I'd scramble some eggs and then go down to the Oak Street beach, a wide band of white sand glowing beside Michigan Avenue with its six lanes of traffic and high-rise apartment buildings. This was the first time in my life I'd ever lived alone, if only for four weeks. The sexy, unknown city was rustling all around me. I'd grab a sandwich and head back to my all-night job loading trucks.

I didn't work long but I did earn enough to treat myself to a hustler. I'd seen them off Rush Street at "Bughouse" Square, an open park covered with old trees where stump speakers harangued small crowds about crank causes. Whereas nearby Rush Street was brightly lit and at night echoed with loud laughter, the sudden gust of jazz, and slamming car doors, Bughouse Square was leafy, solemn, shabby. In the midst of the Trotskyites and vagrants, a few hustlers threaded their way past overflowing trash cans or leaned against a tree, deriving precious sustenance from a cigarette.

I saw a sixteen-year-old with black, wavy hair wearing a well-pressed white shirt, its dandified, foreign collar wide, long, and pointed. He had full lips, soft dark eyes heavily lashed, and a certain luxurious fleshiness of ass inside trousers that were loose in the legs but binding just the right degree across the crotch and hips. He saw me looking at him. My eyes must have been shockingly hungry—the sort of eyes that have lost all self-awareness and glint with only pure emptiness. If someone had whispered, "Ed," in my ear, I'd have had to dial my way painfully back from the boy's handsome face toward earth, toward *me*, like a diver rapturous with oxygen deprivation who is drawn against his will up out of a storm-dark sea.

"Hi there," he said, and even those two syllables revealed he had an accent of some sort, the perilous *th* slurring off into the more universal *z*, the final *r* too faint to be Midwestern. His smile was soft, a bit sad, as if it, too, were a translation filmed through gauze, as if his friendliness had been rebuffed once too often and now hesitated on his lips.

"Hot enough for you?" I asked in a parody of Illinois ordinariness.

He looked puzzled, smiled with his full lips, and shrugged, again in a delightfully foreign way, for Midwestern men dared not risk a gesture that might invoke a sliding shoulder strap—an imaginary flash of pink silk.

"Ed," I said, extending my hand, shaking his warm, yielding hand, which *his* father had not taught him to firm up into a pledge of friendship undermined by an arm-wrestler's strength.

"Roberto," he said, lowering his heavy lashes operatically and nodding slightly off to one side, as if in deference to an unfamiliar but harmless custom of exchanging names.

He wanted twenty dollars, which was what I'd earned crouching all night inside the stifling hold of a truck—the exchange seemed fair, for how else did I deserve talking to this beauty with his small hands that relaxed naturally into a closing curve. His feet were encased in loafers the mellow color of a Stradivarius. When I touched his waist with my right hand as we hurried toward a little hotel he knew about he turned his head toward me, stared, then smiled with an intimate half-smile. I fell just one step behind so I could admire that abundant ass I longed to feel. He was shorter than I, though he held his shoulders back with almost childlike bravado.

"Are you Italian?" I asked.

"Yes," he said, clicking his tongue and jerking his head back to one side in a gesture I discovered only years later was the standard Greek way of indicating agreement.

The room was big and clean and the wide window looked out on the square below, which afforded enough illumination that we didn't need to turn on the overhead light. In the half-darkness his white shirt glowed. He let me unbutton it as we kissed. As soon as we began to touch, Roberto had the sort of gleeful, complicitous smile that says, "Look how wicked we're being." Never before had I associated irony with sex between men. For a moment I even suspected that Roberto might be gay or bisexual and surprisingly I still found him attractive. He held my naked body against his and quaked with silent laughter, then moved without transition into long, languorous kisses, letting his eyes rise and wander along the line between the ceiling and the wall.

Roberto's white shirt and tanned skin, his compact body with the sensual ass, his sense of irony and romantic air—all these properties came together to inspire me. That fall I wrote a novel about him while I was in my junior year at the University of Michigan. Like many novels by young people it was derived more from my reading than from my experience, but the character of the younger brother "Roberto" was based on my very own Lafcadio, my own Tancredi, my own Felix Krull, my own Fabrizio. I had in mind a synthesis of all these gallant young men from Continental literature, plucky characters who had as strong a sense of personal style as my hustler, who were as romantic and long-lashed as a silent movie star and as streetwise as a Neapolitan shoeshine boy. My Roberto (my hustler and my character) was quiveringly and richly fleshed, his smile soft and unfocused, his body instinct with laughter. I knew almost nothing about him but I could keep returning to my memory of having held him in my arms for a moment, and having rented an hour of his time and leased on short term the use of his torso and hips and lightly downed legs and tan arms flung back to reveal his soft, creased, axial paleness. I liked the notion behind the English term *rent boy* more than our *hustler*, since the American word suggested something dishonest and on the make.

Roberto was my first muse, a mental snapshot I worked up into a full-dress portrait in oil. I wanted to recapture that moment I'd bought and present him with a portrait in words. I wanted to convey to the reader as well my fascination with the boy. I was like Caravaggio, who paints in a saint's halo behind the curly head of a street urchin with a farmer's tan and a cynical smile. In my novel an older, richer, blonder brother hires a darker, smaller kid—and discovers they are half-brothers, the offspring of the same father but of different mothers, one fair and legitimate, the other an Italian mistress.

I've never reread the manuscript but as a junior I entered it into a fiction contest at the University of Michigan which I lost. The judge said she found it unbearably facetious. Of course I'm sure it was a grating book to read, partly because it was relentlessly frivolous and supercilious about a subject, homosexuality, that at that time was routinely labeled disquieting or tragic at best. I couldn't subscribe to this lugubriousness and wanted to laugh at everyone's solemnity. The imp of the perverse guided my pen, but I wasn't a mature and cultured European, like my idols, but a bumptious Midwestern teenager. In my failed fantasy the first contact with Roberto had been commercial but before long the rapport was elevated to brotherhood and, finally, impossibly, to an almost marital love. The title of the book was *The Amorous History of Our Youth*, a pedantic fusion of Lermontov's Byronic parody, *A Hero of Our Time*, and *The Amorous History of the Gauls*, a seventeenth-century satire of the court by Bussy

Rabutin, which caused this sharp-tongued cousin of Madame de Sévigné to be banished to his comely little chateau in Burgundy.

Pedantry, satire, literary ostentation, a grating lack of sincerity—none of these faults could conceal from my eye, at least, that I was quite humbly and gratefully in love with an Italian boy I had met once who had a strangely low and almost strangled way of whispering his words into the big ear of a bespectacled American geek, his awestruck client. If in my novel inappropriate emotions kept firing off, all these missteps just revealed how inadequate I was to the occasion.

I looked for him the next summer and all the other times I was in Chicago, but I never found him again. Of course I was looking for an Italian named Roberto and he was probably a Greek named Constantine. And he'd probably vanished, as a million runaways disappeared every year in America. If that Cincinnati hustler had been on the corner with the bus tickets in hand as he promised, I might have ended up like Roberto, a bleached-blond, well-spoken kid too sissy to get more than five bucks on the open market. Surely that was the source of my novel, the fantasy that I could save one of these boys as I myself so easily might have needed to be rescued.

After I graduated from the University of Michigan I lived in Evanston half a summer with my best friend, Steve Turner, a handsome, intelligent, straight guy. Neither of us knew what to do with his life. He was driving a city bus and I was driving a panel truck delivering eggs and fruit juice in a suburb as desolate as its name, Des Plaines. We slept in Steve's basement bedroom, smoked cigarettes, and joked our way through the depression and disorientation caused by graduation, change, lovelessness, and our grueling, low-prestige jobs. I was intending to go to Harvard in the fall to get an advanced degree in Chinese, which had been my undergraduate major.

But one night I went down to Clark and Diversy, a gay crossroads in those days. At a coffee shop I started talking to a hustler with streaked blond hair, a gold lavaliere, and tight black trousers. He wanted me to pay him ten bucks to fuck him, which I did partly because I'd never been with an avowedly gay hustler before. Two days later my penis burned when I urinated and my balls ached. On the third morning my underpants were stiff with a gray creamy discharge. I was mortified and told my mother I had to see a doctor. When she asked me why I said I had a "male problem," my improvised version of the mysterious "female trouble" that once invoked usually warded off all further questions. No such luck. My mother wanted to know everything in detail. I told her as little as possible. Her doctor assumed I'd been with a female prostitute and winked before shooting me full of penicillin and giving me a prescription for a lotion that would rid me of the crab lice I'd also picked up. The whole experience was so shaming that it made me question my life, my values, my future. This one experience with a hustler had major consequences. I decided to take the two hundred dollars I'd saved and fly to New York in pursuit of Stanley, another student I'd met in Ann Arbor and who was now in New York striving to become an actor. A sustained love with someone from my own world seemed far preferable to these fly-by-night encounters with prostitutes.

I stayed in New York, got a job working as a staff writer for Time-Life Books, and eventually started living with Stanley. I skipped Harvard and a Ph.D. in Chinese, and all because a hustler had given me the clap.

In my twenties I seldom hired a hustler, mainly because I didn't know where to find them. Early on I picked up an ugly kid in Times Square. He led me back to a nearby room and to a little alcove separated from the room by a curtain. He was very insistent that I pay him in advance and leave my clothes on the only chair in the main room. He then drew me into the alcove, closed the curtain, and rushed me through sex. Then he dressed me as fast as possible, accompanied me down to the front door, pushed me out of it, and rushed back upstairs. The door closed behind him with a click and the sliding of a bolt. Something made me pull out my wallet and inspect it. His invisible partner had emptied it while I was in the alcove sucking that telltale limp dick. Now I recalled I'd heard the floorboards creak. I didn't know which bell was theirs. Anyway, they were two against one and I had no legal recourse.

One night a friend of mine called me at my office in the Time-Life Building and asked if I'd like to join him on a "double date" with two johns from out of town. My friend was a highly paid advertising copywriter but he liked to work occasionally as a hustler to prove to himself that at thirty he still looked twenty, that as a confident young executive he could still come off as an insecure, skinny little street kid. The thirty dollars he earned turning a trick was worth more to him than his three-hundred-dollar day rate selling vodka and toothpaste. I joined him and two drunk middle-aged businessmen in a hotel room. My hustling buddy had told me to be sure to play dumb: "There's nothing that's more of a turnoff than intelligence." Our customers, who in any event were more interested in mixing more Manhattans than in bedding us, kept trying to explain to us who Beethoven was; they had a novelty tape on which someone had added a congo beat to the *Ode to Joy*. For a moment I'd *almost* grasp what they were talking about but then I'd pretend to get confused and I'd mutter, "Fuck it!" and the two johns would wink furiously at each other over our heads.

I could never have been a professional hustler for even

though I had a beautiful body my penis was too small and I was more passive than active in sex. Bottoms were a dime a dozen; real money was spent only on tops. Occasionally now I'll see an ad for a bottom in listings for escorts, but the fee he's asking is always small—and he's always outnumbered ten to one by those who describe themselves as "VGL XXX horny dominant top WS, FF, C&B torture, BB, verbal"—which for my few heterosexual readers I'll translate as "very good-looking, very well-hung dominant man into water sports, fist-fucking, cock-and-ball torture, a bodybuilder capable of handing out verbal abuse." Now there is a winning profile. God made many masochists and very few natural sadists—no wonder all those bottoms must pay for their tops. To be sure, we read every day about violent men raping women, and that sort of "domination" is neither rare nor sought-after. True, refined sadism is so focused on the victim that it could be said to be selfless; life turns up few disinterested, saintly masters.

Although I only hustled once, that unique experience I'd regularly inflate later into a whole career when I'd attempt to be fraternal with hustlers: "Oh, I used to turn tricks myself," I'd say modestly, "when I was a kid. I know what it's like to be in the business." My hustler of the moment would eye me suspiciously—had I ever been young? he'd wonder.

In the late '60s alternative newspapers like the *Eye* and the *East Village Other* began to run ads for gay escorts. At that moment I entered into a new period of my life that has extended all the way to the present moment—the excitement of ordering up an unknown guy on the phone. In the early '70s I was earning a miserable living ghostwriting college textbooks (I did two psychology books and one U.S. history). I would get $350 for a chapter. I hated the work but I set myself a goal: I'd stay in, type my pages on perception or Bull Run, and then at four in the morning my hustler, who I'd ordered up earlier in the evening, was scheduled to appear. He was my reward.

Half an hour before he was due to arrive I'd empty my overflowing ashtray, make the bed, dim the lights, open a bottle of wine, spray the roaches into temporary submission.

For a while I had a (male) madam, no one I ever laid eyes on but who would call up boys in his stable while I hung on the other line. He'd describe the boys and talk to me in an old-fashioned queeny way: "Now, hon, would you be that rare gay man who just happens to like—not to put too fine a point on it—Big Dick?"

The idea that a twenty-eight-year-old blond, six-foot-two, with an eight-inch penis was headed my way would excite me in advance to the point my hands would shake. I'd force myself to concentrate on my textbook, on the principle of primacy-recency in the chapter I was cobbling together or on the implications of the Dred Scott decision, but if for a moment I dropped the reins, my mind would plunge over the precipice of this secret, this thrill in store for me. As the hour approached I'd convince myself he'd probably fallen asleep or gone out carousing and hooked up with someone at the bar. I'd clattered away at my typewriter hour after hour in order to deserve (and afford) this man, who became taller, better hung, lower-voiced, more crudely passionate by the second.

At last, as I'd listen to those feet pounding up the three flights of wooden stairs, I'd breathe faster, I could feel my nipples stiffening under the friction of my T-shirt and my ass filling out my jeans fractionally. My cock was swelling in the pouch of my jeans and a blush blossom was floating up my chest and neck and invading my face. I became lightheaded.

This was the high point, the instant before he came into sight on the landing below and trotted up to my door.

Sometimes I was already stoned, for even if I risked mumbling and stumbling when high nonetheless that state of mind released my deepest passions; my mood was a bit impersonal but at least intense. If I started fantasizing about doing something with this guy, a second later I found myself actually doing it. There was no membrane between thought and act.

In those days there were suddenly very few taboos against hiring oneself out. Many young gay men in the '70s, at least in New York, thought it was cool, a source of money and adventure and a way to enter other worlds. Grad students who had high tuitions to pay, long, irregular hours, and no time to cruise their equals at bars welcomed the constant possibilities for paid sex offered nearly round the clock. If a medical intern stumbled home at midnight, exhausted from an eighteen-hour stint, his muscles tense and his nerves sparking, he could always plug in his special red phone and answer it, play his friendly cowboy character Jarvis or Will rather than his real Philadelphia persona of Edwin, so intimidating to everyone and so unforthcoming: so unsexy.

I'd get these guys pounding up my steps wearing chaps and cowboy hat, as I'd instructed them, or policemen's uniforms, or work boots and hard hat, which I'd remove as gently as Amfortas assisting Parsifal when the knight returns with the holy spear and must be disarmed.

Of course I was young and attractive, in my thirties. I went to the gym three times a week. I had a powerful chest and strong arms, and my peasant ancestors had bequeathed me their mighty legs. I kept waiting to see how these hired hands would respond to the way I looked with my soulful green eyes, drooping mustache, and shoulder-length hair.

Sometimes they scarcely seemed to register me or my age at all. Later I learned that some hustlers preferred their johns to be old and adulatory. At least the john's gratitude could allow the overhead spotlight to narrow and isolate the hustler in a pool of intense desire, transform him into a St. Michael stabbing a St. Theresa left suitably vague in a swirl of shadows, fold upon fold. The hustler generates the passion, he is the one who drips with sweat, his penis is what he watches swell and stiffen in the mirror. The john merely officiates, like a priest fussing over the chalice. The priest shouldn't be handsome or distractingly young or even too definite an entity; he is just the penumbra around a radiance. The altar boy is the one who should be beautiful.

My favorite hustler was Charles, whom I knew in the late 1970s and early 1980s. I must have seen his ad in an alternative newspaper as a leather-wearing master. He was about thirty, shorter than me, and had an overbite and an emaciated body. His bony face was concealed in the shadow of his visor. His voice was nasal but low.

"Take off all your clothes," he said when he arrived. I stripped and he remained fully dressed, cap, boots, leather jacket, and all. It was an inspired move, since I was entirely exposed and he armored. He told me to kneel on the floor between his legs. He sat on the couch and lit a cigar, turning it carefully to make sure it would burn evenly. He didn't say anything nor was I invited to speak.

The smell of the cigar enraged me, my father!, this stupid hustler polluting my house, how dare he—and suddenly tears were splashing down my face. My father had died just two years earlier and here he was again in the guise of a small, bony sadist. This was the smell of my father's cigar, repulsive and endearing. As Charles inhaled, the tip glowed briefly and lit up his face.

He stood and went over to the hardwood floor and ordered

me to crawl on my knees to him. He pulled out his penis, which was only half-hard. He said, "Pay me."

At first I didn't understand and then I did and I fetched the money I had already laid out on the table. I came back and knelt and handed the bills to him. As I did he became erect. It was a single moment: I handed him the money and he got hard.

I couldn't afford to see him more than once a week, but I had an appointment with him week after week, year after year. He never varied the winning routine. I stripped, he never did. In fact I never saw his body. He'd light his cigar and have me suck him while he smoked, seated. Then he'd stand and become violent, insulting me. He'd kick me with his boots, but he never left any bruises or even created any residual pain. He knew what he was doing. He was a professional. He'd order me to get on all fours and he'd put on tight black leather gloves and stick one finger in me and then make me smell it. Then he'd fuck me hard; he wore a condom, unusual back then, even degrading, as if he were too good to touch my flesh. He never kissed me, though sometimes he'd drool in my mouth from far above as I knelt below him. The long string of saliva slowly unspooled to my open lips. He never smiled, though I smiled at him. He seldom came. Like a Taoist he preferred to conserve his *ch'i*.

I asked him once if our kind of sex turned him on.

"Obviously."

"But do you think of me afterwards?"

"No."

Once I ran into him and his lover outside a leather bar near the docks. His lover was no younger than I nor any better looking. He didn't seem submissive or meek in any way—he was just a big Irish balding blond with some meat on his bones, regular features, and a friendly face quick with curiosity. He was wearing a faded denim jacket and jeans and had a wide but not fat ass. Charles introduced us and acted normally sociable. Though it was a late spring night a cold fog was pouring off the nearby Hudson and swirling dramatically below the sodium-vapor streetlights above us. Half the bar was on the street sipping beers and leaning against parked motorcycles. Charles drove his lover away on his Harley.

Soon after that the hot weather set in for the duration. I was working for the New York Institute for the Humanities, which was housed at New York University. I'd sit in one of the back cubicles attempting to write my novel, *A Boy's Own Story*, fighting the anxiety I usually felt when I wrote. The offices were nearly empty. My cubicle was windowless. The heat and my hangover tempted me to put my head down on my desk and fall asleep. I was so sleepy I would write portmanteau words, which collapsed the syllables of two or three words I'd already sounded in my head. I'd even start to spell phonetically.

My clothes would stick to me. I'd sigh and shift in my chair from one side to the other. One more trip to the water cooler. I'd come back and read through my latest pages and make microscopic changes. I'd sprawl on my desk. Then I'd get fed up with myself, sit up straight, as tall as possible in the chair, and I'd hold my pen as if it were a scalpel. Now, I'd say to myself, I'm going to write a *good* page. Usually my head was so fuzzy with the morning-after effects of wine and marijuana that I was pleased if I could form real sentences, nothing more. But one day I did make a conscious decision to write *well*, and with my scalpel-pen in hand and my perfect posture I felt I was about to *attack* the page, as a conductor might ask the strings to have a cleaner attack on the opening phrases. The stern commands that I issued to myself were the mental equivalent to stabbing my leg with a straight pin in order to stay awake.

I would be horny, if that meant lonely and anxious to such

a degree that only sex could lift me out of this mire with enough immediacy and absoluteness. I didn't have the patience to cruise someone in a bar, chit-chat through three drinks and ninety minutes on the off chance he might ask me back. Anyway it was the middle of the day. I phoned Charles and asked him if I could come over to his house in Prospect Park in Brooklyn. He said yes and gave me careful instructions. In those days middle-class white people thought of themselves as pioneers if they lived in Prospect Park.

He opened the heavy oak door after I rang just once and ushered me into a hallway and stairs gleaming with beeswax and lit by a stained-glass window on the landing above. A small silk carpet glowed under my feet as if it were the light cast by the stained glass above. Charles was dressed in a white T-shirt and black leather vest, which exposed his blue skin and knobby elbows. In the daylight his overbite looked comic, his protruding bones tragic. He asked me if I wanted to see the house. It was all carved massive four-posters and chenille spreads, electrified gas lamps and old wood sewing tables balanced on scrolled, cast-iron legs.

He unbolted and opened one door and showed me a bare room with a mattress on the floor and one small window high up, close to the ceiling. "This is where I'm going to keep you," he said. I didn't know if he was joking, but when I smiled he said, "This is where you'll live."

His words gave me an instant erection—the bliss of total passivity edged with the fear of total passivity. What would it be like to live here, to watch the daylight come and go through the little window, to be led naked in chains to the toilet, to be wiped, to be spoon-fed, to be fucked and threatened with the working end of a cigar?

No more taxes to pay, I thought. No more chapters to write.

Time a blur of longing, excitement, boredom, and loneliness. Come to think of it, that sounded more or less like my life right now but formalized and condensed.

Then after the release of my novel I moved to Paris and lost touch with Charles. I remained in France for the next sixteen years.

Now I live back in New York. When I first returned, after being away so long, I fell into a gloom since AIDS and a tough mayor had closed down all the old familiar sex places, the back rooms and most of the saunas as well as most of the hustler bars.

Freud hypothesized that many of civilization's greatest accomplishments, including acts of altruism, were powered by repressed homosexuality. I thought of that when I first resurfaced in Manhattan. Now that no one would dream of repressing anything, I said to myself, civilization is crumbling, kindness has vanished, and altruism has evaporated. Certainly greed had become more naked, hearts were harder, and there was no repressed desire investing music, painting, or the dance. To be sure my own interest in the arts struck me as evidence against the veracity of Freud's theory, for I had never failed to act on my erotic impulses. Repression had played no role in my acquisition of culture or my accomplishments. Maybe gay life had just been dumbed down like the rest of American society. A duller cultural edge and the new Puritanism didn't add up to an attractive combination for an aesthete and sex addict like me.

I started exploring the gay Internet. One night at 4 a.m. on a rainy Tuesday in February I was staring at a chat-room screen when a new name popped up: "Kevin 20." Although this was not a hustlers' site, I typed in, "I'll pay $150 if you let me suck your dick." Kevin replied, "Nice man." I didn't ask him for a physical description nor did he demand any details from me. He just wanted to know what I expected him to do. I told him I wouldn't even undress—I'd just suck him off. As soon as he gave me his address I went barreling up in a taxi through the deserted streets of the Upper West Side.

The young man who opened the door looked like Michelangelo's David. He had the same deep-set eyes, heavy-browed, square-jawed manly face as the David and a similarly youthful body except for a chest that was hairy and more developed. And in his beautiful sea-green eyes there was something shifty as he'd steal worried glances at me, almost as if he'd grown up mocked by older male cousins and expected me to laugh at him. After our second session, this time down at my place, I wrote him a schoolgirlish e-mail saying I couldn't stop "replaying my mental film of him." He called in a panic: "Dude, did you make a video of me? Was there a hidden camera I didn't notice?"

"Not at all! No, I meant I kept *thinking* about you."

"So, there wasn't a video?"

"Of course not."

"'Cuz if there was... I mean, dude, I might want to run for office some day or be a model."

Soon I was such a weekly fixture in his life that his doorman announced me before I gave my name. I'd realized right away that this boy didn't need my money, that he was a student living in a two-thousand-dollar-a-month studio with an elaborate computer and a plasma-screen TV. Kevin had a private trainer every day at his gym where he went for two or three hours. He'd attended Groton but had not been athletic there. Now, I guess, he was an "athlete" because he pushed heavy weights around.

One day, when I was in his neighborhood by chance, I decided to drop in on him. The woman behind the desk, wearing the livery of the posh building, wasn't content with just the apartment number. She wanted the tenant's name as well.

"It's Kevin something," I said. "His last name has slipped my mind."

"No, sir. Three-C belongs to Paul Thomas."

"Oh. He wants to be an actor—I was remembering his stage name," I said. In any event, he wasn't at home.

I quickly discovered I could please him if I brought him a new porno video every week, which he'd fast-forward and freeze-frame at strategic places as I knelt on the floor between his legs. Once in an e-mail I complained that he never looked at me. He replied, a bit hurt, that he was just trying to be macho and cruel in the way he thought I liked. I quickly conceded he was right. I found his eagerness to please touching. That was the wound in this otherwise perfect man—his granite-hard erections proved that he found our scenario exciting, too.

And yet the slave hopes that in the end the master will be kind, that he'll lift the bruised and flayed slave in his arms and murmur paternal things in his ear, just as the john wants the hustler one day to say, "I don't want your money. I love you." Once I asked an articulate, literary hustler, "Did you ever fall for a john?" And he wrinkled his nose and said, "Are you kidding?" I had hired him and told him he didn't need to climax if he had a client later on. That line ended up in one of his books as an example of unparalleled politeness.

Kevin was never cruel but he could be demanding with all the imperiousness of youth. Sometimes I felt I was a vampire battening off his vitality. I was more than sixty. He was turning twenty-one.

Sometimes he seemed lonely to me, going from school to gym and back again, his habits already old-maidish. He instructed me to remove my shoes at the door and when we had sex on his couch he covered it with an old sheet. If the sheet was pulled even an inch aside in one of our maneuvers, I could see he was worrying about it until the cloth was back in place.

As the months ticked by I learned that the only porno movies he liked were of violent, hairy men in their thirties who thwacked each other on the ass and shouted when they came. A friend of mine gave me a film of a skinny boy bound and gagged and kept in a cage with a red rubber ball strapped into his mouth and round rubber mittens on his hands so that he couldn't masturbate, but Kevin didn't like it. He fast-forwarded all the way through it and handed it back to me reproachfully on my way out.

I think at first he imagined I wanted him to be a tough guy, working-class and taciturn and forbidding, but once he got over that idea he opened up and after sex he'd chatter away about show business. I invited him to a musical; he was quietly dressed and solemnly well behaved. He could have been my grandson if my son had married a great beauty.

I suppose part of what appealed to me was that I was his sole client. I began to click on to other unsuspecting people online and offer them money too. It worked about one time out of thirty. Just yesterday I had a visit from a twenty-three-year-old Aeroflot steward from Moscow who shrugged with bored Slavic indifference when I suggested we move into the bedroom. Only on his way out an hour later did he freeze at the front door and say, "What about our agreement?"

I slapped my forehead. I had forgotten he was one of the men I'd offered money. Suddenly I regretted the extraordinary gratitude I'd felt toward him when I thought I was getting a freebie.

Through my doctor I met a gifted painter my age or nearly who, like Robert Mapplethorpe, devoted his work to society portraits, pictures of flowers, and male nudes at his studio. One by one he hauled out Old Master-sized canvasses of young men sprawling naked in chairs or standing in full command of the wood-slatted floor. Their hands were curving in around invisible rods or scrolls like those held by a kouros.

"You should meet this guy I know," I said. "Kevin. He has the sort of body you like."

"Wait—Kevin? A student? Big guy with muscles and a beautiful face, beautiful butt?"

"Lives on the Upper West Side?"

The painter said, "That's the one. He was here last night. You see, given my great height and big body and beard, I have to pay someone if I want to be topped, and I always want to be topped."

"You paid Kevin?"

"Sure. He's got his own website. Here..." He tapped out the address on his computer. There on the screen was a decapitated photo of Kevin, seated naked on the toilet gripping a fist full of dick. I wondered if our chance encounter, his and mine, had pointed his way toward a career in prostitution or whether he'd accepted my offer that first February night at 4 a.m. because he was already walking on the wild side.

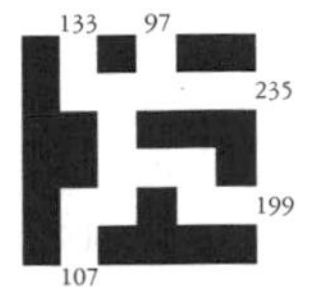

HAPPINESS REMINDERS

by RACHEL HALEY HIMMELHEBER

Make new plans

Early Christmas Eve morning, the cop rolls carefully away from the near-stranger sleeping beside him and types another happiness reminder of his new plans. He tapes this reminder to his bathroom mirror, the wall above his bed, and the dashboard of his car. It says: *Change your attitude and change your life!*

Take time to grieve

It is the robber's first morning in his new home. They left the furniture. The house is livable but has been stripped of personality. Bedding, towels, jewelry boxes, forks, flowers, stereos, dust: gone. When the robber's sister died, her estate went to her brother; however, friends and various other vultures had gotten to the sister's house before the robber. There's no accounting for the ways in which we grieve, the robber tells his dismayed girlfriend when she suggests he go searching for the china or the Oriental rugs.

The house is lovely, but problems abound. For one, there aren't enough sheets.

Last night, the robber tucked a flat sheet under the mattress because he was out of fitted sheets. The sheet untucks, and in the middle of the night becomes a tangled mess.

From this mess, the robber has several choices. He could try right then in his sleepy, sticky-mouthed delirium to extricate himself from this swaddling. Or still in bed, he could half-assedly push the linen under the corners of the mattress and hope it will hold as he rolls around. This never works and he will almost certainly wake up unhappy. Or he could force himself to do it standing, which is slightly more permanent but doesn't last either, but it gets the unhappiness out of the way quicker.

Or he could leave the fabric twisted and adjust to its new dimensions and demands. Some can adjust to anything: their bodies will meld and merge with whatever complications and joys. The robber is somewhat like this; he has bounced back from his sister's death, and he is taking over her house.

The robber brought linens yesterday, but not knowing the sizes of all these enormous beds, he brought only queen-sized sheets. Having eked out a frugal existence for himself over the years, he assumed the beds were queens. And even that had seemed presumptuous to the robber who continued to make love on twin-sized beds well into his forties. He lived below his means. It was a matter of pride for him.

Practice your new choices

The cop returns to his queen-sized bed, which holds the sleeping form of the dispatcher. Surely the dispatcher wouldn't fuck him if the others thought he was gay. The cop is slightly disappointed that the dispatcher was so easy to convince; he isn't sure if he wants to be considered gay or not, and such ambiguity of feeling often causes the reaction the cop is having: he would be disappointed if the dispatcher didn't sleep with him, and he is disappointed that she did.

The cop flicks at the sleeping dispatcher's nipple as if it were something interesting. Lately, he has taken to reading women's magazines. Mostly *Glamour* and *Marie Claire*—they have more substance than *Cosmopolitan*, but the cop doesn't care about substance. *Cosmopolitan* was what his ex-wife read, but he doesn't care about that either. *Cosmopolitan* is always bragging it has discovered a new sex position or the secret to having an orgasm every time, guaranteed. The cop dislikes bragging and he doesn't trust guarantees. *Glamour* is more modest in its promises, and that is attractive to him.

The magazines aren't interested in women. The articles are about pleasing men.

He feels incredible solidarity with the women on the pages; after reading, the cop often gets an urge to call his ex-wife and offer to have a drink with her.

Feed your spirit

Eating breakfast (eggs over hard and rye toast), the robber doodles pictures of the dead sister's home on his napkin. The sky looks like snow, and instead of dreaming of a white Christmas, the robber is thinking of heating systems and leaks. He is thinking of assets and alarms. There is a lot of work and upkeep to this house, which the robber has begun to think of as The Mansion.

In the weeks since his sister's death, the robber has begun to form a plan to rob his own dead sister's home. It is mostly habit, basically a mental exercise, although his plans for The Mansion become more elaborate and sophisticated every day. He desires a plan that could fool even himself, a plan so good that even he would be powerless to anticipate its coming.

The robber has not knocked off a house in weeks. His girlfriend seems impatient with this, antsy when he is home at night.

The robber often sketches in a notebook. Sometimes he uses watercolors in his robbery plans. Sometimes his notebook looks like an artist's and sometimes it looks like a football coach's. The plans for The Mansion look like an artist's. In these plans, the robber has taken liberties with color, he has taken liberties with scale. The plans are beautiful, but he will not consult them when it comes time to rob. They are a stopgap measure, a way to slow down and enjoy the process.

Decide what you need and what you want

Plans were made, but there is no hope. At least this is how the cop feels today. His first Christmas Eve alone, he has to work, he still has presents to buy, he has kicked a woman out of his bed, and it is just 7:30. He is nearing the end of his divorce negotiations but sees no end in sight to his particular despair.

He takes a long time smoothing the plastic wrap over his bowl of tuna fish—the edges have to fit precisely or escaping tuna air might flavor other items in the fridge. Exactness, precision, routine: such is the way he copes with his life in this apartment.

His department doesn't know he's gay, but he thinks his partner does. Well, maybe not gay. Bisexual? The cop isn't sure what any of these terms mean really. He's always been a manly sort.

The cop is virile. He has a daughter. He has desired women,

married and impregnated one, subscribed to *Playboy*, and years ago he and his ex-wife bought the complete Sexy Doctor/Sexy Nurse Kit at Spencer Gifts. However, now at forty-two, he has an inexplicable crush on his partner, another manly sort. His partner may or may not want him, but the cop's crush on this partner helped end his marriage. The cop is not as upset by his divorce as he is by all the changes in his now-single life. He was tiring of marriage for various reasons completely unsexual.

Every day, he fixes tuna for breakfast. He also has tuna for lunch. Sometimes he puts extra onions on his sandwich, and he does not worry about his breath. Real men—whether straight, gay, or playing for both teams—do not have such worries. His partner eats sardines, leftover pizza, salami sandwiches with mustard and sloppy onions and pickles, all kinds of things for lunch, and he does not worry. The partner encouraged the cop to leave his wife. The partner has proved to be understanding.

Embrace everything and let go

The robber's girlfriend is reading a magazine article in the waiting room of the mall hair salon. The girlfriend has her hair cut and styled every year for the Christmas Eve service, although she rarely attends the service. However, the rite of the hair salon on Christmas Eve, warm, wet, and filled with other churchgoing women, crystallizes a feeling within the girlfriend similar to a church service.

The article is about how not to get raped as you are carrying grocery bags up the stairs of your apartment building. The girlfriend is reading the article not because she carries bags up stairs of apartment buildings anymore—she now lives in a mansion—but because she has a morbid fear of rape. She has never been raped, but she imagines her own rape as imminent, and she imagines it a half a dozen times a day. (Her fear is ungrounded; she is extremely careful, and she has taken three self-defense courses. She will not be raped.) She reads every article and book on rape she can find.

This article focuses on the need to be rude—to risk appearing rude—to strange men who offer to carry bags or help in some way. These offers may not come from predators. These offers may come from gentlemen, the article allows, and these gentlemen may say, "Jeez, lady, I was only trying to help," but the article assures the girlfriend that this is okay.

It is better to appear rude than to be unsafe and vulnerable to attack. It is better not to trust anyone; be on the defensive at all times! Be vigilant! Protect your body from strangers! You must believe you are worth protecting before you can protect yourself. The girlfriend finishes and then turns to a humorous article detailing which pickup lines guys use and which they abuse. Finally! the article proclaims, a complete list of which opening lines belong to the losers and which ones to the winners.

When the girlfriend finishes her article, the salon receptionist takes immediate advantage. "Ever think about where things end up?" the receptionist asks. "Like a toy you lost in second grade; if it's plastic or whatever, it hasn't melted away. It must be somewhere. You just don't know where. My Holly Hobby watch."

The girlfriend wonders what she has lost.

Remember that you're more than just a body

Because all criminals are sore about working on Christmas Eve, the cop is able to disappear from the department to work out at the Y for an hour before lunch. (The cop does enjoy exercise, but he leaves mostly because he cannot bear to look at the proud set of the dispatcher's mouth he had kissed only hours before.)

The cop likes to lift weights at the Y. The equipment isn't shiny-new, but the weights are heavy and he is comfortable in the narrow room with its one mirrored wall and one cinderblock wall and its orange water-cooler barrel with the little paper Dixie cups next to it. The cop likes to crush the Dixie cups in one hand. They are easy to crush, but when no one else is in the weight room, he looks in the mirror while doing it. As a boy, his hero was the Incredible Hulk. The cop wants to be so strong that no one could hurt him unless that person had a gun. Even then, the cop could wrestle a gun from most people. He can bench-press three hundred pounds.

The cop is curious about criminals. Violent criminals and repeat offenders. Elementary-school drug dealers. Rapists and murderers. Juvie rapists and murderers. The cop wants people to improve, even when he's angry. His partner talks like the police on a TV show; he uses words like "cocksucker" and "petty thief." His partner views life in terms of good guys and bad guys. The partner's absoluteness and surety is why the cop loves him. The cop views such clarity as being a bit sub-intelligent—and certainly his partner isn't as smart as he is—but he loves it anyway. The cop is not accustomed to feeling more intelligent than others.

Know if you've been bad or good

The magazine the girlfriend reads in the salon has an advertisement featuring a fat and red-faced Santa-suited older gentleman. He grinningly brandishes a plastic bag of California almonds. Residing near his head is a floating holiday table laden with turkey and potatoes, pies and glowing candles, and in the forefront of this feast is a bowl of California almonds.

The girlfriend's mother makes a version of Ambrosia Salad featuring California almonds which the girlfriend has eaten at every family picnic she can remember. As a child the girlfriend didn't like almonds, and she would pick around them. She would eat all the mini marshmallows in her salad portion before eating any of the rest of her picnic: before her hot dog, before her chips, before her popsicle.

The Santa in the advertisement makes the girlfriend think of a visit to the Mall Santa when she was about four. Up on Santa's scratchy lap with its interesting bumps and legs so different from her mother or father or brothers or babysitter or grandmother or uncle or anyone else really, the girlfriend felt happy. She was on a staged platform; she was a person in her own right. She could feel her inside self growing older and she touched the top of her head, felt the crown of it, the silky hair, princess hair, spun gold; beautiful; spectacular. She was taller. Up on the Mall Santa's interesting lap, she knew the world was watching her, and it was as if the dim glare of the Christmas music and shoppers, bags rustling, change ringing, singing, crying—it all receded and she was alone and this mall was her new domain. She began telling Santa about her love for sandwiches made from rye bread. She was thinking of the tiny, thin loaves of party rye that her mother sometimes melted complicated concoctions of cheese and meat and olives and artichokes over for parties. How she loved those loaves! In telling Santa this love, she realized for the first time in her young life that she was going to grow up, that her parents would not always be with her, that their opinions and traditions could be picked up—or not—as she saw fit. Again, she told Santa about the bread. Somehow, and the girlfriend has never been sure how, Santa's message made its way to someone somewhere, and every year, even now, even as an adult living in a different city, her mother dead and her father ailing, she has received one anonymous gift a year every year since she was four: a tiny, thin loaf of her favorite party rye bread wrapped in brown paper and tied with string.

Do what makes you happy

Although the company is closed for the holiday, the robber is in his office looking through files. The robber isn't always a robber. By day he sells insurance, and he and his colleagues make jokes and hear jokes all day long about the thievery of their profession. Ha, ha. Ha, ha!

At first, the robber dabbled in insurance. He was door-to-door, then part-time. Now he's nine-to-five-thirty, and he's more than capable of making the jokes and laughing heartily. He does not see a correlation between his two professions, anyway. People want insurance. They sign up to receive it, its benefits along with its swindlings. After all, it's the customers who make most of the jokes. The robber laughs at these jokes more out of guilt and obligation than true mirth. The robber is not without guilt. He is not without obligation. When people tell you a joke, they are asking for something from you. Would it kill you to give it to them? It is easy to hurt people and also generally easy not to.

Knocking off houses and selling policies are equally lucrative for the robber, and he plugs away at both out of a sense of nostalgia. It isn't necessity; the robber has a healthy savings account, his dead sister's house, and plenty of insurance. He doesn't need to work. But both jobs remind him of his youthful arrogance and earnestness, his faith that he could fuse together two callings, that he could make himself happy through hard work.

Whip your brain into shape

The robber's office window at the insurance company looks onto the busy street. Directly opposite is a five-story building that houses offices and the YMCA where the robber works out. Looking at the YMCA building convinces the robber to take a break. After all, it is Christmas Eve. The large wreath on the Y mocks his work. After all, a break would do him good. At the Y, the robber swims. While he swims, he hums. He hums a tuneless song he has been humming underwater for years. It is a tune made up so long ago he cannot remember when. The robber is not conscious of this tune nor of his humming it underwater. He is happy humming, but he does not hum in order to spur along such happiness. It is more a habit than anything else, a sort of sound tic in his physical being.

The robber is thinking of legs. He is looking at the legs underwater. He does not look at the swimsuits of others. He is looking at legs. All of these legs appear both better and worse under the water: the spongy cellulite and the loose folding sags of the older women look firmer but also paler. The blue veins are more distinct. The robber gets an image of a white-bread roll at the bottom of a fishbowl. The roll is disintegrating and becoming something entirely different. The robber thinks of these legs kneeling in a church or stretching at a yoga class. He thinks of the bones and muscles caught underneath and working hard to carry and move this person. He pictures making love to these legs: the slack or doughy thighs pressing around his back. Their strength surprises him and he gurgles underwater.

* * *

Create intimacy (into-me-see)

"What do you want to do?" the cop asks the partner. They are not in bed. They are not on a stakeout. They are sitting at their desks in the precinct. They want to eat lunch together, but they cannot decide where to go. The cop has a tuna sandwich in the shared refrigerator, but he is willing to waste it to spend more time with the partner.

"What?"

"What do you feel like eating?"

"Food." The partner laughs. He says "food" every time someone asks him, "What do you want to eat?" He doesn't care. The partner likes most foods. He doesn't love Japanese food, but he knows the cop would never suggest Japanese. The cop is meat-and-potatoes, a plain Jane by comparison. In terms of culinary taste, the partner is the more sophisticated.

"Food it is then! And it's on me!" The cop laughs, too. He feels merry and in love with the partner. He thinks his short list of is-something-going-on-or-am-I-misreading-the-signals is steadily growing in favor of a definite attraction. How could he misread such clarity? His partner claps him on the back often. A woman, the cop knows, would hug another woman when she felt closeness. The cop's heart wells up every time he thinks of the partner's blundering way of expressing himself. *He cannot hug me but he wants to be close to me, he wants to be close to me, he likes me, he touches me, he wants to be close to me.*

The cop knows the partner is concerned about him. He goes to lunch with him often. Oftener than before. He wouldn't ask about the divorce, the cop reasons, thumbing through his mind's dog-eared pictures of the partner, if he didn't care.

"What about the diner?" the partner asks.

"Sounds great to me," says the cop. He is hugging and squeezing himself on the inside.

Ask yourself: do you want to be right or do you want to be happy?

The robber's dead sister's lawyer is worried about the robber. He is worried because the robber is no longer going out at night to steal items from the houses of wealthy people. The lawyer is worried the robber has enough now, that he is content with the house and the money and the furniture (many quality Colonial American pieces) from his dead sister, that he will no longer leave at night. The lawyer is concerned with these matters because he is screwing the robber's girlfriend.

Is the lawyer in love with the girlfriend? He thinks so, but how can we be sure? There is no measurement for love; there is no standard definition. People try.

There is a dictionary on the lawyer's bookshelf.

Love suggests—but fails to confirm—a feeling more intense and less susceptible to control than that associated with the other weak words of this group. Affection is a more unvarying feeling of warm regard for another person, so maybe it's just better to say, "Honey, I effect you and I affect you." Devotion is dedication and attachment to a person or thing; contrasted with love, it implies a more selfless and often a less carbonated, effervescent feeling; it's just not as fun. Fondness, in its most common modern sense, is a rather strong liking for a person or thing. Infatuation is extravagant attraction or attachment to a person or thing, usually short in duration and indicative of folly or sexually faulty judgment.

The lawyer tries to compare the definition of love with his feelings for the girlfriend. He is not sure he feels "intense affectionate concern" for the girlfriend; she is quite strong and does not command concern. She is an independent thinker. They do not ever discuss how they feel or just who they think they are.

It is better to give than to receive

The girlfriend's hair is beautiful; she views it in every mall window. She is searching for a present for the robber; or, rather, she should be searching for a present. It is just that she is not sure, not sure what to do. She does not hate the robber; she is not cheating on him out of malice. His sister has died. The girlfriend does not want to hurt anyone, and yet. And yet.

And yet she has no gift for the robber, nor can she think of one suitable.

Her gift for the lawyer has been ready for months: a gift personal, sentimental, full to bursting of her overwhelming feelings for the lawyer, a gift which demonstrates both material and emotional expenditure, wrapped and waiting excitedly in the trunk of the girlfriend's car.

Everything is impersonal. When you have cried, when you have private jokes, when you have rolled naked with a person, should your gift not be more personal than a tie, a paperweight? There is nothing, there is nothing, go the thoughts of the girlfriend, who, like many people, will mistake this difficulty, this revealing of her true feelings (she loves the lawyer and would prefer being with him to being with the robber) as a sign. She will believe it is a sort of divine interpretation of her miserable decision, a way out of her guilt for making her choice. Lawyer beats robber. The end.

And so she exits the mall.

(The robber, who feels intense love for the girlfriend, has painted her a portrait from a photograph. The picture, the

Christmas present, difficult for the robber because of his own grief, is one of the girlfriend's dead mother.)

Write in your journal

The Mansion has thirty-five rooms, not including bathrooms or closets. It has cathedral ceilings. There is a small secret hiding place behind a bookshelf in the library. It isn't noticeable because the library has wooden paneling. The robber hasn't noticed it. The robber's girlfriend hasn't noticed it. The robber's dead sister's lawyer hasn't noticed it, but if he thought hard, he might remember it. The robber's dead sister used to keep her will in this place, but it gradually became the place she would hide what she didn't want anyone to see. It currently contains two Pepperidge Farm Orange Milano cookies, a 24-karat gold chain, retailed at $39.99, and a piece of notebook paper with the fringe torn off and in the dead sister's hand:

Do I want to be distant and make him miss me there's always the chance he won't or try to get the easy friendly feeling back and see where that goes? Both are goal-oriented and me me me. I want, I want, I want him. These are not appropriate feelings. But I feel like making do without is what I always do—I smooth over rough places so I can go back to being by myself because I know how to do that—it's not particularly scary and the only downside is loneliness.

I'm wary of my impulse to want comfort from him. What I want is not what one is obligated to do when I'm sad-voiced or crying. I'm not fabricating being sad, but I'm making it convenient—which feels both dishonest and like settling—I receive an approximation of what I want. And I'm scared it's making me angry and that my anger is going to come out in a dishonest, approximate way and I'll screw everything up.

I hate how willing I am to be by myself—how unwilling to take a chance, I want an insurance policy on everything, against hurt feelings, everything. The shrinks tell me you can't trust others until you trust yourself, and I'm not trustworthy. I feel scared of what other people can do to me because I'm not sure what's there to take—what haven't I already messed up?—and because I have done so much to myself. I don't know if there's something I can present or hand over. Here's me: please take care.

This is nauseating.

self-self-self

me, me, me

but I'm just supposed to be writing it down.

The robber thought of the dead sister as happy alone and would be surprised to read this page, but the girlfriend wouldn't be. The girlfriend is rarely surprised by loneliness. If they ever found it, the piece of paper would make them both wonder why they hadn't paid more attention to the dead sister's unhappiness while she was alive.

Construct your own reality

If someone comes into his office, the robber will have to hide his sketchbook.

He is sketching the kitchen entrance of The Mansion; in his notebook are no fewer than forty-seven sketches of various entrances of The Mansion. Most houses require two or three sketches at most before the robber has a good plan. The Mansion is a challenge, a beautiful challenge to the robber, similar to a Rubik's cube or a game of golf—he is playing against himself, and he doesn't want to lose. The lights, the alarms—he wouldn't disarm a thing.

The robber has been unable to talk to the girlfriend about his plans. He guards his sketchbook carefully. How could the girlfriend understand the robber's need to take from the wealthiest house, even if the house happens to belong to him? If the robber had a plan to steal from the sister while she was still alive, the girlfriend would have considered him heartless and without feeling or loyalty. She would have broken up with him. That problem would be classified as the problem of a jerk, an asshole, a prick who doesn't care about anyone but himself.

But if the girlfriend knew the robber was obsessed with stealing from The Mansion now that his sister was dead, she would certainly have to question the psychological health of the robber. Who would take from his own house? The girlfriend would be worse than angry: she would be perplexed. This state would bring a new level of distance to the relationship of the robber and the girlfriend, and the girlfriend would surely feel disgusted by the robber. (For some women, it is easier to feel disgust than to feel pity or to acknowledge vulnerability.) The robber can sense this limitation in the girlfriend and so he hides his sketchbook.

The sketchbook is open on the wood laminate of the robber's desk. The shrubbery is done in a delicate and sunny orange watercolor, the color the robber made all the trees in his childhood daydreams.

Don't stalk yourself

The lawyer is on the phone. He is on the phone most of the day and evening. He lives alone, orders takeout or has TV dinners. He is the loneliest he has ever been, although he is in love. He talks to at least twenty different people a day: friends, associates, clients, his mother, his ex-girlfriend, the robber's girlfriend, and his brother. He stays on the phone with one person until another calls and he can click over on his call waiting. He checks his work answering machine while at home and his home machine while at work. His cellphone is switched to vibrate during the day, so that the lawyer can take any call no matter the location, and to the loudest ring at night.

He leaves messages for people in between making calls. Someone is always calling back.

Remember, work can actually be fun

The cop is filing papers, but he feels great! He is walking on air. He is replaying The Kiss over and over again in his mind. Sometimes the cop becomes so excited he begins to mimic these kissing movements with the filing cabinet, but the only other person in the room is the dispatcher, and she is trying not to look at the cop.

It isn't the first time the cop has thought about a kiss between himself and the partner, but it is the first time he is remembering a kiss rather than imagining one. The cop thinks of the advice he has received from *Glamour* and *Marie Claire.* Make your own luck. Keep your eyes open when you kiss someone for the first time—it will add excitement and help you get to know each other in a new way!

The Kiss took place in the precinct pisser.

"Sure you won't go to dinner?" the cop had asked. He felt nervous and rejected, even though it was only dinner—and short notice at that!

"Look at me," said the partner. Then... the kiss.

"Wow," said the cop. He leaned in and kissed the partner again, this time letting his hand run through the partner's hair.

"Finally," said the partner. The cop and the partner laughed, months of tension and expectation dissipating instantly.

* * *

Laugh like a bowl full of jelly

On the robber's desk at the insurance office are the plans he is hiding from the girlfriend, a desk lamp, a Palm Pilot, twelve pens, a pencil, and a sheaf of claims he has been sifting through. The desktop also holds three framed pictures: a 5x7 of the robber and the girlfriend hiking, a 5x7 of the girlfriend on the beach, and an 8x10 of the dead sister, age five and nightgown-clad, grinning up at the camera and hugging a stuffed Santa Claus doll. The robber took this picture from the funeral; there was a table of photographs, and the robber knows the picture belonged to someone but he also knows that no one would suspect him of taking it.

The dead sister remains frozen in the photograph. The robber thinks of the day the picture was taken, Christmas morning when he was eleven and the dead sister was five. The robber stood behind the dead sister as they peeked through the bannister rails, trying to get a glimpse of Santa. He had resisted an urge to push his small sister down the stairs. He wanted to crumple her body, to watch it go tumbling down the polished wooden gloss of the staircase, banging against a corner then airborne: bang—air—bang—air. This impulse, born of a feeling that the dead sister would receive more presents, has long been buried in the robber.

Remember your own power

The partner's father died when he was twelve. Today is the anniversary of the death. The partner will visit the cemetery after he gets off work. The partner wants to go to dinner with the cop, especially after The Kiss, but he needs to see his father more than he needs to get fed and laid, so he tells the cop he is sorry and claps him on the back. *Later* is what the clap signifies.

Another time. The partner claps the cop's back because he doesn't feel like telling the cop about his father.

Tell the truth

The girlfriend doesn't feel lust. She rarely masturbates. She does not come in these masturbation sessions, and she doesn't care. She has never had an orgasm. The girlfriend used to care, back in her twenties when she still thought she could have one. Now she has careless, joyless sex with the robber and with the lawyer—more sex than she is accustomed to having—and she fakes with the robber because he wants her to, but she does not always pretend with the lawyer. The lawyer is used to having women fake; he would not believe the girlfriend if she had an orgasm every time. The girlfriend can sense the lawyer's careful skepticism; she does not wish to arouse it in regard to her.

It is too difficult to explain her frigidity.

The girlfriend's friend used to buy her books on orgasms and read masturbation articles from women's magazines to her over the phone, but she has given up. The friend is a feminist, and she has read hundreds of articles on the female orgasm. *Every woman's body is different. You have to know your body before you can please your body. You have to be able to please yourself before others can please you.*

The friend is twenty-nine and she has slept with seventeen people. If she doesn't have an orgasm with a man, she never pretends. The friend suspects the girlfriend fakes every time, regardless of the man's skill. The friend is sure that women like the girlfriend are responsible for the hordes of subpar lovers out there. Honesty is always the best policy when it comes to sex.

* * *

Let every heart prepare Him room

The cop is traveling in the squad car, although he was supposed to be off duty seventeen minutes ago. He's been called to the mall—a gang of kids cornered the Mall Santa and roughed him up. It happens every year, but the cop has never before been called to handle the incident. He hasn't heard of other cities having such a problem keeping their Mall Santas healthy; the cop suspects it may be an initiation of some sort: *Beat the stuffing out of Santa Claus and join our club!*

The cop is grateful for mall security. They are the most incompetent branch of security there is, and the cop knows they will have bungled the investigation so thoroughly that he will either choose to forget the incident and convince the Mall Santa not to press charges or he will be able to send for another officer. After all, it is Christmas Eve. After all, he is not supposed to be working.

The cop is particularly anxious to be off duty because he has dinner plans with the partner. When the partner refused the cop's invitation, the cop was first disappointed but then decided to redouble his efforts—especially after The Kiss!—and the partner, after haggling over the time, agreed to come to the cop's apartment for dinner. The cop's refrigerator holds one bowl of tuna salad, a half loaf of oat-rye bread, two stalks celery, 7/8 jar light Kraft mayonnaise, 2/3 bottle of ketchup, 1/4 bottle of cranberry juice, two Miller High Lifes, and an unopened can of jellied cranberry sauce. The cop has not dated in years; however, he isn't nervous about dinner. After The Kiss, he's confident dinner isn't on the partner's mind either.

It is now twenty-nine minutes after the cop was supposed to be off duty. He is in the mall security office standing over the battered and bloodied Mall Santa. The Mall Santa's nose is broken and leaking red, almost delicately, out of his left nostril.

The cop stares. He has never seen such beautiful blood.

The Mall Santa's lip is swollen and the cop wants to take it gently between his teeth and roll his tongue over it, to feel the slight engorgement, to taste the faint trickle of blood. The Mall Santa's bruised face is changing color, almost every second a new shade, and his broken nose is something the cop wants to hold and love for its very imperfections. The Mall Santa's battered and torn uniform is likewise beautiful to the cop, who in this new mood—this mood of love returned and hope fulfilled and promise everywhere—wishes to kiss and comfort and bandage this other human being, to listen to his problems and hear his desires, to take the corner of a bandage and press it to this man's leaking eye.

Dash through the snow, make an angel, sing at the top of your lungs

The forty-two-inch box in front of the lawyer shows a scene from *Miracle on 34th Street*. In this scene, Edmund Gwenn as Kris Kringle is in the sanitarium. He is speaking with John Payne, who plays the idealistic attorney in love with Maureen O'Hara. The lawyer's TV is playing the colorized version of the 1947 classic, and Kris Kringle's beard is the same color as his hospital gown: a skim-milk blue-white. The color in the colorized version of *Miracle on 34th Street* is never brilliant, and viewers complain about it in a fond, nostalgic way. It would never do to update the color.

As a boy, the lawyer wanted to be an artist. His parents took him to movies or baseball games, and he would come home and immediately begin the process of capturing the event on paper. He had an eye for minutiae, a concentration on details peripheral to the main plot: the sparkles on the dress of Glinda the Good Witch, the look on the face of the fan sitting next to the guy who caught the pop fly. The lawyer was interested in representation—how can you capture that glitter or that disappointment in colored pencil, crayon, or marker? The lawyer's mother keeps his pictures, every one, in old dress-shirt boxes. The pictures are crinkly, curled up like a fried egg. It's sentimental to keep such pictures. The lawyer is the lawyer. He will never be the artist. The pictures are worthless.

Sitting on his sofa in front of *Miracle on 34th Street*, the lawyer waits for the girlfriend. It is snowing outside, but he isn't worried about her driving. She has snow tires and so far the snow isn't sticking. The lawyer stares at the beard blending into the gown of Kris Kringle and thinks about his future: a wide-open space ahead in which he isn't alone. He loves the girlfriend, loves her for her insecurity and her body and the way she can beat anyone at Scrabble and the way she pumps gasoline into the car, keys dangling from the gas tank, her face turned toward his, her tilted chin dimpled from her smile.

The lawyer isn't worried about the girlfriend crashing her car; he's worried about what her entrance into his life this Christmas Eve will mean. Because he has asked her to leave the robber, she has. Because he has asked her to move in with him, she will. Because he has asked her to come and spend Christmas with him, she is on her way, three streets down, now turning, her tire sliding from contact with frozen water. Now she is in his driveway. She will leave her bags, come up the walk crunching snow on glad boots, and he will open the door to embrace her.

Take deep breaths

The cop was right: the contents of his refrigerator were not important. Now he and his partner are in bed together. It is time for pillow talk. They are swapping humiliations. The partner's humiliation goes something like this:

> When I was in ninth grade all my friends—'cause my friends were cool. I was the only one not smoking, you know? They all smoked outside by the library windows 'cause the library windows were the highest and no one on the inside could see them. Anyway, all my friends did drugs. They were getting into, you know, misdemeanor shit, no one was dealing. Shit, they were just little punks, but I was hanging on. They were cool. But I was hanging on by a thread, you know? I could fall any minute. My jeans weren't right, I was kinda scrawny. Nothing special. No reason they *would* hang with me except they already were. I was a habit from junior high. Anyway, one day in Earth Science they were all talking about smoking weed and dropping acid and all this other shit and I started talking, too, and I didn't know my head from my ass in these talks. I guess they weren't really my friends or I woulda been hanging with them, doing drugs after school. My life woulda turned out different, I guess. Anyway, I said something about smoking a bunch of acid over the weekend and how fucked up I got and how I was already having flashbacks and shit. How was I to know that you didn't smoke acid? I'd never even seen the shit. Anyway, these kids were real nice to me, asked me a few questions and probably laughed their asses off after school but they didn't say a word to me then. And I sorta wish they had, you know? I don't think I woulda liked it, it woulda been embarrassing to be found out like that, but it mighta cured me of bragging and it woulda saved me thinking about it now. Now I keep cringing inside, I get this real awful feeling, you know, whenever I think of what a dumbass I was and how those kids didn't even make fun of me. Man, they didn't ever even try to make me feel bad about it.

* * *

'Tis the season to be jolly

Because the cop fell asleep, sated and slobbery, trusting drunk, and because the snow has started to drift down through the air and settle in the lower places of the ground, and because he feels active and alive rather than sleepy after sex, the partner has snuck away from the cop's bed and he now stands at the mall's lighted map contemplating. The mall's lighted map is a large black-backgrounded signpost with small green dots and letters and lines delineating the locations of the mall's vendors. The partner touches YOU ARE HERE with his right thumb. The fingers of the partner's left hand run down the green list of stores; there are seventy-seven stores on the lighted map.

In his teenage years, the partner was considered by mall authorities a mall rat; that is, a young person with no discernible reason to be at the mall who nevertheless frequented the mall on Friday and Saturday nights, lurked in corners with other young people, and rarely spent money at any of the mall's vendors. The partner hung out at the mall every weekend and participated in various aspects of mall-rat culture, hairstyle trends and getting high in the parking lot of Sears—all for the purpose of looking at and potentially securing dates with girls.

However, the partner had a secret mall-rat life: he met older men at the mall, their particulars obtained from the personal ads of the local newspaper; it was difficult, weekend after weekend, to trick or lose track of his friends without arousing their keen teenaged suspicion, but the partner's desire was a match for the finely tuned force of the high-school social hierarchy. It was hard on his nerves, however, to pretend to be someone else with every new person. (It is hard on his nerves today, too, The Kiss with the cop and all it will mean from now on. It takes guts to kiss another man in the precinct pisser. This fear was not a thrilling fear, not the thrill of blowing some guy in his musty Ford at the lonely edge of the parking lot, not the thrill of the cruise. No. It was more the horrible thrill of getting in a rickety car on an old wooden roller coaster, getting on because you wanted to—but only if you could be assured that you'd emerge later, safe and whole.)

Walking through the food court brings back a flood of memories for the partner. He sees the Mall Santa with a child on his lap. Something in the graceful line of the Santa's nose or the powerful arm that lifts the child convinces the partner that this Mall Santa is a young man, a man familiar to the partner, perhaps the last lover the partner had: a cruel and hard body with a weak mind, an unemployed mechanic who could fuck like nobody's business. The partner knows logically that the Mall Santa is not his ex-lover, but the slight resemblance gives his mind permission to think of his ex-lover, a permission the partner does not usually receive, a permission he craves deeply with every part of himself. In the glassy food court, the partner feels himself getting hard, the speaker softly breathing "Deck the Halls," the lights twinkling in the parking lot, catching the small bits of metal in thousands of cars and reflecting light up into the snowing sky. Shutting himself in the stall of the dirty bathroom, the partner jerks off and comes almost immediately, an exhalation of feeling that has been pent up and waiting, biding its time until it must break forth—the picture of a hard chest with stomach padding strapped beneath, a set of white whiskers dangling from a baby-smooth upper lip.

Think about what you really want (Hint: You may already have it!)

The robber's girlfriend is in love with the robber's dead

sister's lawyer. (In a scene that can be described only as horrible—that *horrible* fight—the girlfriend will leave the robber for good. After, sometimes, the girlfriend will think, "He wasn't bad, that robber, just not the right time, I wasn't ready, or he wasn't, it hardly matters now. I wish him well." The robber will suffer a severe depression and will question his existence.)

But these are not necessarily problems. These are facts of the robber's life. How is it a problem if the girlfriend falls in love with someone else?

Love is scarce, and maybe the lawyer's sperm will travel inside the girlfriend to its destination and make a baby. Maybe the baby will grow to be a great doctor. Or maybe the baby will travel and fall in love and read books and eat hamburgers and shave hairy areas of the body and will be a good person who tries to do good things and has babies who also grow into good people who try to do good things.

But right now this is all too philosophical for the robber. He sits on a stool in the kitchen of The Mansion.

The girlfriend has left to spend Christmas with the lawyer. At this moment, on the stool, the robber is not sure what he wants. He thought he would marry the girlfriend.

Now he doesn't know who he will be without his plans. He has a drink, yes, and he isn't crying.

They say, *You can be happy, no matter what.*

He is too afraid to cry.

Cope, don't mope

The cop cannot believe the partner has left him. The partner is not in the bathroom. He is not in the kitchen drinking a High Life. He is not in the garage, nor is his car in the driveway. Maybe, the cop reasons, the partner is merely out in search of sustenance. After all, they were supposed to have dinner. After all, the cop does live two streets down from an all-night Chinese buffet. Maybe, the cop reasons, the partner did not want to wake him. Maybe, the cop reasons, the partner was being thoughtful. The cop decides to take a drive, just to see if the partner would like his company now that he is awake.

The robber is on a ladder. He is not yet ready to rob The Mansion, but neither is he prepared to wait any longer. The robber is antsy. Grief has altered his usual careful planning, and he is staging what is referred to as a dry or trial run. The robber does not usually stage such runs; it is not wise, not prudent. But the robber is distraught, and he is beyond caring about following protocol. He will climb to the roof, he will creep along the north side of The Mansion, he will unlatch the great room's smallest skylight, and he will drop safely down onto his own ottoman. There, he will be face to face with the tree the girlfriend decorated, he will be staring at his lonely presents to her, and he will force himself to confront this new life.

Speeding by The Mansion, his siren blaring, his stomach muscles clenching and unclenching, his dick hard, his brain intent upon finding the partner, the cop sees the robber on the ladder, sees him in his robber gear, sees him as the robber. The cop sees, but he does not see. In his mind's eye, the robber has been transformed, perhaps to a regular homeowner, checking the chimney, perhaps to a workman, called to fix the antenna, perhaps even to the partner, dick also hard, waving to him and blowing kisses down from this vantage. In any case, the cop is speeding by, and soon he is in front of another mansion, soon he is seeing another resident of this wealthy neighborhood, soon his eye is focused completely inward, soon he is out of sight.

* * *

Sleep in heavenly peace

Flying over the rooftops of this snow-covered, light-twinkling, tucked-in-cozy city, Santa sees the robber collapsed on his ottoman.

The robber, surrounded on all sides by reminders of the girlfriend, has begun to cry with the sort of gusto that can lead only to the gift of dreamless sleep.

Santa sees the cop driving.

The cop is dazed. Why did the partner sleep with him? And why did he leave? The cop's mind seizes and discards answers. Perhaps he was too eager, perhaps he did something wrong.

Santa sees the partner in the bathroom stall.

The partner is depressed by his actions, depressed by the decisions he has made on the anniversary of his father's death. Why did he sleep with the cop? Why did he come to the mall? Why does he do anything? He thinks of his father, thinks of his father's response to the behavior of his only son, and he begins the sort of gulping crying which betrays its own long wait.

Santa sees the girlfriend cuddled with the lawyer in front of the TV.

Both are falling asleep, half-waking, half-dreaming, and, for this moment, both states are the same: the promise of love, the unexpectedness of every new day.

Santa is taking note of who is naughty and who is nice, and he will distribute gifts accordingly.

Of course, it isn't fair to distribute toys and sugarplums and expensive electronic equipment based on the one moment of observation. But he won't change his flight schedule or his manner of distributing gifts: Santa doesn't give a shit. His nose is cold, his thighs ache from their position in the sleigh, he wants only to get home to Mrs. Claus, who has roast beef and baked potatoes waiting. When he arrives, Mrs. Claus may greet him warmly and dine with him: a white damask tablecloth, candles, an apple pie baking. She may ask about his day; she may have his slippers waiting.

Or maybe Mrs. Claus will choose today to find religion, in which case there will be no dinner, and perhaps Santa will need to go back out in the snow to the Wendy's drive-thru after fielding a series of questions and accusations about his contribution to the spirit of mall commercialism that permeates this most sacred of holidays, the birth of baby Jesus, the Holy Son of God. For Chrissakes. That isn't what he needs to hear tonight.

Or she may have become a raging feminist, she may want to be Ms. Claus, or even to return to her maiden name—an expensive and time-consuming legal process—and how will he ever explain the change to their friends, much less all the businesses that capitalize on the popularity of the icon of sweet Mrs. Claus. And the children, my God, the children! The children would never understand.

It's possible, too, that she could be upset by his broken nose, it's possible she will cry and worry and rage now that he's lost his mall job—"Who will believe you're Santa looking like that?"—the job that was paying their rent, not to mention their liquor and their dog.

But he knew they shouldn't have adopted a dog. Two rarely employed alcoholics—what business do they have taking in a stray dog? But she'd looked so cute, holding the puppy on her lap, and he did love her; he couldn't refuse her much.

Sometimes Santa is in the right place at the right time and sometimes not. If his nose hadn't been broken—who knows? Santa and Mrs. Claus could have started AA the next day, they could have opened a bank account and saved money and then moved somewhere warm and tropical with their dog. They could open a dog kennel, and he could watch his wife play with puppies all day, life a constant opportunity to take cute photographs of the person you love. But flying home, Santa understands none of these options is open to him. Too many people depend on him, too many children cling to his legacy, too many adults point to the moment they learned he wasn't real.

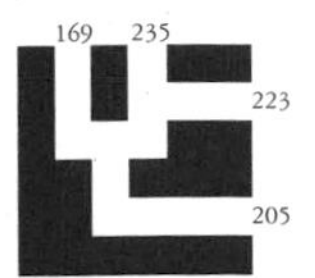

IN A BEAR'S EYE

by YANNICK MURPHY

SHE HEARD the bear. It hooted like an owl, only lower, sounding like an owl far down in a well or in a cave. She looked out the window. There it was, in the field above the pond on its hind legs. It shook the apples from the apple tree. Her boy did not look up at the bear in the field. He was by the pond. The bear was not so close but neither was he far away. If the bear had wanted to, the bear could run to the boy and the bear could be on her boy in no time at all, in the time it took an apple to fall from the branch and onto the field.

She ran outside with her gun.

Her boy had brown hair that over summer had turned almost blond. In the light of the setting sun she imagined how her boy's hair would look golden, how when he moved about, as he never kept still, how the color of his hair would surely catch anyone's eye, even a bear's.

When she was a girl she wanted her hair to turn that color. She cut lemon wedges and folded them around the strands of hair and pulled down on the lemon wedges, all the way to the ends. She would then lie down and bathe in the sun. She spread her hair out behind her on the towel. The strands were sticky. There was lemon pulp clinging to them in places. Bees flew close to her hair. The color stayed a light brown.

The gun was heavier than she had remembered. There was probably some muscle in her arm that was once stronger when she had carried the gun with her husband through the woods. They had hunted grouse every season. Now the muscle was weak. To get to her boy she knew that she would have to first crouch behind the rock wall and then, like a soldier, she would have to run and hide behind trees. She would have to be in some way like a snake. Serpentine, her pattern. Isn't that what a soldier would say? Serpentine, she would have to run down the line of trees that bordered the field for a few hundred feet. She did not think she could do it. She would eventually be seen. The bear would stop shaking the apple tree and look around, sniffing the air. The bear might come at her.

Her husband was the one who always shot the grouse. He was a good shot. She always aimed too high. Her husband, while she was aiming, would put his hand on top of her gun, to lower it down, but still she never shot a grouse.

The boy took some small rocks from the pond's shoreline. He stood up and threw them into the water.

"Sit down," she said out loud in a whisper that didn't sound to her like her own voice.

The boy was not doing well in school. He liked to read during class. Beneath the desk he would hold an open book. A book about beavers or silk moths or spiders. The teacher sent him home with notes for his mother. The notes said the boy must pay attention. Her boy would sometimes read to her from his books while they ate dinner. There were things she had never learned as a girl. A silkworm female moth is born without a mouth. It does not live long enough to eat. It only lives long enough to mate and lay its eggs before it dies. Her boy would stop and show her the pictures. She would shake her head. She was amazed at how much she had never learned as a girl her boy's age. Was she just too busy squeezing lemon wedges onto her hair? Her boy never said he was sad that his father, her husband, had died. But she knew he was sad. Her husband was like a book that could talk. At the dinner table he would tell their boy about science and math. He talked about zero. "Zero scared the ancients," her husband said. "No one wanted to believe that there could be nothing."

He walked into the ocean one day and he did not stop walking. She liked to think he was still walking under the water. Skates stirred up sand and rose to the surface as he walked by them. Water entered his shirt cuffs and his shirt back ballooned. She and her boy sometimes talked about it. Her boy said how the hair on his head must be floating up and wavering like the long leaves of sea plants. Her boy said how his father must be reaching out to the puffer fish, wanting to see them change into prickly balls. His father must be touching everything as he walks, the craggy sides of mouths of caves where groupers lurk and roll their eyes, the white gilled undersides of manta rays casting shadow clouds above him. "My father must be in China by now," the boy said to his mother.

China because after he had died and the boy and the mother cleared out the father's drawers, they found a travel brochure for China. They had no idea the father was interested in going to China, but the words "See the wall" were written on the outside of the brochure.

The mother now saw how the sun was going behind the hillside. Its last rays hit the black steel of her gun and it hit the very top of her boy's hair before it sunk down. The bear was finished. It had knocked almost all the apples to the ground. He began to eat them. The mother thought how the boy would be safe now, the bear would eat and then leave and she would not have to run closer to the bear, going from tree to tree, looking for a shot she would probably miss because her husband was not there to put his hand on her gun, pushing down, keeping her from aiming too high.

Not long ago the boy's teacher had come to see her. She held open the screen door for the teacher and told her to come in. They sat in the kitchen and the teacher asked the boy if she could speak with his mother alone. The boy nodded and slid a book off the kitchen table and left the room. The mother could hear the boy walk up the stairs and close the door to his room.

"Your boy is a smart boy," the teacher said. "The death of his father must have come as a shock. But still," the teacher said, "there is school."

She looked into her refrigerator to offer the teacher something. There wasn't much. She hadn't been to the store in days. She opened the bottom bin and found two lemons. She took them out and put them on the table where they rolled for a moment. The mother got her wooden chopping board and placed the lemons on it and cut each lemon in four. She pushed the chopping board toward the teacher. "Please, have some."

The teacher did not say anything. After a while the teacher said, "I'm sorry. I'll come back another day to talk about your son." When the teacher left, the mother went upstairs to her boy. He was reading a book about spiders. Together they lay on his bed and looked at the pictures.

She would take her boy on a trip. They would go to China. They would see the wall. They would look for signs of him. She had yet to tell the teacher how her boy would miss days of school, even weeks.

Now, at the pond, the boy thought he would try it. He walked in slowly. The brown water filled his tennis shoes. It was cold. The boy knew from his books that beavers had flaps of skin behind their front teeth. They could shut the flaps when underwater, sealing the water out of their mouths and lungs. When the water came above the boy's eyes and finally over his head, the boy imagined he had these flaps. He opened his eyes underwater. The darkness was like four walls all around him. Maybe he could reach out and touch them.

The bear stopped eating. It sniffed the air and lifted its head. It went toward the pond. When it walked it looked like a man who was sauntering. She did not know before how bears hooted like owls, how they sauntered like men. She followed it. She did not run from tree to tree. She ran in a straight line. "No, no, you'll never shoot anything running at it like that," she could hear her husband say. Where was her boy? Where was her husband?

She saw ripples in the pond where her boy had gone in and then she noticed that the bear was looking at her. Its upper lip was curled. It had white on its chest, the shape of a diamond, but not perfect, a diamond being stretched, a diamond melting. She let the gun drop. She ran fast through the milkweed. The butterflies flew ahead of her. She ran past the bear. She dove into the water on top of the ripples made by her boy. She wanted to save him. She wanted to tell him he did not have to drown. She swam down, wishing she could call to him underwater, wishing she could see through the black silt. She had not taken a breath before she went down and she could not believe she did not need one. She thought for a moment how everyone must be wrong, there was no need to hold your breath underwater. She now knew it. She thought her boy knew it too. They had both found out a secret. She could stop thrashing about in the water now, looking for her boy. He would come up and out when he was ready. When she came to the surface she realized the pond was shallow. She was standing with the water only coming to her hip.

Her boy was on the other side of the pond. He was sitting on a large flat rock on the shore. He was holding something in his hand. The bear was watching them, his lip no longer curled. She walked to her boy while still in the water. It dragged her shirtsleeves and her pantlegs behind her. She moved her hair away from her eyes.

The boy had mud in his hand that he had scooped from the bottom of the pond.

"What's that?" she said.

"Maybe some gold," the boy said, moving the mud around and poking at it in his palm.

"Look over there," the mother said, pointing to the bear. The bear turned and sauntered away.

"Yes," said her boy. "I saw him ages ago. He likes the apples from our apple tree."

That night she told the boy that maybe they had better not go on their trip to China after all. There was school to think about. The boy nodded. "All right," he said.

She thought how she missed her husband. She thought how she would now miss him the way other women must miss their dead husbands. She would wear his shirts. Isn't that what other women did? They took long walks and thought about their husbands and when they sweat the smell that came up to them was not the smell of themselves but the smell of their dead men?

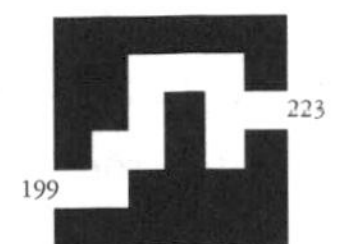

BAD HABITS

by JOYCE CAROL OATES

THEY CAME FOR us at school. They didn't explain why. In their faces was the warning *Don't ask.*

Uncle S., Aunt B.

Hurriedly they took us from school. In the corridor the principal stood staring. *What is? Family Emergency? Why...?*

Faces of alarm, disbelief.

A. was the youngest, he tried not to cry. There was T., he was eleven. There was D., thirteen.

Uncle S. was driving. Aunt B. was staring straight ahead.

In the back seat, D. sat between us. D. was our older sister and held our hands tight.

Don't ask. Don't ask.

A. was whimpering and wiping at his nose. A. knew Mother was dead.

T. was staring out the car window. T. believed it had to be Father, they were going to the hospital to see Father who'd had a heart attack at work.

D. shut her eyes. Trying not to think that both Mother *and* Father were probably dead. Trying not to feel a thrill of excitement, how special it would make her at school: an orphan.

In the front seat of the vehicle, Uncle S. and Aunt B. conferred in lowered voices. A decision was made. Uncle S. turned onto our street. Except after a few blocks the street was barricaded.

Uncle S. demanded to be let through. Uncle S. showed a police officer his driver's license. Camera flashes were aimed at Uncle S. who held his hand in front of his face. Uncle S. was pleading. Uncle S. spoke in a cracked voice. We heard Uncle S. say *No I am not his brother, I am hers.*

Uncle S. was allowed to drive through the traffic barricade.

Our neighbors stood on their lawns shading their eyes, staring. Strangers milled in the street and on the sidewalks. There were many uniformed police officers. There were photographers running beside our car. Yellow tape had been posted around our house.

Yellow tape had been posted around our house! Out to the very edge of the grass our father kept trimmed short and free, or almost free, of nasty crabgrass and dandelions. Out to the very edge of our property where there was a three-foot chain-link fence, Mother kept covered in climber roses, in the summer.

Our house looked so strange. A blinding light of many flash cameras. Strangers' faces like masks of stretched skin. A din of voices we could not hear.

Aunt B. instructed us *Keep your windows rolled up! Keep your heads down!*

Uncle S. turned the car into our driveway where the strangers were not allowed to follow. Police officers stood on the walk leading to the side door, by the carport. Quickly then, Mother appeared. Quickly then, Mother hurried to the car. Mother was hunched over shielding her face with her hands.

Mother crowded into the back seat with us and lifted A. onto her lap. Uncle S. shut the car door that Mother was too weak to shut. *Take me away. Out of here. Oh God.*

By a circuitous route we were taken to Uncle S.'s and Aunt B.'s house that was just miles away. Yet in the street, on the lawn, and in the driveway strangers were already there, waiting.

Reporters. Photographers. TV camera crews. A single police vehicle, parked in the driveway.

There they are! His wife! His children!

Aunt B. began to scream. Uncle S. cursed. In the back seat of the car Mother clutched at us, all three of us, as if trying to shield us even as she buried her tear-streaked face in D.'s hair.

Uncle S. protested the trespassers onto his private property but still they came rushing at us. Still they came clamoring after us. The police officers did not seem sympathetic. Mother clutched and pulled at us as we hurried into the house. Already we knew to duck our heads and shield our faces with our hands. Already we knew to run bent over, trying to ignore the cries pitched at us like stones.

Ma'am! Will you say a few—

—your husband innocent d'you think?

—guilty? Do you think?

—are you surprised—

—did you suspect—

—any hint, in his behavior—

—marital relations—

Inside the house we hid. We hid upstairs. The windows of the house were always shut. The window blinds were drawn. Mother lay in bed with the covers over her head. We could hear Mother praying. *Oh God dear God help. Help him, help us. Help this to be a mistake.* We hid in our beds. We were not allowed to watch TV. The house wasn't safe. On the street, strangers had a right to congregate. There were television crews: WBEN-TV, WWSB-TV, WTSM-TV. A. could not sleep alone. Yet A. was likely to wet the bed. T. could not sleep. D. could not sleep. We were given food. We were in a room together. We slept like puppies together. We asked where Father was. We were told Father was away. A TV helicopter circled overhead. Mother hid beneath the covers. For a long time Mother was silent. Mother began to cry. Mother began to scream. Mother was in a state of shock, it was explained.

In a state of shock, poor woman will never recover.

Has got to be a mistake. Could not possibly…

Married to the man for fifteen years, what a…

…silly woman, not to know. Not to suspect.

The children! Think of the children.

Bad Habits' children? Or…

We were not allowed to leave the house. We were not allowed to return to school. We were told that our presence would be "distracting." We were told that nothing we had done was bad or wrong or nasty or evil but still we were not wanted back at school. Mother made us kneel with her. *Pray! Pray to God for mercy.* D. refused to kneel. D. refused to pray. D. begged to be allowed to return to school. D. had just been elected to the student council when we'd been removed from school. D. had just been elected to represent her eighth-grade homeroom on the student council. D. screamed it was unfair. D. screamed she hated Father. Mother began to shake. Mother had chest pains and could not breathe and was taken by ambulance to a hospital. We were not allowed to visit Mother in the hospital. We were not allowed to visit Father in the place where he was incarcerated.

Incarcerated! This was a word new to us.

There was another house we were taken to. We were followed. A WXCT-TV van thundered alongside the vehicle in which we were riding. TV cameras were aimed at us. Bullhorn voices shouted. Microphones were shoved at us. *Were you surprised at your dad's arrest? Do you believe your dad is innocent? Do you love your dad? Was your dad a strict disciplinarian? Will you attend the trial? Do you feel sorry for the strangled children? Do you pray for your dad? Is there a favorite memory you can share with our TV viewers, of your dad?*

We were living now with Grandpa and Grandma. This was a different house in a different city. We had not seen Father in a long time. When we asked about Father we were told *God's will* and *Don't ask!* Mother had returned from the hospital. Mother smelled of the hospital. Mother wished to hug and kiss but we shrunk away from her. Grandpa and Grandma were Mother's parents. Grandpa covered all of the windows of the house on the inside with aluminum foil so that strangers could not peek in at us. Grandma drew the blinds down on all the windows. It was never daytime, only night. The TV was for adults. The newspaper was for adults. We were taken to church here. We were allowed to go to church here with Grandpa, Grandma, and Mother. It was not our old church but the same prayers were said. The same hymns were sung. In our old church, Father had recently been elected president of the church council. In our new church, the minister prayed for Father and for Father's family. Mother was *the wife of*, we were *the children of*. There were fewer photographers now but still we had to be vigilant for strangers rushed at us when we least expected them. Grandpa became very angry. Mad as a hornet, Grandma said of him. Grandpa refused to go outside without a hat on his head. Grandpa began to cover his bald, dented head with aluminum foil in the shape of a little cap before he put his hat on to go outside. Grandma kept all the blinds on the windows drawn. Grandma could no longer knit or crochet, for her arthritic hands trembled. Grandma was found wandering in the neighborhood in her nightgown, barefoot. Grandma was heavily medicated for a condition called dyskinesia. We were very embarrassed of Grandpa and Grandma and wished they would die soon.

Bad habits. We were acquiring bad habits.

We did not remember Father very clearly. Sometimes entering a room one of us saw his shadow on a wall, looming to the ceiling. Sometimes in the middle of the night one of us heard him prowling downstairs muttering to himself. There was a gassy-bad smell of Father in the upstairs bathroom sometimes. There was a memory of Father in Mother's weepy eyes.

It is all a bad dream, children. A terrible mistake. I pray for this revelation and so should you.

We hated Mother. We loved Mother but we could not bear the hospital smell.

We were forbidden knowledge of Father because it would be "too upsetting"—"distorted"—"exaggerated" for us, but of course we came to know certain facts. We knew that Father was frequently on TV and in the newspapers because in all the Midwest no one was more famous than Father. No one was more talked of, discussed. No one was more prayed-for by Christian congregations. No one was more reviled. When the old people were napping we slipped from the house. In the 7-Eleven store we stared at newspaper headlines. A tabloid magazine cover. Front-page photographs of Father who was "Bad Habits." Here was a man we might not have recognized immediately, older than we recalled, unshaven, eyes glittery and shrunken beneath grizzled eyebrows, a downward twist to his rubbery lips like a smile of secret merriment. *"Bad Habits" Indicted on 19 Counts of Homicide. Alleged Serial Killer Stands Mute at Arraignment. 12-Year*

Rampage of Torture, Murder, Terror and Taunts by "Bad Habits": Why? Utilities Worker, 53, Longtime Local Resident, Arrested in Sadistic Murders. Notorious "Bad Habits" Revealed as Husband, Father of 3, Ex-Boy Scout Leader and "Devout" Church of Christ Member. Suddenly D. began to laugh. T. who'd been staring with widened eyes began to laugh. A. who wasn't sure that this was Father anyway gave a cry of anger and knocked over the newspaper rack sending all the papers flying and we ran out of the store before the astonished clerk could stop us.

Bad habits that summer.

D. who'd been vain about her hair, began plucking single hairs from her head. T. began to bite his nails. Thumbnails first, then fingernails. Sometimes in his sleep. Poor A., the nosepicker. He'd been apt to pick his nose before Bad Habits came into out lives, now his fingers could not seem to stay away from his face, poking into his nostrils, savaging the soft interior skin of the nostril, provoking nosebleeds.

Prowling the house at night. Searching for the room where Father's shadow might be waiting.

Slipping from the house while the adults slept. Rummaging through neighbors' trash. Behind the 7-Eleven.

Serial Killer Unrepentent: "God's Will"?

Bad Habits Hints to Police: More Victims' Bodies?

DNA Match Linked to Semen at Crime Scenes: Sex Pervert?

There were court hearings. There was to be a trial. Mother was brave and hopeful for she believed, if there was a trial, Father's name (which was our name) would be cleared. *The evil cloud will lift. The nightmare will be over.* We were made to pray with Mother. We did not expect the nightmare to be over.

We were the children of Bad Habits. For us the mystery was *Why had Father chosen those he'd chosen.*

It was the key to everything! If only we could know *why.*

Yet in secret we liked it, that Father refused to cooperate with his captors. It was said of Bad Habits that he was an "enigma"—"the face of evil." When he was questioned, Bad Habits remained "mute." Bad Habits showed "no remorse." We came to believe that it might be meant for us, the children of Bad Habits, to crack the code of his silence.

Poor Grandpa died of a sudden stroke. The aluminum-foil head-covering could not save him. Poor Grandma became too infirm and confused to live without nursing care. Mother wept, committing Grandma to a facility.

One day, I will bring Grandma home to live with us. One day, your father's name will be cleared.

Mother took us to live in another city, with more distant relatives. Mother was grateful and taught us to be grateful. We would never complain. We would execute our household duties in the home of Uncle G. and Aunt C. as instructed. We would eat meals in the kitchen and clean up after ourselves without fail. D., the eldest, would oversee T. and A., her younger brothers, when Mother was not present. In this new household we were, at the start at least, more hopeful.

Still we slept restless and agitated as creatures being eaten alive by fleas. Still we slipped from our beds, prowled the night-time house like feral cats. Dolores, Trevor, Albert: children of Bad Habits.

Dolores wished to believe *We can be like other kids. Nobody knows us here.*

Yet Dolores wished to crack the secret code of Bad Habits's silence. *Why had Father chosen those he'd chosen?*

Trevor and Albert could not assist her much. Trevor maintained a belief that Father maybe wasn't Bad Habits, exactly.

Bad Habits was someone who'd taken over Father in some way, like a carjacker? Albert was too young to know what to think, what not to think, what was real, and what was bad dreams, why poor Albert picked his nose until the nostrils bled staining his fingers.

It happened that Uncle G., who was a light sleeper, was beginning to be wakened by Bad Habits's children prowling the house at night. Uncle G. wasn't happy with such behavior though Mother tried to explain we meant no harm, and would not do it any longer. Still it happened, Uncle G. heard creaking on the stairs, footsteps in the downstairs hall. Cautiously he made his way downstairs, switching on a light to expose our faces: *What are you doing awake at this hour? Go back to bed!*

A glisten of fear in Uncle G.'s eyes.

Father's shadow had not yet appeared in Uncle G.'s house. We could not find it and did not wish to find it yet felt the compulsion to search.

It was summer. There was no school. We worked hard, even Albert, who was small-boned for his age and tired easily, at our household tasks, and ate all our meals in the kitchen and cleaned up after ourselves tidy as hungry mice, yet we began to hear Aunt C. complain of us to Mother behind closed doors.

Your children. Bad habits. Can't you control!

Mother came to us, wept over us. Mother embraced us, kissed us, prayed *Jesus let my children be spared. Help my children to be good. Jesus come into their hearts, save them from sinful ways.*

Sometimes, seeing our eyes on her, staring at the wild-haired stark-eyed wraith-woman she'd become, Mother gave a little cry of hurt and seized our shoulders in her talon-fingers, shook us until our teeth rattled in our heads.

Bad! How dare you! This is a test God has put us to.

Our bad habits began to run together. Trevor picked his

nose as well as bit his fingernails. Dolores bit her nails as well as plucked at her hair. Albert began to bite his nails, pluck hairs from his head, leak urine into his bedsheets even as, helplessly, he picked his nose until the tender nostrils bled.

It began to happen that, in one of the upstairs bathrooms, a faint gassy-bad odor began to be detected. Against the farther wall of a room entered without caution, a man's shadow looming to the ceiling began to appear.

Dolores hid away. Dolores drew up lists. While her brothers played in the backyard kicking a soccer ball, imitating the actions of normal boys by running and squealing like deranged little dogs, Dolores printed columns of names in her school notebook. Thinking *I will be the one to break Bad Habits's code.*

None of is could recall Father very clearly now. Before Bad Habits.

Gloating Dolores thought *I will see Father, and tell him: that I know why. Only me!*

But when Mother went to visit Father in the detention facility, none of us were allowed to accompany her. When Mother returned from the visit, exhausted and unsteady on her feet, she pushed past us without a word, hurried upstairs, and locked herself in her room. Uncle G. refused to speak of the visit. Consequently we learned from eavesdropping on the adults that Mother had not been able to speak with Father for Father has been "distant"—"cold." We learned too, the shocking news that Father's attorney was entering a plea for him of not guilty by reason of insanity which was an admission of guilt and which could not possibly be true, for Father was not insane.

Just stunned by circumstances, overwhelmed and confused, Mother believed.

We were incensed. Even Albert, who scarcely recalled Father any longer. Our father is not insane!

A half mile from Uncle G.'s house was a municipal park. Part of the park was playing fields, picnic groves, woodchip trails. Trevor drifted into the park dreaming of how he would lose himself in the wetlands and never be found until his bones were picked clean and white by vultures. Thinking vaguely *He will be sorry then. For what he has done to us.*

Now Trevor was squatting in the grass watching boys playing soccer a short distance away on an open stretch of land. Next day, Trevor returned. And the next day. The boys were Trevor's age and a little older. They were husky rowdy energetic boys who shouted as they kicked the soccer ball from one end of the playing field to the other, laughing and cursing in imitation of older adolescents. They began to be aware of Trevor watching in yearning. Suddenly Trevor was astonished by jeering voices, *Go back to hell where you came from!*

Trevor stayed away from the park for several days. When he returned, the boys were waiting for him. Ambushing him with pebbles, sharp stones. Rushing at him shouting *Freak! freak! go back to hell!* and Trevor turned to run, struck on the back, on the side of the head, bleeding from a cut over his eye.

Mother was nearly recovered from her nervous collapse after the visit to Father. Mother was determined to take us on nature outings. Long ago, before she'd met Father and had what she called "my babies," she'd been an avid bird-watcher with friends who rose early, tramped in marshy places to see migrating birds through binoculars. Several times that summer Mother led us on nature walks in the wetlands but our outings ended disappointingly soon. Mother tired easily and we were sullen, anxious, and distracted by our bad habits of picking, biting, plucking at ourselves, which followed us everywhere we went, like frantic shadows.

Yet again, Trevor returned to the park. To the soccer playing field. The boys were astonished and outraged to see him, squatting in the grass as before. When they ran at him, Trevor rose in a crouch and threw a jagged chunk of concrete the size of a hubcap at the nearest boy. Fortunately, the concrete struck the boy's shoulder and not his jeering face where Trevor had aimed.

A shriek of pain, a trickle of bright blood. *Now you know* Trevor laughed.

Hiding in the basement of Uncle G.'s house. Behind the furnace until a patrolman came to the front door with a warrant from juvenile court for Trevor's arrest.

Some days, Dolores believed she was close to cracking the code.

Other days, Dolores despaired of ever cracking the code.

In secret, Dolores had assembled the names of Bad Habits's (known, alleged) victims. These she listed in columns. Her notebook was filled with columns. Before she'd become the daughter of Bad Habits, Dolores had had little time for intellectual pursuits, hadn't been a particularly thoughtful or sensitive girl, certainly not a girl to ponder the inscrutable motives of others. Now Dolores spent most of her time alone, brooding. Tirelessly she hand-printed columns of names in her notebook, always in new arrangements. The first had been a column simply listing names of victims in the chronological order of their deaths, dating back to August 1993 and ending March 2005:

Suzanne Landau
Tracey Abrams
Duane Fitch
Gladys Zelmer
Eli Nazarene
Willis Rodman
Donna May Emory

Alfred Myers
Thomas Flaxman
Steven Etchinson
Melissa Patch
Alice Taub
Carrie Miller
Sallie Miller
Dennis Miller
Bobbie Dix
Allan Sturman
Molly Sturman
Ginny Hahn

Other columns reflected alphabetical order, names in ascending order of ages (youngest seven months, oldest sixty-two years), means of death (strangulation, stabbing, "blunt force trauma"), whether singly or with other victims, whether indoors or outdoors, distance from our house (the farthest was ten miles, the nearest only a few doors away on our side of the street), which side of the Mississippi River, months of the year, days of the week and so forth.

It was maddening to us how the media continued to report that police could discover "no logic" to Bad Habits's actions and deemed him "senseless"—"randomly vicious." There was heated debate in the media about Bad Habits's alleged insanity. We did not accept it that Father was insane as we did not accept it that Father had led an "ordinary"—"average"—"Midwestern small-city" existence though we could not have said what Father's truer life had been.

In our church it was said *The kingdom of God is within.*

In the public world, Father was a man named Benjamin S. Haslet, Jr. He was fifty-three, five-foot-nine, weighed one hundred eighty pounds. He had been a "competent" public utilities worker, a "devout" member of the local Church of Christ, a former Boy Scout leader, a husband, father. Sources not wishing to be named spoke of his reputation for being "difficult to know"—"withdrawn"—"minding his own business." Dolores twined single pieces of hair around her fingers and plucked them from her scalp that was reddened and stinging. Coin-sized bald spots glimmered through what remained of her hair. She'd begun to wear a scarf over her head when she left the house, but for days at a time Dolores didn't go outside, preferring to brood over her notebook, neatly recopying, reprinting columns of the names of Bad Habits's (known, alleged) victims, in ever new arrangements.

At last, in the waning days of the summer, we were taken to visit Father.

Remember to look hopeful, children. Smile at Father all you can.

Father had pleaded guilty. Father was now in a maximum-security prison for men in the southern part of the state, less than two hundred miles from Uncle G.'s house.

It was believed that Father's attorney had coerced him into pleading guilty to nineteen counts of homicide and to providing the police with names and descriptions of other victims for which Bad Habits had not claimed credit, dating to January 1988, in exchange for a sentence of life imprisonment instead of death by lethal injection. Everyone who knew Father believed this, or nearly everyone. Mother insisted he'd pleaded guilty to bring the tragic case to a close. *To bring peace to the survivors of the victims. But one day Father's name will be cleared. I know this.*

Though we were only a few feet from Father, we had to speak with him over a phone. As Mother spoke in her animated, eager way, we saw Father's eyes drift from her and onto us with a look of vague surprise and discomfort. As if he'd forgotten who we were! For months Father had had no word for us, his children. It had never been suggested that we might speak with him on the phone. Mother had conveyed to us Father's words for us: *I love you* and *God's will be done.* Even Albert had wondered if these were Father's authentic words.

Mother did most of the talking, for Father had little to say. As at home Father had frequently muttered and grunted in vague response to Mother's conversation, so in prison. Mother had aged a decade in the past several months yet bravely she'd dressed as if for a Sunday, in cheerful colors. With a shaky hand she'd applied a mascara brush to her eyelashes and her tremulous mouth was a pert coral pink. Mother's eyes snatched at Father's through the Plexiglas partition. Though Father's chest hunched inward, he'd gained weight in his midriff. There was a settled, fleshy contentment to him we had not recalled. Behind his glasses, his eyes were shrunken and without luster, lightly threaded with blood. His nose was larger than we recalled, like a putty nose, with a filigree of broken capillaries.

In the car on our drive to the prison Dolores had whispered to us her theory of why Bad Habits had killed the individuals he'd allegedly killed: the secret was that certain of the victims corresponded to us and to Mother. For instance, one of the first victims was named Gladys, which was Mother's middle name; and another of the victims had the surname Miller, which resembled Mother's maiden name, Muller. Another of the female victims had been thirty-nine at the time of her death, which had been Mother's age at that exact time. There had been a nine-year-old boy killed in a particularly savage assault at the time Trevor had just turned nine. There was a child Allan to correspond with Albert. Clearly, Dolores was mirrored in Donna and Duane.

Tracey and Thomas were obvious matches for Trevor. Bad Habits had the identical initials as Benjamin Haslet!

But the man in the baggy prison uniform, shoulders slumped and chest collapsing into his belly, bored gaze drifting past our heads, did not seem capable of any of the acts of Bad Habits.

Mother's eyes shone with tears. Impulsively, though perhaps it was a premeditated gesture, Mother brought her fingertips to her lips and pressed them against the Plexiglas at about the level of Father's downturned mouth. Mother now alarmed us by handing the phone to Dolores who fumbled to take the receiver from her and could only mumble inaudible words. Next, Mother handed the receiver to Trevor who mumbled similarly inaudible words, and next the receiver was held out to Albert who shrank from it with a look of terror. An expression of annoyance flickered in Father's face, but he said nothing. He seemed now to know us, at least to know who we were in relationship to him. He might have said *A man's seed is sucked from him, to take root where it will.* But he did not, for Mother was weeping now, saying *One day your name will be cleared, Benjamin. I know this. I have faith.* Before we left, Mother insisted that we all kneel in prayer. Father took his time lowering to the floor, for his knees were stiff. Mother led us in the Our Father. Our lips moved numbly. A yawn played about Father's mouth and his eyelids dropped with a peculiar sort of contentment. Bad Habits was no more. Father was no more.

As we left the visiting room we turned to look back, but already Father was being escorted away by a guard, his back to us.

We moved from our uncle's house but remained in the area. Within a few months, Mother would change our family name.

We would not see Father again. One autumn morning Mother roused us early, to hike with her in the nature sanctuary. Birds were migrating. Warblers, robins, red-winged blackbirds. Trees quivered with the poised bodies of hundreds of starlings. There was the harsh smell of brackish water, organic rot. There were mudflats where turtles sunned themselves. There were shore birds picking in the mud. There were dragon flies, butterflies drifting like the most random of thoughts. Mother had discovered a trail through the wetlands. It was hardly more than a deer path but it was a trail. *There is another side* Mother said. *We can get to the other side.* We began our hike through the marsh. We hiked through the marsh.

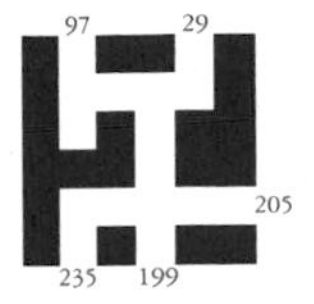

THE RAILWAY NURSE

by Nelly Reifler

Becoming a railway nurse was not easy.

She remembers walking down the long hall in the old Railway Hospital, those slick tiled floors, and the sound her rubber soles made as she hurried toward the room where the screening test was to be administered. She remembers that she was carrying her white tote bag. She remembers pushing open the wide swinging door at the end of the hallway. And then entering the room. It was a long, narrow room. Its windows had been draped with heavy black fabric. At the distant end of the room stood a tall podium with a dim green lamp upon it. In the middle of the room was a small desk attached to a chair with a wooden seat. A bright spotlight, mounted on the ceiling, was focused on the desk.

A door opened in the far corner, behind the podium. She squinted to see beyond the spotlight's bright circle. The administratrix had arrived.

The young woman curtseyed.

"Please sit," said the administratrix. Her voice bounced off the limestone walls.

The young woman unbuttoned her white cape and folded it over the back of the chair. She pressed herself onto the wooden seat of the chair, blinking in the stark white light.

"The written section of the exam," came the administratrix's voice, "is in the cubby before you. You have one hour to complete the written section of the exam."

The young woman reached into the cavity beneath the desk and pulled out a sheaf of mimeographed pages. She had been studying for a year. She had arrived at the Railway Hospital certain that she knew the answer to every possible question that might appear on the Railway Nurse Screening Examination's written section. Still, holding the pages, she started to sweat. She was trembling. Her breath was shallow. They were all counting on her. Her mother. Her brother. *Her brother.* She remembered what he'd said to her that morning as he'd fastened her cape at the throat: do it for me. *Do it for me.* She looked up toward the human shape at the podium, hoping to catch an eye, hoping for some expression of encouragement. But she received no sign. She looked down at the paper. She pulled her pencil from her pocket. She took a deep breath and began answering the questions—true or false, multiple choice, and essay questions—one by one, methodically. Then, just as she was composing the final sentence of the final essay, a grinding metallic alarm sounded. She dropped her pencil and heard herself yelp. She blushed. Her hands were shaking. Her heart pounded.

When the alarm ceased, the administratrix intoned, "Place the written section of the exam back in the cubby hole before you."

The young woman did so. Oh, how she wanted to be a railway nurse.

"Stand up," came the voice from the end of the room.

The young woman, the would-be railway nurse, inched her way out of the tight space between chair and desk. Her synthetic dress clung to her new white hose. She stood up.

"Step forward" The administratrix's voice raised on the last syllable. For-*ward*.

The young woman felt a chill travel up her spine to the base of her skull. The hairs on her arms raised. She stepped forward.

"It is now time," said the administratrix from the darkness at the end of the room, "for the oral segment of the exam. This will last one half hour."

She nodded.

"Please clasp your hands behind your back, and I shall begin presenting your questions."

For half an hour, the young woman stood there, chilled to the bone, forcing herself to speak. Each time she opened her mouth, a tiny puff of frozen breath hovered before her and then disappeared. The questions were not difficult. Still, with every word, the young woman felt more doubt and grew colder and colder, until, at the last question, she was shivering, teeth chattering, shoulders shaking, hypothermic.

She was forcing out her final answer when she was almost knocked off her feet by the alarm. This time, the noise was so loud, so high-pitched, it was impossible to know where its source was: it seemed to come from the very center of her head. What had sounded before like hammering metal was now a screech. She stumbled backward and leaned on the desk for support.

The alarm ceased.

Silence for ten seconds.

Finally, the young woman's body returned to its normal temperature. Her shoulders stopped shaking. She stood up straight and faced the podium, the boxy outline of which she could just make out, with the silhouette of the administratrix behind it.

"Well," came the voice from the podium, and the young woman thought for a moment that it sounded ever so slightly softer, "now it is time for the final segment of the exam. Now," the administratrix paused, then announced, "it is time for the Practical Segment."

With that, the door in the far corner of the room swung open, and the young woman heard voices, and footsteps, and a thud, and then more voices. She felt the approach of several moving bodies, and something being dragged along the floor, coming closer. Then they entered the outer rim of the white circle of light, and the young woman, the would-be railway nurse, could make them out: three tremendous men with black stockings over their faces, so that their features were flattened. All three had wet spots between their mashed lips. One of the men was bald, and his scalp shone a little in the light, even through the black nylon, but the others had thick hair, pressed down over their eyebrows. They were pulling something with them. But what was it? They gave it a shove.

It tumbled into the spotlight.

It was a fourth man. He was small and stooped. A bandanna had been wedged in his mouth and tied at the back of his head. He looked at the young woman with wide-open, bloodshot eyes. His hands were tied together, wrists crossed, and he began to raise them toward her, but one of the big men slapped his arms down. His clothing was ragged; his trousers were hanging off his hips, his hipbones jutted out over his waistband. A straight line of gray hair traveled from his navel downward. The young woman found her eyes following that line of hair.

One of the big men spoke from inside his stocking: "You'll

be needing your first-aid kit," he said in a wet, gurgling voice.

"Oh, yes," she said, and curtseyed. "Thank you," she added, and she reached into her tote bag. She pulled out her first-aid kit. Touching the soft pink leather of its case, she thought of her brother, who had given it to her for her birthday. Then she thought of how her brother used to visit her in the middle of the night to play bunnies. Once again, she leaned back on the desk for support.

"Begin," came the administratrix's voice. The young woman righted herself.

"You might want to open that," said the big man who had spoken before. He nodded toward the kit. His hands were busy holding the small man still. The small man twisted in the big men's hands.

The young woman caught a whiff of a pungent odor, the sweet smell of fear and decay. It came from the struggling man's body.

"Thank you," she said again, and began to unzip the first-aid kit.

As she did, the big bald man reached into his pocket, pulled out a pistol, and shot the struggling, skinny man three times.

Three deafening bangs.

The young woman's eyes clamped shut, and her hands flew up and covered her ears.

"You have one hour," the administratrix's voice traveled through the echoes of the shots and the smell of gunpowder.

When the young woman opened her eyes, the big men had disappeared, and there was blood everywhere. She felt hot, wet droplets seeping through her stockings. She looked down. Her white dress was spattered with red. And before her, on the floor, was the skinny man. The wounded man. He lay, twitching, covered in blood. One of his arms was torn open. He had another hole, a tidier one, like a puncture, near his ribs. And he was bleeding wildly from the right side of his head. Where his right ear used to be, there was gore. His face was contorted, his eyes rolled back in his head, his mouth was moving, he was panting. His hands had been untied. The bandanna was gone. The young woman, the would-be railway nurse, slowly moved her hands down from either side of her head. She could hear him, whimpering and moaning. She looked at that line of gray hair on his stomach. It was now soaked with sweat. A large wet stain spread across the crotch of his pants.

She reviewed the lessons from her textbooks and tried to recall the charts that hung on the walls of the classrooms where she had studied. She had dissected a guinea pig and a worm.

She lowered herself to the floor. She knelt, carefully placing the first-aid kit beside her. The man was panting. His inhalations were whistling little wheezes, his exhalations harsh, puffing moans. His eyeballs rolled forward, then stopped. The young woman saw him focus on her face, on her own eyes. She leaned forward and looked into his brown pupils. If he were not wounded, incapacitated, the look in his eyes would have frightened her; he looked like he wanted to eat her.

Blood gushed from the side of his head and pooled on the floor.

As the young woman finished unzipping her first-aid kit, she couldn't help smiling a little at the ingenious stringency of the Railway Nursing Examination Board. She surveyed the man's body. She considered the bullet that was lodged in his ribs. Was there one in his arm as well? His ear had been blown off. She'd need to do some patching. She pulled out her golden scalpel, her long tweezers, her golden clamps, her packet of golden surgical needles, golden scissors, a pile of her fluffy white gauze pads, and her spool of sterile black thread. She admired the color of the gold—it glinted in the stark white light—and pictured her brother, her handsome brother with his strong arms and his clean dungarees, her brother, who had given her the gift—and then she set to work.

The man writhed and moaned. She noticed he was turning gray. She thought of her textbook: *gray skin, gray skin… blood loss…* His panting had become a little shallower. He twitched as she clipped the skin around his chest wound back with her delicate little clamps; he gasped as she plunged in with her tweezers. She dug around, probed the bloody mess. She furrowed her brow as she used up most of the gauze pads soaking the red slop that kept pooling in the hole.

"Aha," she said when she felt the tips of her tweezers touch metal. She dug in just a bit deeper. She felt something inside the man's chest tug and shred as she pulled.

Then she heard the voice from the far end of the room, "You have thirty more minutes to complete the practical section of the examination."

At that, the man's unhurt arm jerked up and grabbed the shoulder of the young woman. She almost toppled forward. He clutched. His eyes locked on her eyes, more fiercely than before. His fingers dug into her skin through the fabric of her sleeve. She shook her head at him. "No," she whispered. "No." She peeled his fingers away. She couldn't waste any more time.

The bullet was slick and bloody, tinier than she would have thought. She twisted around and set it on the desk behind her. Then she unspooled some sterile thread, snapped it off, wet the end between her lips, and threaded it through her golden needle. She bent over the man's chest wound and slowly, methodically began sewing up the hole. It was hard work. The skin slid around on top of the layers of muscle, the scanty fat and the bones. So different from a guinea-pig cadaver.

The man wouldn't stay still. He writhed. He was turning whiter and whiter.

"Stop it!" the would-be railway nurse heard her own voice say. For a second, she thought of her mother, how her mother used to chide her and her brother when they wrestled too vigorously on the carpet. The girl remembered the feeling of her brother's muscular hand on the small of her back, her own face pressed into his armpit. The scent there, his musk. The way her shoulders and thighs felt, stretched into unfamiliar positions beneath her brother's weight. And their mother's voice: *stop it, children, that's enough, stop it...*

A gurgling sound came from the man's throat. The young woman blinked. *Pay attention*, she muttered to herself. She wiped her palms on her dress, smearing more sticky blood on the fabric. She would have to have the dress cleaned. *Pay attention*, she muttered again. Her whole future was at stake. She had to pass the examination.

She finished sewing up the wound. She pulled her little crystal jar from the first-aid kit and dribbled some antiseptic around the stitches. She snipped the thread with her golden scissors. "All right," she said to the man, whose tongue was lolling, dry and flecked with something white. "All right, that was the worst one." She remembered something a doctor had said once on a television show she used to watch with her brother when he came home sweaty from lacrosse practice on Thursday evenings. "Hang in there," she said to the man now, just as the kindly television doctor had said. She remembered leaning into her brother's side while they watched the program. He'd smell like the grass and mud of the lacrosse field.

"P... p... p... please..." It came from somewhere deep inside the man.

"All right," she said. "I'm doing my best. I want this to

work as much as you do. Stay still." The man's eyes had been fluttering for a few minutes. Now they closed.

How much time had passed since that last announcement? Every moment counted, but the young woman had no sense of how many minutes were left, how many seconds made up a minute. She unspooled another length of thread and started on his ear, or the place where his ear had been. Although this was the bloodiest wound, it was the shallowest. The skin there was thinner, easier to handle. She sewed quickly, admiring her own efficiency. She watched her hand, moving quite naturally. She wished she could see the look on the administratrix's face.

His arm wound slowed her down a bit, but she didn't lose confidence. *Breathe*, she told herself silently. She was smiling while she worked. *Will I get an A?* She thought. And then she shook her head. She nearly laughed as she hooked the last few stitches. *Silly girl*, she said to herself, like her brother used to say to her when she hung on him in the morning as they parted to go to their separate schools. *It doesn't matter if I get an A*, she reminded herself. *Anything above a B-minus, and I'll get to be a railway nurse.*

"There," she said. Suddenly, she was seized by panic, and she felt for the man's pulse. He still had a pulse. She giggled. *Silly girl.* "I did it," she said. One of the man's eyes opened slowly and seemed to search the space in front of him. "I mean," she said, overwhelmed with a feeling of good will toward her patient, "I mean, *we* did it." She smiled.

She sat there for about a minute, looking at the man. His stomach moved in and out, haltingly. It was a lean stomach, and that line of hair traveled straight from his fly to his sternum. Like railroad tracks, she thought.

She savored the moment. And then she looked up and squinted toward the far end of the room. She shielded her eyes with her hand, knowing that even then she wouldn't be able to see anything more than a shadow. "Done!" She called out.

The alarm sounded, even louder than before, but this time she was expecting it. She smiled and let the sound enter her; she could feel it penetrating her marrow. But then the screeching turned into the ringing of bells. One bell began to clang, and then another, and then several more—all different timbres, at different speeds. This was a joyous noise, she realized, it was like being in a church tower. The lighting changed, became softer, yellowish, shifting, gently illuminating the whole room. The young woman's body filled with warmth. A spasm of pleasure shook her. She closed her eyes for a second, then looked at the podium. In the distance, a small woman with spectacles and a gray topknot bent over, gathering a thick notebook and some pencils into a briefcase. And then the railway nurse—for that's what she was now, a railway nurse—saw a hint of a smile on the administratrix's face just before she turned to leave.

From the door in the corner, the three big men entered. No longer were their faces masked by stockings. She saw that one had a dimple in his chin. Another had curly blond hair. They ambled over to the railway nurse and helped her to her feet. The bald one stood in front of her. She looked into his blue eyes. He raised his arm and paused for a moment; then he cupped his hand around her cheek. She nudged her face into his hand, just once.

The other men were rolling the patient onto a white stretcher. When they lifted him, the stink rose from his body. His feet twitched and his legs flopped open. His white hands gripped the edges of the stretcher. He was covered in drying brown blood.

The girl imagined the bath she would take when she got home. She would use her honeysuckle bath salts, and she would soak there for a long time. She deserved it.

Until this moment she had always felt as if something were missing, as if everybody else had something she didn't. She put on her cape and gathered her things into her tote bag, and every movement she made seemed to her to carry a new importance. She opened the door and stepped onto the tiled floor of the Railway Hospital's hallways. She nodded to the portraits of Railway Hospital founders and donors that hung on the walls, and their faces seemed to look back at her with satisfaction. She hummed as she walked past the security guard and through the metal detector in the lobby. When she got outside, she stood between two stone columns at the top of the pink marble steps that fanned toward the sidewalk below. She looked up and down the avenue, at the tall limestone buildings and their awnings. Perhaps, now that she was a railway nurse, she would have her own apartment, maybe even in one of these grand places, and her brother could come over whenever he wanted. They could play bunnies again. Her lips stretched into a wide smile. She hurried down the steps, crossing her arms against the first autumn chill. She broke into a run, and the wind bit at her cheeks. Her smile grew larger. Then a swirling gust whipped up from nowhere, and her mouth was filled with the dry grit of the street.

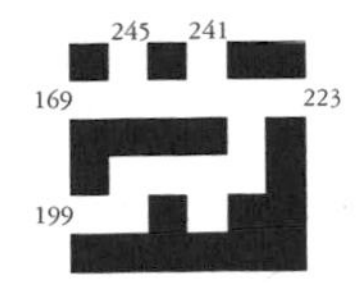

PEOPLE ARE BECOMING CLOUDS

by JOE MENO

PEOPLE ARE BECOMING clouds nowadays. Each time John goes to kiss his wife, Madeline simply laughs politely into the palm of her hand and immediately turns into a puff of soft, white vapor. The vapor is odorless and can assume various sizes and shapes. It can still understand when it is being spoken to, the vapor. It can understand whenever John begins wordlessly crying. One time, while holding hands at the airport, John, without thinking, kissed Madeline's soft cheek and immediately she turned into a puff of charming whiteness that resembled a young pony leaping over a fencepost. It seemed that the pony was neighing from the way its long neck was stretched and raised.

As a cloud of vapor, Madeline will remain transparent for upwards of an hour or more. Her appearance varies greatly, depending on unknowable factors such as the weather, what she has eaten that day, what she happens to be wearing. When she is not a cloud of white smoke, Madeline is a first-grade schoolteacher who is greatly loved by her first-grade school students as well as almost everybody else, including strangers who pass her on the street. She is that type of striking young woman. She has short red hair and bright eyes like a pixie. She laughs the way you imagine a toy dog laughing. It should be noted that Madeline did not ever turn into a cloud before the couple was married and this new strange, unplanned development has been a source of silent frustration for John.

A partial list of the strange shapes Madeline has taken as a cloud of vapor: a dove with enormous wings blowing a large trumpet, an intricate snowflake with castles for feet, a swan with an impossibly long neck sewing a blanket made of clouds, a fairly accurate representation of an angel with rings of spoons for a halo, a gigantic apple being swallowed by a ghostly white tiger.

Madeline claims turning into a cloud is totally beyond her control. John does not entirely believe this. Right before she transforms, she seems to be laughing, and her laughter is what leaves John unconvinced. But he refuses to argue about it. He loves her and he thinks she loves him and he believes it is just one of those things that will have to work itself out. *Couples go through these kind of things*, he thinks.

John and Madeline will still sometimes try to be intimate. They will turn off the lights and put on some soft music, maybe jazz, sometimes not. John will lie there in their white bed and close his eyes and wait for his wife to touch his body and when she does he will try to stop himself from running his fingers through her hair. He will be able to resist her for a little while, but if she is wearing the pink and brown nightgown he will eventually grope at her and within moments she will be drifting high above him. He will lie in bed then and stare up at her, a white cloud of happiness, condensing and expanding. He will reach his hands up to grab her but he will be unable. He will try to draw her in, to breathe her into his lungs, but his face will only turn red. He will turn on his stomach and want to cry into the pillow but he will not. He will be too embarrassed to cry. When he finally turns over, he will see Madeline has become a snowy-white falcon eating a peach or a series of lovely hills decorated with a miniature cloud town. He will wait, laying there in bed, and fumble with her discarded nightgown until she drifts back down.

John will call Madeline from his office sometimes, where he works as an accounts representative for a paper company, and ask her, "Are you a cloud right now?"

"No," she'll say laughing. "Of course not, honey."

"What about now?"

"Um, no."

"What about now?"

"Nope."

Other times, John will go on business trips to sad places like St. Louis and Cleveland and he will call Madeline from his motel room and they will try and talk dirty, like they are only dating.

"I am climbing in the window and sneaking up on you," John will say. "I am dressed like an old-time bandit with a striped shirt and a mask."

"Okay. What am I doing?" she will ask.

"You are doing the dishes. You are wearing a white, frilly apron, like a maid."

"How about I'm wearing the apron but I'm not a maid?"

"Okay, that's good. You're doing the dishes in your apron and I am sneaking behind you and touching your shoulders and arms and the back of your legs."

"Then what?" she will ask.

"I dunno. Um... I am carrying you off into my jet and we are flying away now. I have kidnapped you maybe."

"You're a bandit with your own airplane?"

"Yes, I'm independently wealthy. I chose a life of crime to relieve my boredom."

"I see," she will laugh. "What are you doing to me now?"

"I am..." Someone will be listening to the television too loudly in the motel room next to his and John will whisper into the phone softly, "I am blindfolding you. I am blindfolding you and feeding you a lot of frosting and candy."

There will be a pause where John will be unsure if his wife has hung up or is still listening. After some time, he will whisper, "Are you a cloud now?" and there will be silence, only be the sound of air, which is no sound at all, which means, yes, she is a cloud now, and John will imagine kissing his wife right then and he knows he will be unable to. Instead, he will kiss the phone, and it will be the closest he can get to the actual thing, the kissing of his wife, and then he will say goodnight and place the receiver back in the small plastic cradle before closing his eyes and fighting to go to sleep.

At work, John finds himself searching the internet for clues, hints, suggestions, stories of similar weather-related problems happening to other normal, red-blooded men. There is nothing. There are only endless pictures of girls in wet T-shirt contests and site after site of affordable radar-tracking devices which give three-dimensional depictions of storm clouds hovering above far-off cities. He comes across a photograph of a Gulf Stream hurricane tearing the roof of a small white house and thinks he recognizes Madeline drifting in the nearby gray sky. He stares at the photo on his computer for a long, long time.

On the bus ride home from work, John fantasizes about the lips of various nondescript strange women. He imagines what he would do with a pair of hot lips if given a chance. He stares across the aisle and a question forms from nothing in the vessel of his mind. *Would he still love his wife so badly if she was not so impossible to claim? Would he still want her if he could have her whenever he wanted*? He does not know. He isn't sure. He does not think so, suddenly. But maybe kissing her might be worth all the boredom in the world as well.

When John arrives home, he finds Madeline has become a large sparkling building. She is as tall as a skyscraper and is made entirely out of a strange silvery material like glass, both precious and transparent. The building is standing in the yard, rising high and mighty and reaching up into the infinity of the evening sky like a futuristic needle. He sets his briefcase down and sighs, then takes off his jacket, folding it over his arm. "Great," he says, looking up. "This is just great." He finds the façade to the great silver building, spins in through the revolving door, takes an elevator up to the highest floor, and stands staring out at the stars, finding their glowing spots above the rest of the world.

The horizon is so big and dark and sad that John can barely lift his head. In the silence of that very great height, he can hear the echo of his own breathing.

"Madeline?" he asks and then leans against the silver railing.

Somehow he knows his wife is listening. He unties his tie, taps on the railing once, and then says, "It looks like you had a bad day."

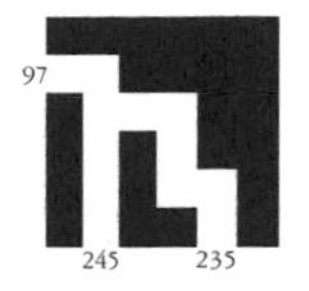

DEB OLIN UNFERTH

by DEB OLIN UNFERTH

NO ONE IN Wyoming thinks that Deb Olin Unferth is a fuckup.

No one in Alaska, Tennessee, Texas, or Wisconsin thinks that Deb Olin Unferth is a fuckup. Nobody in Morocco, Hungary, or anywhere in South America thinks that Deb Olin Unferth is a fuckup. Nobody in Mexico.

There may be someone in Alabama who does. There may be someone in New York. Maine. Members of her family may (Arizona, Illinois).

In many democratic nations where the opinion of the individual is a matter of consequence, no one thinks that Deb Olin Unferth is a fuckup. In many fascist nations, in countries with dictators, failing oligarchies, puppet parliaments, poverty, and crime, people, many many people, do not ever have the thought that Deb Olin Unferth is a fuckup.

No king or any member of any royalty thinks or ever thought that Deb Olin Unferth is a fuckup. There was a man who people thought was a prince and who may have thought that Deb Olin Unferth is a fuckup but it turned out he was not a prince although he did live in a castle and the word "prince" was part of his last name. In any case it isn't certain that he thought Deb Olin Unferth is a fuckup but it is possible.

Many famous writers never thought that Deb Olin Unferth is a fuckup. Gertrude Stein, Marcel Proust, Balzac.

Many thinkers of all sorts never thought that Deb Olin Unferth is a fuckup. Margaret Mead, Plato, Wittgenstein. Thucydides. Kant.

Nobody who fought in World War I, the Crimean War, the Fenian Invasion, ever thought that Deb Olin Unferth is a fuckup. There may be a vet or two from the Gulf War or Panama who think that Deb Olin Unferth is a fuckup.

Nobody in Ethiopia thinks that Deb Olin Unferth is a fuckup.

No one who lives on a little boat on the ocean thinks that Deb Olin Unferth is a fuckup.

There may be a few people in Florida who do, and a man in El Salvador has his doubts, along with a couple in Cuba, but otherwise the Caribbean latitudes are safe.

Nobody in any time zone where it is midday when it is midnight where Deb Olin Unferth is thinks that Deb Olin Unferth is a fuckup.

Nobody who ever washed up on dry land, bloated, gutted, chewed through, nobody who ever fell over, shot or hacked up, thinks that Deb Olin Unferth is a fuckup. Nobody who time-travels, no double-dimension people or Klingons, think that Deb Olin Unferth is a fuckup.

That she knows of. It must be admitted that somebody may have sailed off without telling. Somebody may have moved to Morocco. It is likely, in fact. Or it is possible that somebody, a stranger, saw her from a distance and knew what she was (fucked up) and that stranger may still be out there, with that thought, but doesn't have a name, only the face. The thought is attached to nothing, floats, alone: that woman, that odd-looking woman, what a fuckup.

The number of people who do think Deb Olin Unferth is a fuckup is statistically insignificant. In fact the thought that Deb Olin Unferth is a fuckup occurs in so few minds and in so few places and when one considers the bucketful of thoughts pouring off the earth, all the thoughts, all the minds, and how even those who do think that Deb Olin Unferth is a fuckup think it rarely, only perhaps when she is present or her name is, when one considers this, then that thought—that she is a fuckup—is hardly there at all, is not even a weak whine in the scream, is softer even than the wavering thoughts of those who think that Deb Olin Unferth actually is *not* a fuckup: I do not, you do not, we will not ever believe and never did, couldn't believe that Deb Olin Unferth is a fuckup because she is not fucked up, or a fucker, or fucked, not then and is not, will not be ever.

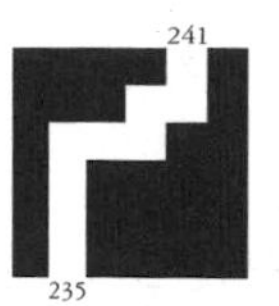

CODA / CREDO

WE JOIN SPOKES TOGETHER IN A WHEEL

by LAWRENCE WESCHLER

SOMEHOW I KEEP coming back to Nicholas of Cusa, that late-medieval Renaissance man (1401–1464), a devout church leader and mathematical mystic who was at the same time one of the founders of modern experimental science, propagator, for example, of some of the first formal experiments in biology (proving that trees somehow absorb nourishment from the air, and that air, for that matter, has weight) and advocate, among other things, of the notion that the earth, far from being the center of the universe, might itself be in motion around the sun (this a good two generations before Copernicus)—and yet, for all that, a cautionary skeptic as to the limits of that kind of quantifiable knowledge and thus, likewise, a critic of the then-reigning Aristotelian/Thomistic worldview. No, he would regularly insist, one could never achieve knowledge of God, or, for that matter, of the wholeness of existence, through the systematic accretion of more and more factual knowledge. Picture, he would suggest, an *n*-sided equilateral polygon nested inside a

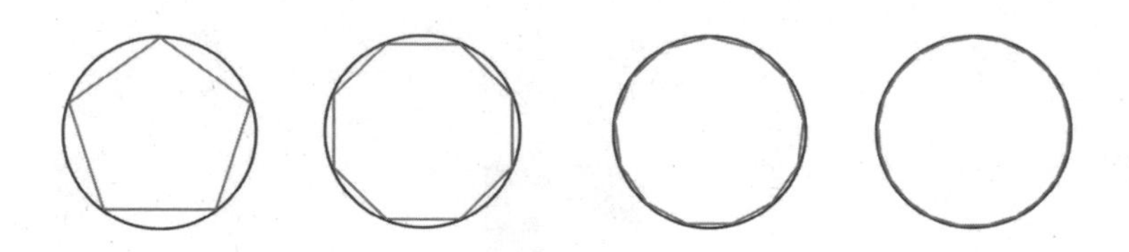

circle, and now keep adding to the number of its sides: triangle, square, pentagon, hexagon, and so forth. The more sides you add, the closer it might seem that you will be getting to the bounding circle—and yet, he insisted, in another sense, the farther away you will in fact be becoming. Because a million-sided regular polygon, say, has *precisely* a million sides and a million angles, whereas a circle has none, or maybe at most one. No matter how many sides you add to your polygon (ten million, a hundred million), if you are ever going to achieve any true sense of the whole, at some point you will have to make the leap from the chord to the arc, a leap of faith as it were, a leap which in turn can only be accomplished in or through grace, which is to say in some significant way *gratis*, for free—beyond, that is, the *n*-sided language of mere cause and effect.

And all of that rings true to me (the ring of truth, indeed, it seems to me, being one of the ways you might know you had popped past the *n*-sided polygon and into the realm of the circle).

And yet I also find myself holding with the late Carl Sagan, who, in his 1994 book *Pale Blue Dot*, insisted that

> In some respects, science has far surpassed religion in delivering awe. How is it that hardly any major religion has looked at science and concluded, "This is better than we thought! The universe is much bigger than our prophets said—grander, more subtle, more elegant. God must be even greater than we

dreamed"? Instead they say, "No, no, no! My god is a little god, and I want him to stay that way." A religion, old or new, that stressed the magnificence of the universe as revealed by modern science might be able to draw forth reserves of reverence and awe hardly tapped by conventional faiths. Sooner or later, such a religion will emerge.

Nicholas and Carl

That, too, seems profoundly true to me, evinces the ring of truth. But can Nicholas of Cusa and Carl of Cornell both be right? Phrased another way, I suppose, is it possible to imagine a science that, while remaining true to its own principles and methods, nevertheless manages to break free of the *n*-sided polygon and toward the circle whole?

One morning, a while back, over NPR's *Morning Edition*, somebody was reporting how scientists have determined some of the mechanisms whereby staph bacilli mutate (evolve) with astonishing rapidity so as to outwit antibiotics, sharing DNA ("information") across the entire process in ever more novel ways.

It sounds almost as if staph as such is thinking, or rather maybe daydreaming, or anyway musing—letting its thoughts (all that genetic information) meander into whatever available channels present themselves (that the attempt to counter this tendency in effect is an effort "to keep" nature's "mind from wandering, where it will go—ooh—ooh—ooohhh... oh oh oh oh oh").

The mind/body split may constitute a misguided formulation, as for that matter in a sense may the split between the in-itself and the for-itself, between the world and consciousness.

It may not be a matter of *cogito ergo sum*—in fact, in a sense, perhaps it's that formulation's very opposite: *sum ergo cogito*. Or better yet: *esse est cogitare.*

Being is itself thinking: the world is daydreaming.

Hence the German word: *Glaube*. Faith, belief, as in *das glaube ich* (I believe this; This is what I believe). But also, *der Globus*: the globe.

The globe glaubes.

All that is, wonders—and just goes on marveling.

And then, just the other day, there was this startling image staring up at me from the pages of the science section of my morning paper and spearing me in its gaze (I momentarily felt the way I imagine some microbe might, gazing back up the barrel of a microscope—or, then again, the way Szymborska's "darling little being with its tiny beating heart inside" must have, plastered that day across the giant screen). "The crash of

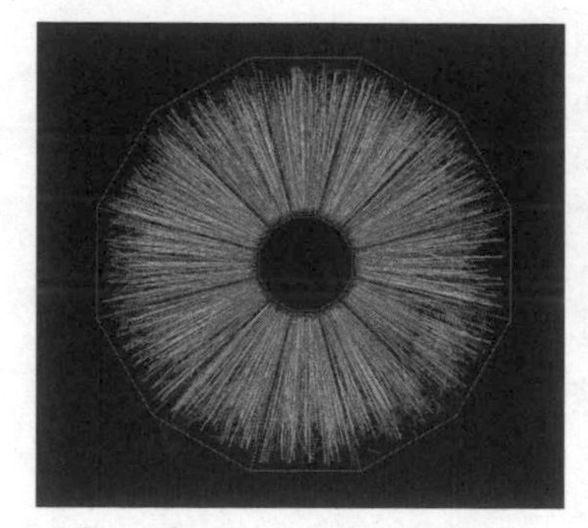

The crash of two gold nuclei traveling at nearly the speed of light

Supernova remant photographed by the orbiting Chandra X-ray Observatory

two gold nuclei traveling at nearly the speed of light," the picture's caption explained, "produces a shower of debris that is detected by a house-sized detector that is part of the Relativistic Heavy Ion Collider at the Brookhaven National Laboratory on Long Island." The article itself went on to note how, "according to one theoretical physicist, the collisions have even been creating a sort of tiny, short-lived black hole" (granted, "very, very tiny and very, very short-lived," lasting "less than one-10,000,000,000,000,000,000,000th of a second").

By now I suppose you know me well enough that you won't be surprised to hear how all that got me to thinking about black holes and vision, or more precisely about what comes in and what goes out when we see. The history of thinking about vision is in fact a history of a continual rejiggering of the relative importance of those two vectors: is it that light rays enter the eye through the corneal lens (whereupon they get sprayed onto a sort of tabula rasa screen at the back of the eye)—or rather, in some sense, that the brain's, or the mind's, or anyway the self's attention courses out to the world through that lens (actively grasping and even shaping what it sees, or rather looks at, or rather chooses to tend to)?

To the extent that something is going in, what is it going in *to*? Recall how Sartre characterized voracious consciousness as Being's very obverse, which is to say, Nothingness—in that sense a (perhaps not merely conceptual) mirror of the sorts of actual physical black holes cosmologists posit out there in the actual physical universe. Consider, in this context, Rilke's melancholy Panther at Paris's Jardin des Plantes, padding in his cramped circles behind those perpetual bars, its will by now almost completely paralyzed, how (in Stephen Mitchell's marvelous translation),

> Only at times, the curtain of the pupils
> lifts, quietly—. An image enters in,
> rushes down through the tensed, arrested muscles,
> plunges into the heart and is gone.

Then again, as I say, maybe the vectors go the other way around, and mind is more like the black hole's physical obverse, the extravagantly spewing supernova, with wave-particles gushing forth at the speed of light. Which in turn raises the question of whether the outgoing attending gaze moves at the same speed as the incoming light, which is to say, the speed of light? Or faster? Or slower?

Beats me. Maybe it's some combination of all of the above. After all, as the great sixth-century B.C. Chinese master Lao-Tzu parsed things in the eleventh of the poems that make up the *Tao te Ching* (again this time in Stephen Mitchell's superb translation, with a slight tweak of my own there at the very end):

> We join spokes together in a wheel,
> but it is the center hole
> that makes the wagon move.
>
> We shape clay into a pot,
> but it is the emptiness inside
> that holds whatever we want.
>
> We hammer wood for a house,
> but it is the inner space
> that makes it livable.
>
> We work with being,
> but non-being is where we live.

Maybe it just takes a circle to know a circle.

CONTRIBUTORS

ALAN ACKMAN is a graduate student in the MFA program at the University of Arkansas, where he is currently completing his thesis. He is a former editor of the *Evansville Review*. This is his first publication.

CHRIS ADRIAN is a pediatrician and divinity student in Boston. His novel, *The Children's Hospital*, will be published by McSweeney's next year.

RODDY DOYLE's latest novel is *Oh Play That Thing*.

RACHEL HALEY HIMMELHEBER works as a freelance editor and caterer. She lives in Las Cruces, New Mexico.

ADAM LEVIN's fiction has appeared in a number of publications, including, most recently, *McSweeney's* (No. 16) and *Tin House*. He received his MFA from Syracuse, and currently lives in Chicago, where he teaches at Columbia College and the School of the Art Institute.

JOE MENO is a fiction writer from Chicago and a winner of a Nelson Algren Literary Award. He is the author of several novels, including *Hairstyles of the Damned* (Akashic 2004) and the short-story collection *Bluebirds Used to Croon in the Choir* (TriQuarterly 2005).

PHILIPP MEYER lives in Austin, where he is a fellow at the Michener Center for Writers. He previously worked as an EMT and a carpenter in Baltimore. A report of his experiences as an EMT during the New Orleans hurricane was published on Salon. He is currently writing a novel and has a story forthcoming in the *Iowa Review*. This is his first print publication.

YANNICK MURPHY is the author of *Stories in Another Language* and *The Sea of Trees* (a *New York Times* Notable Book). She has received a Whiting Writer's Award, a National Endowment for the Arts fellowship, a MacDowell Artists' Colony Fellowship, a Sewanee Writers' Conference fellowship, and a Chesterfield Writing Program Fellowship. She lives in Pasadena, California, with her husband and three children and is in the process of moving to Reading, Vermont. Her novel *Here They Come* will be published by McSweeney's this spring.

JOYCE CAROL OATES is the author, most recently, of *Missing Mom*, a novel, and *Uncensored: Views & (Re)Views.* Her forthcoming *High Lonesome: New and Selected Stories 1966–2006* will contain work previously published in *McSweeney's*.

DANIEL OROZCO's work has appeared in the *Best American Short Stories*, the *Best American Mystery Stories*, the Pushcart Prize anthologies, and in *Harper's*, *Zoetrope: All-Story*, and elsewhere. "Somoza's Dream" is part of a collection in progress. He teaches in the creative writing program at the University of Idaho.

NELLY REIFLER is the author of *See Through*, a collection of stories. She lives in Brooklyn.

DEB OLIN UNFERTH's fiction has appeared in *Harper's*, *Conjunctions*, *NOON*, *Fence*, *3rd bed*, *StoryQuarterly*, and other publications. She lives in Lawrence, Kansas.

LAWRENCE WESCHLER, author of *Mr. Wilson's Cabinet of Wonder* and *Vermeer in Bosnia,* directs the Institute for the Humanities at NYU. *Everything That Rises: A Book of Convergences* will be published by McSweeney's this February.

EDMUND WHITE is the author of eighteen books, including the biography of Jean Genet, for which he won the National Book Critics Circle Award. He lives in New York and teaches at Princeton.

ISBN 1-932416-38-2
52200>
9 781932 416381